Flora Harding began writing over 30 years ago to fund a PhD on the disposal of waste in Elizabethan York, and has juggled fact and fiction ever since. Under various pseudonyms she has written more than 75 novels, histories and other forms of non-fiction and continues to be fascinated by the relationship between the past and the present, whatever she happens to be writing. Flora still lives in York with the city walls and the Minster at the end of her street, and is a freelance project editor as well as an author. Much as she loves the historic city, she yearns too for open horizons, and is a keen walker, preferably in wild, open spaces.

🐦 @AuthorFlora
f @FloraHardingAuthor

Before the Crown

Flora Harding

OneMoreChapter

One More Chapter
a division of HarperCollins*Publishers*
The News Building
1 London Bridge Street
London SE1 9GF

www.harpercollins.co.uk

HarperCollins*Publishers*
1st Floor, Watermaque Building, Ringsend Road
Dublin 4, Ireland

This paperback edition 2020
21 22 LSC 10 9 8 7 6 5 4 3 2 1

First published in Great Britain in ebook format by
HarperCollins*Publishers* 2020

A catalogue record for this book
is available from the British Library

Ebook ISBN: 978-0-00-838753-2
US Paperback ISBN: 978-0-00-843841-8
Canada Trade Paperback ISBN: 978-0-00-841170-1
UK Audiobook ISBN: 978-0-00-840644-8
US Audiobook ISBN: 978-0-00-841207-4

This novel is entirely a work of fiction.
The names, characters and incidents portrayed in it are
the work of the author's imagination. Any resemblance to
actual persons, living or dead, events or localities is
entirely coincidental.

Set in Birka by Palimpsest Book Production Ltd, Falkirk Stirlingshire

Printed and bound in the United States of America
by LSC Communications

Chapter 1

Windsor Castle, December 1943

He's not there.

Elizabeth has her eye pressed to the chink in the curtains. The velvet is worn and smells musty. It reeks of mothballs and greasepaint, of old productions carefully rehearsed, suppressed giggles, and first night nerves.

In front of the stage, she can see the audience beginning to fill up the rows of chairs. Some are taking their seats in deferential silence, others look around, defiantly casual about finding themselves in the castle. The splendid gilt of the Waterloo Chamber is dulled now by neglect, its walls stripped of famous portraits, but it retains plenty of its original grandeur. The carpets had been rolled up and stored at the beginning of the war, and now the great hall echoes with the scraping of chairs, the subdued burble of conversation, and the clearing of throats.

The front row is empty still.

'Is he here?' Margaret whispers, crowding at her shoulder.

1

'Not yet.' Elizabeth steps back from the curtains, disappointment a leaden weight in her stomach which is already rolling queasily with anticipation and stage fright. This will be the fifth performance of *Aladdin*, and though she knows all her lines, still there is that moment when the curtains are hauled back and the terror of failure clutches at her throat.

'Let me see.' Margaret elbows her sister aside and takes her place at the curtain as if she can conjure Prince Philip of Greece into space by the sheer force of her will.

Sometimes Margaret's will is so strong, Elizabeth almost believes she could succeed but on this occasion her sister's drooping shoulders indicate failure. She lets the curtains drop back into place and turns back to the stage, kicking at her satin skirts.

'Papa *said* Philip would come,' she pouts.

'For Christmas,' Elizabeth reminds her, trying to disguise the dullness in her voice. 'He didn't promise to come for the pantomime. Something may have come up.'

Margaret stares. 'Something more important than joining the King and Queen to watch their two daughters perform?'

'Philip's a prince. He's not going to be impressed by a couple of princesses.' It is Elizabeth's secret worry. She has spent her whole life being special, and now, the one time it matters, she may not be – at least, not for Philip.

It's been two years since Philip of Greece took tea with the King and Queen. Elizabeth and Margaret sat enthralled as he entertained them with his wartime experiences at sea, deliberately making light of his own part and playing up the funny side of things. For Elizabeth, whose only memory of Philip up to that point had been of a bumptious cadet who had showed off terribly, it had been a revelation. The swaggering boy had been replaced by a young man who was everything a prince should be: brave, witty, charming.

And handsome. The memory of those penetrating blue eyes has been a tiny, insistent throb inside her ever since.

Not long afterwards, the royal family were invited to a party at Coppins, where Philip was staying with his cousin, Marina, Duchess of Kent. Philip asked Elizabeth to dance, either out of kindness or out of duty. She knew that much. She was fifteen and tongue-tied, burningly aware of his hand at her waist, his palm pressed against hers.

She is seventeen now. She longs for him to see that she has grown up.

'He *ought* to want to come and see us,' says Margaret stubbornly. She's been looking forward to impressing him with her acting skills. 'Especially you,' she adds, uncharacteristically ceding centre stage to Elizabeth. 'He's been *writing* to you.'

'Sometimes.' Ever cautious, Elizabeth won't even admit to her sister how she has pounced on Philip's rare letters, how many times she has read and reread them, smoothing out the creases in the paper. They have told her nothing because what could they say? That he has remembered her, that's all. But it has been enough. 'He probably writes to lots of people.'

'Lilibet, you're going to be Queen of England one day. You are *not* "lots of people".' Exasperated, Margaret stalks across the stage, her heels clacking on the wooden boards.

'Margaret!' There is a hiss from the back of the stage where Crawfie, their governess, is beckoning. 'You too, Lilibet. The King and Queen are just coming in now. You need to take your places for the show.'

Elizabeth draws a breath. It doesn't matter that Philip isn't here. She will not be disappointed. He is coming for Christmas. She will see him soon.

Beyond the curtains she can hear the rumble and scrape of chairs being pushed back as the audience stands for her parents.

'Quick, into the basket!' Cyril Woods scampers across the stage. Elizabeth likes him. He is jaunty and bright-eyed, and he dances and sings nearly as well as Margaret. The two of them carry her scenes, Elizabeth knows. She learns her lines and moves when she is supposed to, but she doesn't have Margaret's dazzle. Next to her sister, she is muted, dull. That is how she feels, anyway.

But she is the elder; she will be Queen. So she has the starring role. It is Elizabeth who is playing Aladdin, in a shockingly short jacket and tights that make her feel very exposed. Margaret is Princess Roxana, which she doesn't mind as she gets to wear a gorgeously embroidered silk robe and a tiara.

For the opening scene, they are to jump out of a huge laundry basket. The back has been cut out so they can crouch behind it. There isn't much room and Cyril keeps touching her leg by accident. 'Sorry,' he mutters. 'Sorry.'

Elizabeth's heart is thudding. Oh, how she hates this moment before the curtain goes up! Her mind has gone blank. Her costume is too tight and she can't remember a single line. The wicker basket is tickling her cheek and her legs are already stiffening. As the Guards' orchestra strikes up the fanfare, she is gripped by the longing to leap up and bolt from the stage, to run out into the Upper Ward and down to the stables. To ride far, ride fast, to a place where there is no one to fail and no one to please and no duty to be done.

But she cannot do that. The show is one of the few contributions she can make to the war effort. Proceeds will go to the Royal Household Knitting Wool Fund to provide comforts for the troops who are fighting for their country, Elizabeth reminds herself sternly. They aren't allowed to run away. All that is being asked of her is to sing and dance. What kind of example would she set if she were to refuse even that?

It is too late now in any case. The orchestra is reaching a crescendo, the drums are rolling and there is a swishing of velvet and a creaking of ropes as the curtains are hauled back.

'You're on!' Cyril jabs Elizabeth in the side and she springs up, tossing the lid of the basket aside. Her sudden appearance provokes laughter, which increases as Margaret pops up beside her, but Elizabeth doesn't even notice.

Philip is in the front row, sitting next to her mother, and he is looking right at her. His expression is astounded and a smile is just starting to curve his cool mouth.

Elizabeth's heart swells. Her doubts are forgotten. All at once she can sparkle like Margaret. Her feet are lighter, her smile brighter. She can dance, she can sing. She can arch a brow and cast a knowing look at the audience.

She can make Philip laugh.

He is there. That is all that matters.

Chapter 2

Next to the Queen, Philip is trying not to make it obvious that he is nursing the hangover from hell. Why in God's name did he drink so much last night? But it was his last chance to see Osla before Christmas.

It was fun, at least what Philip remembered of it. They danced at The 400 and then somehow a party congregated in Osla's flat where they ate the Russian salad she made with powdered egg. Last night it hadn't seemed disgusting, but the liquid paraffin dressing is still roiling in his stomach. He slept on the sofa and he should have stayed there instead of making the fatal error of returning to the flat in Chester Street where he found a letter from Mountbatten urging him to present himself at Windsor Castle as soon as possible.

Letters from Uncle Dickie are hard to ignore.

'Your grandfather was a king,' Mountbatten said the last time Philip had seen him. 'You're a prince, connected to most of the royal houses of Europe. But what have you got to call your own? Barely more than the clothes you stand up in.'

'And that sweetheart of a car you gave me for my twenty-first birthday.' Philip loves his MG.

Mountbatten was not to be diverted. 'You know what I mean, Philip. You're a personable fellow, and Lilibet will be Queen one day. Make yourself agreeable to her, as I hear you're more than capable of doing. Dammit, you owe it to your family and to yourself. The war won't last forever, and then what will you do? You're not a British citizen and you won't be able to stay in the Navy.'

Philip can't imagine the war being over. It seems to have been going on forever. If Philip is as honest with himself as he tries to be, he has been enjoying the war.

There are flashes of terror, of course, but more of adrenalin and anticipation. In unguarded moments, the screams of injured men echo, and memories of flames and thrashing limbs and the vicious rat-tat-tatting of machine guns surge and spin in his head, leaving him stranded on the edge of an abyss, temporarily unable to catch his breath, but when that happens he simply pushes them away. It is war, that is all, and he hasn't suffered so much as a scratch.

Philip prefers to think of the pitch of the ship and the dazzling Mediterranean light. The sense of liberation as they ease away from the quay. The stomach-clenching excitement when the order for battle stations crackles out of the speakers.

It is harder here, he thinks. The country is exhausted,

its cities bombed, its people grey-faced and worn down by rationing and blackouts. In London, Philip walks past ruined buildings without noticing them anymore. Once, he was with a party heading for the Café Royal only to discover that it had been bombed barely minutes before. Dust still hung in the air. There were bodies lying on the pavement, men in evening dress, women in furs and diamonds that glittered in the moonlight. The looters were already there, stripping away jewels from the dead and dying, pulling up satin dresses to rip off nylon stockings.

Philip remembers stepping past and going on to The 400 instead.

That's how it is during a war. Nobody knows when the next bomb will drop, when the torpedo will hit, when that Messerschmitt will slide out from behind a cloud and shoot you down. There's a febrile edge to socialising. The knowledge that each night might be the last time you dance, or laugh over cocktails, or kiss a girl, makes it hard to be sensible and go home early to bed. So they stay up, determinedly dancing and drinking and laughing, squeezing every last drop of enjoyment out of an evening.

It is a world away from Windsor Castle. Here, in the Waterloo Chamber, there is little sign of the chaos and destruction elsewhere. The famous Lawrence portraits have been taken down and in their place – Philip squints to make sure he hasn't imagined this – are bizarre cartoon characters. But otherwise little seems to have changed since the previous century. The King even leant across the Queen to tell Philip that the stage and curtains are the very same ones used by Queen Victoria's children for their theatricals.

Philip's head is aching, a ferocious grinding that jabs every time anyone shifts in a chair, sending it scraping across the floor. He feels fuzzy and stale. Perhaps he really is coming down with the flu that was his excuse for not arriving until last night?

'Go and help with the pantomime,' Mountbatten urged.

'I'm not prancing around on stage making a fool of myself in front of the King!'

'Make yourself useful backstage, then. There must be something you could do. It'd go down very well. The King and Queen like that kind of thing.'

The more Mountbatten pushes, the more Philip digs in his heels. He's like a dog being dragged to a bath.

'Philip, you're halfway there.' Uncle Dickie can't understand why Philip is so reluctant to press his case. 'The King said Lilibet was very taken with you when you saw them in '41. She's been writing to you, hasn't she?'

'Occasionally.' Philip knows he's being contrary but he can't help himself. Elizabeth's letters have been more than occasional. Written seriously in a childish hand, he has found them obscurely touching, though he will never admit as much to his ambitious uncle. He is deliberately keeping things light. He is grateful that she hasn't embarrassed him by asking for his photograph, and he has been careful never to suggest that he would welcome one from her. That would be taking things a step too far. 'She's just a young girl, Uncle Dickie. She hasn't got much to say.'

Mountbatten waved that away. 'I hope you're writing back?'

'When I can. I don't know if you've noticed, but there's a war on.'

'You seem to have time to go drinking and dancing on shore leave,' his uncle had pointed out.

'I do write.' Not that he had much to say either.

The truth is that he has struggled to remember much about Elizabeth. A quiet girl, sturdy and sensible, she has always been there at various family events like his cousin Marina's wedding to the Duke of Kent and naturally she had been at her father's coronation, which Philip remembered clearly. They had played croquet together at the Naval College in 1939 when Uncle Dickie, that old intriguer, had somehow arranged for Philip to look after the two princesses while the King and Queen attended chapel. There had been mumps, or measles, or some medical reason why Elizabeth and Margaret hadn't gone too.

Philip wouldn't be surprised if Mountbatten had engineered the whole outbreak just to put his nephew in front of the King's oldest daughter. Not that Philip thought it had done much good. Elizabeth was painfully shy, he seems to remember, and rather chunky. He had hardly been able to get a word out of her. There had been a good tea on the royal yacht, though. He remembers *that*.

Good Lord, his head hurts. If only he'd been able to

find an aspirin but it wasn't the kind of thing you asked for the moment you were ushered into the Crimson Drawing Room where the King and Queen were greeting their guests for the pantomime.

The last thing Philip wants to do right now is to sit through a pantomime. The Waterloo Chamber is so big it must be impossible to heat at the best of times but with the royal family anxious to share in the country's wartime privations there isn't so much as an electric bar to warm the air and the cold is penetrating. He envies the Queen her fur coat.

In spite of the cold, he's very tired. Osla's sofa isn't the most comfortable of beds. The effort of suppressing a yawn leaves the muscles in his cheek aching. Surreptitiously he pinches the bridge of his nose between his thumb and forefinger. The last thing he can afford to do is nod off. For all his recalcitrance, he knows Mountbatten is right and he needs to make a good impression on the King.

'And the Queen,' his uncle warned. 'You'll have to work harder with her. It's not at all helpful of your grandmother and great aunts to keep referring to her as a common Scottish girl!'

So far the Queen has been charm itself, but Philip is aware that her sweet smile is at variance with her sharp blue eyes.

At last, the main lights go out and the orchestra gets going. There's some rousing music and just as Philip is seizing the opportunity to slide down in his seat, the curtains are dragged open. The drum roll bangs a conclusion, the lid of the laundry basket on stage is tossed aside and up pops none other than Princess Elizabeth, heiress presumptive to the English throne.

There's a tiny moment of silence when she seems to be looking straight at him, and he's so taken aback that at first he can only stare back, his headache forgotten, before he starts to grin at the sheer absurdity of it.

Then she smiles – another shock, as he doesn't remember her smiling like that – and starts to sing as she comes out from behind the basket. She is wearing a red and gold Chinese jacket and filling it out very nicely indeed. The jacket reaches her thighs. Beneath it, she is wearing only a pair of satin shorts and silk stockings that reveal surprisingly shapely legs.

Philip whistles to himself and sits a little straighter.

He watches with new interest as Elizabeth tap dances across the stage. The show is better than he had expected, he has to admit, and he even finds himself laughing out loud at the more groan-worthy jokes. Princess Margaret is very pretty and undoubtedly the better performer. She has a better voice and is a better actor, but Philip's eyes keep going back to Elizabeth. She is positively sparkling.

She must be seventeen by now, he calculates. He hasn't realised what a difference two years can make. Uncle Dickie's exhortations to fix his interest with her suddenly don't seem quite as tiresome.

Chapter 3

Elizabeth feels as if she is smiling with every cell in her body as she joins hands with Margaret and the rest of the cast and bows. The curtains fall into place with a dull swish. Never has she danced so well, sung so well. Dressed as a washerwoman in a sackcloth dress and an apron, she sang 'We're Three Daily 'Elps' with Margaret and Cyril and thrilled at the sight of Philip throwing his head back and laughing. No tight smiles or simpers for Philip of Greece.

She is trembling with excitement and anticipation as they leave the stage, but when Philip comes backstage to congratulate her, her confidence evaporates abruptly. After dreaming of him for so long, the reality of him is intimidating. He is taller than she remembers, the lines of his face harder, the icy eyes bluer. He seems to take up more than his fair share of air so that her breath shortens and she feels twitchy and exposed.

He comes in with the King and Queen and his intimidatingly elegant cousin, Marina, Duchess of Kent with her languid, tilted smile and exotic accent. Elizabeth remembers being a bridesmaid at Marina's wedding to her uncle George. Philip was there, too, but he was just a boy then, an alien creature Elizabeth watched out of the corner of her eye. Uncle George was killed on active service last year, and Marina is facing her widowhood with courage. She is effortlessly beautiful and has a warmth, a kindness and an easy charm that Elizabeth admires and envies.

'What fun that was!' Marina kisses Elizabeth warmly. 'You were marvellous, darling.'

Elizabeth smiles and thanks her, and kisses her parents, but all the time she can feel her gaze being dragged to Philip, who is standing a little behind them. She doesn't want to look at him, she is determined not to, in fact, but it is as if her eyes are iron filings being sucked remorselessly towards a magnet. When the others move on, he lingers, and she doesn't know whether to be delighted or terrified.

'I say, that was terrific,' he says warmly. 'Very funny indeed.'

'Thank you.' The old terrible shyness clamps around her throat. She is still wearing the costume with the jacket and tights and she turns the saucy cap she has worn on stage between her hands, keeping her eyes firmly fixed on it. 'Mr Tannar, the headmaster of the Royal School, wrote the script, so it's nothing to do with me really.'

'I don't agree. A script isn't any good without good actors. I enjoyed it. The laundry scene was very funny.

Especially with the iron burning through all those "unmentionables".'

His eyes drop to her legs. Elizabeth orders herself not to fidget but she feels ridiculously exposed and her smile is stiff.

'Yes, Margaret and Cyril are very good.'

What has happened to the sparkle she felt on stage, she wonders miserably. She had been so determined to show him that she was no longer the gauche fifteen-year-old he had met before, but look at her: her tongue feels thick and unwieldy, any hope of witty repartee shrivelling in her throat. It was hopeless.

'I thought you were very good, too,' says Philip, but Elizabeth can't help wondering if he would think she was good if she weren't the King's eldest daughter.

'That's kind of you,' she says with a stiff smile, 'but it's Margaret who is the performer.'

'You're determined to turn aside any compliments, aren't you?' he says. He's not exactly smiling but when Elizabeth risks a glance at him, she sees that the crease in his cheek has deepened. The sight sets warmth trembling inside her. She can feel it spreading outwards, blotching her throat and staining her cheeks beneath the greasepaint.

'I don't like being complimented when I don't deserve it.'

Philip seems amused rather than daunted by her priggish voice. 'What *do* you deserve to be complimented for?' he asks, as if he's really interested.

17

Being dutiful, that's what her parents would say.

'I have a good appetite,' she says and remarkably, he laughs.

'We have something in common then. I still think of the tea on the royal yacht when you came to the Royal Naval College in '39. I had two banana splits.'

'And platefuls of shrimps, if I remember right,' says Elizabeth, encouraged by his laugh. 'I'm surprised you weren't sick.'

Philip grins at her. 'It would have been worth it.'

His smile burns behind her eyelids and she looks away.

'It's hard to imagine a banana split now,' she says after a moment. 'I haven't seen a banana since the start of the war.'

'I've got friends who say that they dream of fresh fruit now.'

'For me it's soap,' Elizabeth says and he raises his brows.

'Soap?'

'Before the war, when the soap got thin, we'd have a new bar to unwrap. It always smelt lovely, of roses or lavender. But now we have to use it down to the last tiny sliver, when it's all cracked and grimy, and then it gets put together with other slivers so we can keep on using it. It makes us feel that we're doing our bit, though it's little enough compared with what most people have to do. So I always feel guilty about longing for a new bar all to myself. It's a dream for when the war is over!'

Why had she told him that? Elizabeth cringes inwardly.

Philip has been fighting. He has seen the reality of war. He is hardly going to be impressed by a silly girl yearning for soap.

But he doesn't sneer, which is kind of him. 'We all need a dream for when the war is over,' he says.

Realising that she is still fidgeting with the cap, Elizabeth drops it onto the table behind her. 'I'm awfully glad that you'll be joining us for Christmas,' she says bravely.

'Not as glad as I am,' Philip says. 'Dickie and Edwina are away and I have nowhere else to go. It would have been a very sad Christmas for me otherwise.'

Elizabeth doubts that. She is not a fool. She is sure Philip has lots of girlfriends who would be delighted to invite him to share Christmas with them. She knows he is only here at Mountbatten's bidding. His uncle's plans for an alliance with the House of Windsor are common knowledge but what Philip thinks of the idea is less clear.

Elizabeth knows what she wants.

'Well, we'll be a very small party so it's lucky for us that you're not at sea,' she says, willing the stiffness from her voice.

'My ship's being refitted so I'm on shore duty for a couple of months.'

So he has been around for several weeks without coming to see her, Elizabeth notes dully. But then, what was she expecting? Yes, he writes sometimes, but they are not friends. They hardly know each other. He has filled a large space in her life, but whatever he may plan for the future, for now she occupies only a very small space in his.

Elizabeth may not know how to flirt but she has not been hosting lunches for the Guards officers at the castle without learning how to make conversation, and she has her pride, after all.

'How do they keep you busy?' she asks Philip.

'Instructional courses mostly.' If Philip notices the coolness in her voice, he gives no sign of it. 'Deadly dull, to tell you the truth. I can't wait to get back to sea. It feels all wrong to be kicking my heels here when other chaps are still out there fighting.' He stops. 'I'm sorry, that sounded rude and ungrateful. I didn't mean that I'm not glad to be here,' he says. 'Here at Windsor, I mean. With you.'

There is a tiny moment of silence. *With you*. Elizabeth is very conscious of the stickiness of the greasepaint on her face. The satin tights have become crumpled and twisted at one ankle and the collar of the jacket is chafing her neck.

'I understand,' she says, achieving a stiff little smile. Crawfie is hovering and the babble of overexcited voices from the cast behind them is growing louder and more boisterous. Her parents must have left.

She gestures down at her costume. 'I'd better change,' she says, hardly knowing whether she is glad or sorry to bring the conversation to a close. There is something about Philip that makes her nervous. She is drawn to him almost against her will. He reminds her of a stallion, alluring and dangerous at the same time, a horse she longs to ride but one which might easily bolt.

'Of course.' Philip steps back. 'I'll see you later, I hope?'

'Yes.' Her mouth stretches into an artificial smile. 'Yes, I'll look forward to it.'

Chapter 4

Uncle Dickie must have got it wrong, Philip thinks as Elizabeth turns away. He's seen little evidence that the princess is 'very taken' with him. She strikes him as stiff and serious ... and yet ... and yet, he is sure that he caught an intriguing flash or two of warmth and humour, quickly buttoned down.

It might be pleasing to try and coax out that side of her, he muses as he strides along the dark, frigid corridors.

Elizabeth has grown up, that is for sure, but she is still very young. She isn't a beauty like Osla, Philip thinks, but she has a curvaceous figure, wonderful skin and her eyes are extraordinary – a clear, true blue. And when she was on stage, her smile lit up the Waterloo Chamber. Philip finds himself hoping he can make her smile like that again.

He stops at the end of the corridor. Left or right? The corridors in this part of the castle seem to go on forever, firmly closed doors on either side. Windsor Castle is subject to blackout regulations as much as anyone else and there is only the occasional, dim bulb to light his way after he has brushed aside the offer of an elderly footman to carry his bag.

'I've got a pair of hands,' he said shortly.

The footman looked offended, but he must have been over seventy by Philip's reckoning. Is he supposed to walk empty-handed along miles of corridors while an old man struggles with his bag?

Only sheer stiff-necked pride prevents Philip retracing his steps to ask the footman for help after all.

When he eventually finds his room – HRH Prince Philip of Greece is printed by the door – he unpacks his bag and lays his meagre wardrobe out on the bed. Thank God for uniform, he thinks, picking up his much-darned socks with a grimace and tossing them onto the chest of drawers with his underwear. His dinner jacket is shiny with age and the trousers patched. Whichever footman has the dubious pleasure of looking after him will not be impressed.

Shifting the clothes aside, he throws himself down onto the bed and lights a cigarette.

Well, the country is at war, he reasons as he blows a circle of smoke into the chilly air. They can't expect him to turn up in an immaculate outfit. There is no way he can afford new clothes even if he could get the clothing coupons. The royal family will have to take him as he is.

It's not as if Windsor Castle is the lap of luxury either. It might be imposing from the outside but its thick stone

walls make it unforgivingly cold inside and with its treasures in storage it feels more like a grim fortress than a
royal palace. The chandeliers have been taken down along
with the great paintings. The state rooms are shrouded in
dustsheets or converted into offices. No fires are allowed
in the castle bedrooms, he's been told, and all he has for
light is a single, flickering electric lightbulb. Between the
blackout and rationing and the need to set an example of
sharing the country's misery, the conditions are far less
comfortable than at the Mountbattens' flat.

But he's not here to be comfortable, Philip reminds
himself. He's here to make himself appealing to a princess.

He smokes for a while to distract himself from the cold.
The truth, Philip can acknowledge to himself, is that he
is slightly miffed that Elizabeth didn't seem more delighted
to see him. After all those painstakingly written letters, he
has assumed she would fall over herself to welcome him.
That may have been a mistake.

It's galling to think his uncle may have been right about
the need to come to an understanding with Elizabeth
sooner rather than later. There's a coolness to her, a reserve
Philip recognises but didn't expect. He may have to work
harder to charm her than he thought.

He doesn't need to commit himself yet. Philip stubs out
his cigarette and links his hands behind his head on the
pillow. Nothing is going to happen until the war is over,
in any case, and he is far from ready to settle down. He is
only twenty-two.

On the other hand, he is a prince. Elizabeth is a princess. He will need to marry one day, as will she. There might be worse fates.

He thinks of his father in Monte Carlo, with his fraying collars and cuffs. Of his mother living in that bare flat in Athens, pawning her jewels to buy food for those even poorer than herself. Philip has known since he was nine that he would have to look after himself. He will come into no vast inheritance. He has his title and that is it.

Elizabeth, on the other hand, will succeed to the throne of England and all the lands, wealth, and treasures that go along with it. If he marries her, he will have all the security he has never known.

At a cost.

The cost is marriage to a girl he barely knows. A lifetime of behaving well, of playing second fiddle.

Philip doesn't know if he can bear the thought of that.

And then, of course, Elizabeth might not want him.

He scratches his chin while he thinks about how that prospect makes him feel.

She will need to marry and give the Crown an heir. How many eligible princes can there be? Why wouldn't she choose him?

With a sigh, Philip swings his feet to the floor. It is time to get changed.

He knows what he needs to do. He just doesn't want to do it.

Chapter 5

A fire has been lit in the drawing room where the King
and Queen's guests are gathering for drinks before
dinner. By unspoken consent they all huddle in front of
the mantelpiece to make the most of the meagre warmth
from the flames.

Elizabeth is talking to Porchey, one of her oldest friends
and as passionate about horses and racing as she is. Porchey
is easy company. She never has any trouble talking to him.
Her tongue doesn't tie itself into knots when she is with
him. Her smile doesn't stiffen and her stomach doesn't
churn.

Not like when Philip is there.

She refuses to let herself watch the door for his arrival
and deliberately turns a shoulder away from it, adjusting
the fur stole she wears against the chill. It is only recently
that she has been included in evening engagements and
she still feels a little as if she is dressing up in her mother's
clothes.

She is laughing with Porchey when a prickle in her spine

makes her look over her shoulder in spite of herself to see Philip walk in. He's wearing his naval uniform and brings an energy with him, almost as if he is charging the air by standing there. The sight of him clogs the breath in Elizabeth's throat and her heart starts to slam uncomfortably against her ribs.

Instinctively everyone turns to look at him. Philip seems quite unfazed by the short silence that greets his arrival. It is broken by her father who goes over to welcome him and introduce him to his private secretary, Tommy Lascelles. Tommy has a stern gaze and a quelling manner but Philip gives no sign of being intimidated, chatting easily as he accepts a glass proffered by one of the elderly footmen who have been persuaded out of retirement for the duration of the war.

The King stands with them but he looks tired and diminished next to Philip's vigour, Elizabeth can't help noticing.

'Who's that?' Porchey asks, following her gaze.

'Oh, that's Philip.' She is proud of how steady her voice sounds.

'One of the Mountbattens, isn't he?'

'His mother is. He's part of the Greek royal family. His cousin, George, is King of Greece but they're all in exile at the moment.'

Porchey studied Philip's fair hair. 'He doesn't *look* very Greek,' he commented dubiously. 'He looks like a bally Viking!'

'I think they're connected to the Danish royal family too. And the Russian one.'

Porchey doesn't look impressed. He is an aristocrat, heir to the Earl of Carnarvon, and sturdily British.

'Come and meet him,' Elizabeth says, just as Philip turns away from Tommy and the King and heads determinedly towards her. The slam of her heart picks up and she pins on a bright smile.

'Hello,' she says.

'You look very nice,' says Philip and his pale eyes rake her from head to toe. 'Blue becomes you, ma'am,' he adds with a small smile that drives the colour into her cheeks. She feels Porchey stiffen beside her.

'Thank you,' she says nervously. 'Honestly, I'd rather be in jodhpurs and a jumper.'

Philip's brows rise in amusement as she clears her throat. 'I don't think you've met Henry, Lord Porchester? Everybody calls him Porchey. Porchey, this is Philip.'

When the two men shake hands, they put Elizabeth in mind of two dogs circling each other, bristles up.

'In the Guards?' Philip asks, nodding at Porchey's uniform.

'Yes.'

'Seen any action yet?'

There is a touch of gritted teeth in Porchey's reply. 'Not yet, no. I'm with a training battalion of the Grenadiers. My first stint is here, guarding the sovereign.'

'And the sovereign's daughter,' says Philip, looking from one to the other.

'Porchey's a terrific horseman,' Elizabeth puts in quickly in an attempt to defuse the antagonism.

'Is he?'

'Do you ride?' Porchey asks Philip.

'No,' he says. 'I'm more of a speed man. I like fast cars and fast boats.'

'I like speed too,' says Porchey, 'but I like fast horses.'

'So do I,' Elizabeth says quickly. 'I remember my grandfather taking me to his stud at Sandringham and being allowed to pat Limelight, who was one of his favourites. And it was only last year that I went with Papa to the Beckhampton stables and said hello to Big Game. I promise you, I didn't wash my hand for the rest of the day.'

'What about you?' Porchey looks at Philip with a trace of hostility. 'You're a long way from the sea for a naval man, aren't you?'

'I'm on shore leave. I've been on convoy duty, escorting merchant ships from Rosyth and Sheerness.'

'Isn't that route the one they call E-boat Alley?' she asks.

Philip's brows rise in surprise. 'You're well-informed.'

For a girl, or for a seventeen-year-old? Elizabeth is both those things, but she is more, too.

'I feel I must be.' She doesn't want to tell him how carefully she has followed his movements with every letter. She has a map of the world with pins marking his route. It has felt like the only way she can connect with him.

Two years ago, when Philip came for tea at Windsor, she and Margaret had been enthralled by his devil-may-care attitude and the entertaining way he talked about his experiences. Afterwards, she shyly offered to write to him, and of course was thrilled when he said he would be delighted to get a letter from her. But then, what else could he say? He had even replied occasionally. It was kind of him to find the time to write at all, Elizabeth always told herself as she read and reread his letters in vain for any indication he thought of her as anything other than a remote member of his extended family.

'I try to keep up with what is happening in the war everywhere,' she adds, wincing inside at how pompous she sounds.

It is true, though. All round the world, people are fighting in her father's name, and one day they will fight in hers. The least she owes them is to know what is going on.

It is almost a relief when her mother, arriving late as usual, beckons Porchey over. He is a favourite with the Queen. Elizabeth is not supposed to know, but her mother has a 'first eleven' list of potential husbands in mind for her, and Porchey is on it. It's no secret that she wants Elizabeth to marry an aristocrat from a background similar to her own.

Elizabeth is very fond of Porchey but she can't imagine marrying him. He's a friend. He would be safe. He would be kind. Those are good qualities to have in a husband, she can see that, but marrying Porchey would mean that everything in her life would carry on exactly as it has always done. Elizabeth is ready for a change.

She doesn't want safe, but she's not sure she is brave enough for danger either.

Philip isn't safe.

He's not doing anything threatening. He's just standing there with a glass of whisky in his hand but still she feels as if she is teetering on the edge of some precipice, half fearful, half tempted to step out into the unknown.

It's not like her to be fanciful, but something about Philip leaves her feeling spooked, edgy as a young colt, beneath that icy blue gaze.

And more alive than she has ever felt before.

'Have you known Porchey a long time?' he asks and she could almost swear that he is jealous.

'Since we were children. We both love riding, and racing. We can talk about bloodstock lines for hours. We'd both rather be in the stables than at a party.'

'Maybe the parties you've been to haven't been enough fun.'

Elizabeth's eyes slide from his. 'Maybe.'

'I was glad of your letters,' Philip says abruptly.

'Oh ... good. I'm afraid they must have been very boring.'

'Not at all.'

He's being polite, Elizabeth thinks and when she risks a glance at his face again, she is sure of it. His expression is carefully neutral. What else can he say, after all? How could he possibly have been interested in anything she had to say?

'We don't have a very exciting life here so there's not

much to talk about,' she says to show him that she understands. 'Lessons. Riding. Walking the dogs. Sometimes we invite the officers to lunch, and Papa and Mummy come back at weekends, which is nice but ... well, it's very tame compared to what you've been doing.'

Chapter 6

Tame? It sounds unbelievably tedious to Philip. Her letters have indeed been very bland, but for the first time he thinks about what life must be like for her, trapped in the castle for the duration of the war, surrounded by over-protective servants determined to keep her safe and stop her from having any fun at all. Entertaining officers for lunch seems to be the social highlight. If they are all as stuffy as the young Lord Porchester, it must be deadly, Philip thinks.

He hasn't taken to Porchey. There was something damned proprietorial about the way the younger man had been standing next to Elizabeth. Philip doesn't care for the easy way she and Porchey were talking when he came in. The first thing he saw was her unshadowed smile and it gave him, not a shock exactly ... Philip struggles to explain it to himself. It had been the tiniest of checks, an unexpected jump in his breath, that was all.

Her smile dropped when she saw him. He didn't like that either.

He wants Elizabeth to smile at him the way she smiles at Porchey.

It occurs to Philip that he may have to work a little harder than he thought. 'I was very glad to hear from you, whatever you wrote about,' he says. 'And your parcels were always welcome.'

'I hoped it would be nice for you to have a word from home,' Elizabeth says.

Home. That word always settles like a stone in the pit of Philip's stomach. Everyone uses it so easily. *Home*. It has so many connotations of comfort and security, of familiarity and belonging. Somewhere you can be yourself, where you do not have to sing for your supper or watch what you say. At least, that is how Philip imagines a home. He hasn't had one since he was a small boy in Paris.

Not that he will tell Elizabeth that. He wants her to think of him as strong and steadfast, not as a little boy longing for somewhere to belong.

'It was indeed,' he says instead, and she flushes a little with pleasure.

'I'm glad. It's good to feel that *something* I can do makes a difference. I feel so frustrated sometimes that I'm not allowed to do more for the war effort. I've asked Papa if I can volunteer for the ATS, but he thinks it's safer for me to stay here, where all I can do is knit for the Wool Fund.' She makes a face. 'And I hate knitting! I do try, but I am very bad at it.'

Philip laughs. 'All I can say is that the comforts we get – the socks and scarves and things – are all very welcome.'

'Still, I wish I could do more. Other girls my age are out there, doing their bit.'

Philip thinks of the ruined streets, the houses where wallpaper flutters sadly from exposed walls. Of the grime and the grind of daily life and the looters lurking in the shadows. Of groping through the dark or tensing at the stutter of sirens breaking into their inhuman wail. Listening to the desperate fire of the anti-aircraft guns as the searchlights rake across the night sky. Worse, hearing the fiendish whistle of bombs falling and the eerie second of silence before the air explodes.

Once, he and his cousin David were weaving their way carelessly back from a nightclub when they came across a house that had suffered a direct hit only minutes before. They had gone to help but they had been drinking and had probably got in the way. Philip doesn't remember much about it, only the sight of a disembodied hand lying as if discarded in the smoking rubble. One finger pointed right at him as if accusing him, though of what Philip couldn't tell. For a moment he can almost smell the stink of smoke and terror.

He is not stumbling around a bombsite now, Philip reminds himself. He blinks himself back to the present – Windsor Castle, a drink in his hand, a princess to court – to find Elizabeth looking at him. Her eyes are very clear, very blue. They seem to see far more than they should.

He musters a smile. 'Don't wish to be out there. It isn't safe.'

'*You're* out there.'

'I'm not as precious as you.'

Elizabeth sighs and pushes a wisp of hair away from her face. 'I just wish I could *do* something.'

'You are doing something,' Philip surprises himself by saying. 'You're representing hope for the future. We all need you more than you know.'

'Thank you,' she says softly after a moment. 'That makes me feel less useless.'

'Besides, it's not as if you're completely out of danger here, are you? I was given my instructions on how to find the bomb shelter. Although I doubt I'd be able to find it again – it was hard enough finding my bedroom,' he goes on, coaxing a smile out of her at last.

'It's not an easy place to find your way around, is it? Especially not in the blackout. In the early years of the war we used to practise what would happen if there was an invasion and we had to escape,' she tells him. 'We had to run down to the armoured cars in the darkness. There's only enough room for Margaret and me and Crawfie and some luggage. They told us we'd only be allowed to take one corgi.'

'It must have been a dilemma wondering which dog to take.' Philip tries to lighten the conversation, and Elizabeth smiles back at him.

'Well, it was!'

He feels like punching the air. Her smiles are rare, but worth waiting for.

By unspoken consent, they turn the conversation away from the war.

'Where *are* the dogs, anyway?' Philip asks. 'You talk about them so much in your letters, I was expecting to have to fight my way through them to get at you.'

Get at you. That wasn't the right way to talk to Princess Elizabeth, Philip berates himself mentally. Uncle Dickie would have his hide if he could hear him!

Subtlety, my dear boy, subtlety. Philip can practically hear Mountbatten's voice.

Fortunately, Elizabeth seems to realise he is teasing, though the faint colour that tinges her cheeks suggests she might have been a little taken aback at his forthright reference to why he was there.

'They're cattle dogs,' she says, shifting her stole up onto one shoulder. It promptly slithers down her other arm. 'They like to herd people up and nip at ankles, and they can be a bit naughty. Consider yourself fortunate that they're shut away tonight.'

'Lucky for me,' Philip murmurs, but he is distracted by the slippery stole that is dragging his attention to her bare arms. He wonders what it would be like to draw the stole up into place for her. Her skin would be warm, the fur would be soft. His fingers twitch with the urge to touch and his mouth dries so abruptly that he takes a slug of his whisky.

It is unexpectedly intriguing, the way she swings between shyness and sensible conversation, the way she turns aside compliments and talks of dogs and knitting, apparently unaware of the lures at her disposal: the creamy skin, the enticing figure, the curve of her mouth.

'I'm glad you're coming back for Christmas,' she says abruptly and Philip smiles.

'So am I.'

Chapter 7

They eat in the State Dining Room. With the velvet curtains drawn against the winter night, it could almost be as it was before the war, Elizabeth thinks. The log fire may be meagre in the magnificent fireplace and the elaborate gilding on the walls and ceiling dulled, but the light is so dim one can hardly tell. The great mirrors on either side of the fireplace are warm with the wavering candlelight; the silver gilt gleams, while the mahogany table is polished to such a high shine that one can see the immaculately set crystal glasses reflected in it.

The meal itself is hardly a match for the setting, but her parents pride themselves on being rationed like everyone else, and at least they have access to game from the royal estates. Some pheasants have been sent down from Sandringham and are served roasted with vegetables grown in the castle gardens. Like everyone else in the country, the cook does his best with what he can get.

For Elizabeth, it is a change from the usual nursery

suppers. She is content to sit and let the conversation flow around her. She wants to think about Philip. What was it he had said about the dogs? *I was expecting to fight my way through them to get at you.* She still doesn't know quite what to think of that. A part of her is affronted: Philip sounded as if he assumed he could just walk into a room and claim her like a parcel. Elizabeth is not someone who can be 'got at'. She expects to be treated with the deference due to her as heir to the throne.

Another part of her, she reluctantly admits to herself, felt an unwilling thrill at his arrogance.

Philip isn't like the other men. Listen to him now, telling Papa about his ship being dive-bombed somewhere off Sicily.

'There were three of the blighters coming for *Wallace*,' he is saying, and she is not the only one listening. His expression is alert, amused, his gestures expansive. Compared to the deferential courtiers whose every movement is discreet, he is overwhelming, but her father doesn't seem to mind.

'We all dived for cover at first,' Philip goes on, 'but the first Stuka missed us completely. We thought that was a lucky escape and we kept our heads down as the second one came in low.' His hand swoops over his plate in demonstration. His smile glimmers. 'But he missed, too, and then blow me down if the third pilot didn't strike out as well! They were at it for about half an hour and they didn't get a single hit!'

The King is laughing. He likes Philip, Elizabeth notes with relief.

'We ended up standing on the deck jeering at them,' says Philip. 'Eventually they gave up or ran out of ammunition. I don't think they can have been the Luftwaffe's finest. I can only think they must have been flying with shocking hangovers.'

'No one was hurt?' Elizabeth asks and Philip turns to her.

'Not a scratch on any of us. I can't say the same about the pilots' feelings! They must have had a boll— A dressing down,' he amends, 'when they got back to base.'

'You didn't have such an easy time of it later, I hear,' her father says.

Philip picks up his knife and fork. 'No, there were some hairy moments.'

'Dickie was telling me some story about a raft,' the King prompts.

'Oh, that … Just a lucky ruse.'

Elizabeth can see he is trying to shrug off any attempt to cast himself in a heroic light. 'What happened?' she asks.

Philip hesitates, but at her father's urging he tells the story. '*Wallace* was covering the Canadian landings on Sicily,' he begins. 'As you can imagine, the Germans weren't very happy with that, and their Stukas were on us the whole time, so we were at action stations pretty continuously.'

'That particular night, it was still and very bright. A beautiful night at any other time, but the worst possible conditions for us then. The moon lit up our wake and turned it into one long, shimmering trail. We might as well have had a flaming sign pointing towards us for a pilot to follow. A German bomber found us, of course – he could hardly miss us! – and we took a hit to the side of the ship. He took off then, but we knew it was only a matter of time before he came back with reinforcements. At that point we'd be sitting ducks.

'There was no way of knowing where they would come from. In the dark, they could see us on the water, but we couldn't see them. It's like being blindfolded and knowing someone is coming to get you.'

Elizabeth lays down her knife and fork. She is picturing the men silent on the ship, their shoulders hunched in anticipation of the next attack, straining their eyes at the night sky, listening for the sound of aircraft while the sea slaps unperturbed against the hull.

Conversation around the rest of the table has fallen silent and they are all listening to Philip's story. 'What did you do?' the Queen asks.

'We got the men to knock up a wooden raft,' Philip goes on. 'We knew we didn't have long. It took them a matter of minutes until we could haul it over the side and set fire to it. Then we hightailed it out of there, full steam for a good five minutes before we felt safe enough to cut the engines.'

'So that the wake subsided?' The King nods. He was a naval officer in his time, too.

'Yes, sir. Or we might as well have taken out a sign saying "Look, we're over here".' Philip takes a sip of wine. 'We lay there in the darkness. I remember the ship rocking gently, and the silence. Nobody said a word. We were all waiting for the Germans to come back. I don't know how we long waited,' he says. 'It felt like hours and hours but it can't have been. And then we heard the aircraft.'

He pauses and Elizabeth realises she is holding her breath.

'I don't mind telling you I was terrified to breathe in case the pilot noticed us,' he says with a ghost of a grin, almost as if he had read her mind. 'Not that it would have made any difference! The next thing we knew a bomb was screaming down ... but it wasn't anywhere near us, thank God. The pilot must have seen the flaming debris and thought he had done for us the first time, so he was finishing off all that was left of *Wallace*.'

'Exactly what you wanted him to think, in fact,' Elizabeth says.

Philip sends her a glimmering smile. 'Quite. We were lucky he fell for it. We lived to fight another day.'

'T-thanks to you,' says the King, whose stammer still surfaces occasionally even when he is relaxed.

Philip holds up a self-deprecating hand. 'You don't want to listen to Uncle Dickie, sir. You know yourself how it works on a ship. It's never just one man's idea, especially not under circumstances like that. You don't have time to think, just to act.'

'Well, we're very grateful to you for doing both. What's next for you, Philip?'

'I'm heading up to Newcastle, of all places, I believe. They're commissioning a new destroyer, *Whelp*, and I'm to oversee the finishing touches before she's ready for active service. After that, I hope I'll see some action again.'

Chapter 8

Philip's footsteps echo along the stone corridors as he gropes his way back to his room later that night. Kicking off his shoes, he yawns hugely and wrenches at his collar so he can fall backwards onto the bed. Whatever other changes the war has foisted on Windsor Castle, it hasn't affected the excellent wine cellar.

The evening has gone off quite well, he decides, pleased. The King seems disposed to like him, although he may have to put in a bit more effort with the Queen, just as Uncle Dickie warned.

More importantly, he has made some progress with Elizabeth. He didn't miss the admiring way she looked at him when he was talking about that nerve-wracking night on *Wallace*. Uncle Dickie will be pleased with him.

Best not to push it, Philip muses. He will go back to London tomorrow. There are still a few days to go until Christmas and he doesn't fancy spending them on his best behaviour at Windsor. He and his cousin, David Milford Haven, are invited for Christmas itself, so they can come back together on Christmas Eve. In the meantime, there will be parties and maybe a chance to catch up with Osla, although he senses a certain cooling there.

He will need to go carefully with Elizabeth. Isolated at Windsor, she is unlikely to pick up on any gossip, but still it behoves him to be discreet, Philip realises. He has seen how quickly she withdraws, like a snail shrinking into its shell at the slightest brush of familiarity, but he is sure he can coax her out, given time.

Philip thinks about the fur slipping down her arm, the blood running warm beneath her skin. How tempting it had been to reach out and adjust the stole for her, to take the opportunity to trail his fingers over her shoulder.

Just as well he hadn't tried it, he reflects wryly. She might be disposed to admire him, but she would need to feel a lot more than that before he would be allowed any closer.

Courting Elizabeth may turn out to be harder task than Philip thought, but then, he has always liked a challenge.

'It's bloody freezing,' Philip tells David, raising his voice above the sound of the engine. They're in his beloved MG, heading back to Windsor Castle. It's Christmas Eve and a hard frost has left the countryside edged in glittering white. Philip settles his sunglasses one-handed on his nose. The sky is a thin, washed blue, the light low and glaring.

'Everywhere's bloody freezing at the moment,' David grumbles. His cousin likes his comforts.

'But Windsor Castle takes cold to a whole new level.

It's probably freezing in a heatwave. Something to do with all that stone.'

In spite of his complaints about the cold, Philip is in a cheerful mood. The last few days have been fun: plenty of socialising, plenty of drinking and solitude when he needs it at Chester Street, where he sleeps happily on a camp bed in the dining room and Mrs Cable, the rough-tongued cook, spoils him.

The Mountbattens' home is a haven, and so much more comfortable than staying in Kensington Palace with his cousin and their grandmother, the formidable Dowager Duchess of Milford Haven, who is grand enough not to care what anyone else thinks but has plenty to say about what she thinks of her grandsons. She has ears like a bat, David claims, and no matter how quietly they try to tiptoe past her apartment, she always calls them in with her harsh smoker's voice to berate them for their lateness or lack of consideration while the ash trembles on the end of her inevitable cigarette only to fall onto her skirts and be brushed impatiently away.

'I don't care how cold it is, anywhere would be better than staying with Grandmama,' says David, following his own train of thought. 'I tried to sneak Robyn in the other night. I thought there was no way Grandmama would be awake, but I swear she took up the carpets deliberately to listen out for that creaking floorboard.'

'You should know where it is by now.'

'I ended up shoving poor old Robyn into the broom

cupboard.' David sighs. 'I wish we could get Lynden Manor back. You wouldn't catch Mama making a fuss about bringing a girl home.'

Philip gives a crack of laughter. David's mother, Nada Milford Haven, is notorious for her affairs with men and women. She is exotically beautiful and glamorous and generous, one of the most interesting and intriguing people Philip knows. It was Nada and her husband, his uncle George, who first gave him a home when he was a small boy in need of one and Philip adores her.

Lynden Manor has been requisitioned like so many other stately homes for the duration of the war, but at least David will be able to claim it again when the war is over. Philip will have nowhere to go home to.

'Then you should enjoy Windsor Castle. The wine is good too.'

'And what about the company?' David swivels in the passenger seat to study Philip's profile. 'What's she like?'

'Who?' As if he doesn't know who David means.

'Elizabeth. She was just a little girl the last time I saw her. All tweedy skirts and sensible shoes with socks. Has she grown up?'

Philip changes down a gear as they come up to a sharp bend. 'She has,' he confirms with a sidelong grin.

'And?'

'And ... she's nice.'

'*Nice?*' David scoffs. 'I didn't think you liked nice girls.'

'I like Elizabeth. I do,' he insists when his cousin rolls

his eyes. 'She's not like other girls. She's serious. She holds herself back. I don't think she lets many people close.'

'Should be a good match for you then,' says David with a wry look.

'Quite.' A long, straight stretch of road comes up and Philip puts his food down, enjoying the feel of the little car beneath his hands. The hedgerows flicker past and the road is striped by the low winter sun. 'She's still very young, though.'

'Is she a looker? It's hard to tell in photographs.'

'She is when she smiles. She's got lovely skin. A nice figure. Very blue eyes.'

'Sounds promising. I might have a crack at her myself. Cut you out.'

'Ha! You wouldn't stand a chance, David,' says Philip, grinning.

'Why not, pray? I have plenty of charm and address when I choose to use it.' Which was, of course, all too true.

'Forget it. You're not a prince.'

'I would be if George V hadn't made my grandfather renounce his royal title.' David settles back into his seat, unfazed by the speed at which they were travelling. 'What a fuss that must have caused, the transformation of the princes of Battenberg into mere Mountbattens. No wonder Grandmama never got over it. Mind you, I'm damned glad not to be saddled with a Jerry name now we're at war again.'

'You don't do too badly as Marquess of Milford Haven,' Philip pointed out and David gave a smug smile.

'I suppose not.'

'Anyway, you're not Elizabeth's type.'

'And you are?'

'I could be.'

David stares at him. 'Good God, Philip, you're not *serious* are you? I thought that was just one of Dickie's barmy ideas to restore the Mountbatten fortunes.'

'Well, as he's always pointing out, I don't have a lot of options. I'm a prince without a country. I've barely been to Greece even if the monarchy were welcome there, which it isn't. Uncle George is still in exile and likely to remain there. I feel British, but I'm not, so I can't stay in the Navy. All I've got is a title and a lieutenant's salary for the duration of the war. You've got to admit that marrying the greatest heiress in the world would solve some of these problems.'

'And create a whole lot more,' says David. 'I can't imagine you settling down, especially not as a Prince Consort. You're too restless. And you're an awkward bugger. You'll rub everyone up the wrong way!'

David knows him well, it has to be said, but Philip only laughs as he swings the car onto the Long Walk. The trees in Windsor Great Park stand stark and rigid in the frosty air, and the avenue undulates, reminding him of the sea with the castle perched on the highest wave.

Swathes of the park have been dug up for vegetable

growing but it is still an imposing entrance. Philip, though, has spent his life visiting magnificent palaces and castles across Europe and he barely notices the soldiers on guard as the little car buzzes through the George IV Gate. The tyres kick up a spurt of gravel as Philip stops the car in the Upper Ward and pulls on the handbrake.

'Don't worry, David. I'm not going to commit myself yet, but there's no harm in keeping my options open, is there?'

Chapter 9

There are only nine of them for Christmas lunch. They are served venison and a Christmas pudding bulked out with breadcrumbs which is flaming as a footman carries it into the dining room to oohs and aahs all round. The pudding is decorated with a sprig of frosted holly that sparkles in the candlelight.

'Apparently it's done by dipping the holly in Epsom salts,' the Queen tells them. 'Isn't it clever?'

Elizabeth can't help feeling guilty. She has been reading about the lengths ordinary housewives are going to in order to make Christmas lunch special. Few families will have access to venison, she knows. The lucky ones who live in the country may celebrate with a rabbit or even a chicken, but others will be making do with mock goose, which is apparently some kind of potato casserole, and a Christmas pudding based on grated potato and carrot.

Their lunch is a feast in comparison.

The food makes a nice change from nursery suppers

but Elizabeth has unaccountably lost her appetite. Something in her jumped when she saw Philip arrive with his cousin and there has been a jittery feeling in the pit of her stomach ever since.

David is darkly handsome and glossily self-assured but Elizabeth prefers Philip's rougher-edged charm. He made a beeline for her when he came into the drawing room and his assumption that they are friends has sent warmth simmering along her veins.

Both men are on terrific form and between them keep everyone laughing. That evening Margaret insists on playing charades. She has a flair for acting and loves to stand up and show off, while Elizabeth prefers to be the one guessing, but Philip makes sure that they are in the same team, and under his encouragement she can feel herself blossoming. Once or twice she sees the Queen watching him with an indecipherable expression.

Philip himself is funny as a fit when it is his turn to act out an outraged dowager being caught in the bathroom and Elizabeth laughs until she is weak. Wiping her eyes, she lifts her head to find her mother looking at her closely but the moment Elizabeth meets her gaze, the Queen puts on a bright smile and leads the applause.

'Bravo!'

Afterwards, they turn out the lights, extinguish the candles and sit around the fire to tell each other ghost stories. Elizabeth is aware that Philip is manoeuvring to sit next to her in the shadows. Having got himself into position, he moves his chair closer until his knee brushes hers.

'You can hold my hand if you get scared,' he says, his smile glimmering in the firelight.

'I'm not easily frightened,' Elizabeth says, but she doesn't move her chair away. She can feel his knee pressing against hers. Her insides are tangling themselves into a trembling knot and she is preternaturally aware of her own body. It is as if she has never felt the slow slam of her heart before, never been aware of the silkiness of her stockings or the way her satin dress shifts over her skin. The fire has a crisper spit and crackle than she has realised before, while the wind pokes and rattles at the windows behind the blackout curtain.

Luckily the stories are not very scary. When it is David's turn, Philip keeps interjecting comments to make everyone laugh until Margaret gets cross. 'You're spoiling it, Philip!' she complains. 'Ghost stories are supposed to be frightening and these are just *not!*'

Boxing Day is a disappointingly wet, grey day but Philip agrees with alacrity to Elizabeth's suggestion of a walk that morning. She has been thinking, and there is something she wants to say to him, although she is not entirely sure how she will find the words.

Her parents are resting, Margaret wants to play the piano, and David excuses himself, whether by prior arrangement with Philip or not, Elizabeth is never sure.

'I'm not much of a walker,' he says.

'David's like a cat,' Philip scoffs. 'He can't bear getting his feet wet.'

Elizabeth looks out of the window. 'It doesn't look very nice,' she says dubiously, dragging on an old coat and some rubber boots. 'But the dogs could do with a proper walk.'

And the conversation she wants to have will be easier outside.

'Let's go,' says Philip. 'If I get wet, I get wet.'

Outside, a raw wind snatches at the scarf she has tied over her hair and throws petulant handfuls of icy rain into their faces. They walk with their heads down to avoid the worst of it but Elizabeth is very aware of Philip beside her, matching his long stride to her shorter steps, while the dogs bustle around them, snuffling through the longer grass or circling each other skittishly.

It's hard to talk at first but they pause at last in the shelter of an oak standing doughtily atop a rise and look back at the castle through the murky light. It looms massive and austere in the distance, the Round Tower skimmed by the lowering clouds.

'There's something reassuring about that building,' Philip comments after a moment. 'It's seen so many wars, so many changes, and it's still there.'

Elizabeth nods, her eyes on the grey walls. 'Even though it feels now as if this war will never end, one day it *will* be over and it will be part of history, just something children learn at school. It's good to remember that.'

'Except that means remembering one day *we'll* just be notes in a history book too,' says Philip with a grimace.

'Well, it's true.'

'You'll have a rather bigger note than me.'

There is an edge of something Elizabeth can't quite identify in his voice. She glances at him and then away. That, too, is true. There is no point in denying it. Does it bother him that her inheritance is so much greater than his could ever be?

'Do you ever wonder what it's like not to be royal?' he asks abruptly.

'Sometimes.' Elizabeth pulls the collar of her old coat closer against the chill as they start walking again. 'When Uncle David abdicated, we moved to Buckingham Palace. We were horrified at first. We loved our cosy house in Piccadilly. That felt like an ordinary way to live, although I don't suppose it is. The palace isn't the most comfortable of places but it has a lovely garden with a hillock in it. Margaret and I used to climb it so we could look over the wall at the people walking past. We liked watching the children especially and wondering where they were going, where they lived, what they would have for their supper.'

'Did you envy them?'

'Not really. We were just curious. It's hard to imagine what life is like for other people, isn't it? Probably those children were walking past and wondering what it was like to live in a palace, but for us it was just the way things were. How they are.'

'You're lucky,' Philip says, and she smiles faintly.

'It doesn't always feel that way. I know how privileged I am, but it does come at a price. I don't have a choice about the life I get to lead.'

He looks down at her. 'What would you choose if you could?'

'Oh ... nothing exciting. Just to live in the country with dogs and horses.' She sighs a little. 'I suppose you think that's very dull,' she adds, flushing a little.

A smile twitches the corner of his mouth. 'Well, it's not what I would choose, I have to admit. But if it's what you want ...'

'I might want it but I'm not going to get it,' Elizabeth says. 'I might have been able to if Uncle David had done his duty, but he chose to put his personal feelings above that. Papa has had to pay the price for that decision, and I will too. Of course there are worse fates, but no, I don't always feel lucky.'

Philip has his hands jammed into the pockets of his tweed jacket. 'Actually, I was thinking about your family,' he says. 'About how close you are. Your parents, your sister. It's been very nice for me to see that. I do envy you that.'

'Yes, I am lucky in my family,' she acknowledges, her face softening as she thinks of her beloved father, her bright, charming mother, and Margaret, so quick and so talented, so funny and spirited. Too spirited, sometimes. 'Of course, Margaret and I have our moments, but I suppose all sisters have those.'

One of the dogs has dropped behind as it determinedly investigates some scent. Elizabeth turns and whistles for it, and after a moment, the dog grudgingly leaves the smell and trots towards them.

'Jane,' Elizabeth says fondly. 'She's getting on now and she likes to do what she wants. She's the matriarch,' she explains, glancing around at the corgis. 'That's her daughter and granddaughter ... and over there is her great-granddaughter.'

Why is she talking about dogs? Philip can't possibly be interested. She is just putting off the moment.

The water is dripping from the peak of his cap and the shoulders of his jacket are spangled with rain. She has been enjoying the walk but he must be soaked, she realises with a guilty look. 'Shall we turn back?' she asks.

Chapter 10

Philip is glad to agree. There is rain trickling down beneath his collar and his hands are frozen. He has never thought that he would remember with nostalgia those sweltering days aboard *Valiant* after the Chinese stokers jumped ship in Puerto Rico. Stripped to their shorts, stinking and sweating, he and his fellow midshipmen had to shovel coal into the ship's furnaces all the way to Virginia and he had dreamt of a cold, wet winter day.

No longer.

'You have sisters, don't you?' Elizabeth asks after a moment. 'Are you close to them?'

She doesn't ask about his parents. She must know that they have lived separate lives for many years.

'I wouldn't say close. I'm the baby of the family and my sisters are all much older than I am. They're very ... boisterous.'

In his memory, his ears ring with the noise his sisters create when they are all together. They're all restless movement, jumping up and down, and swirling their skirts, a mass of swooping scented kisses and talking over each other and shrieks of laughter. Their conversation is a vibrant mixture of English, French, and German as forgetting a word in one language they would switch to another and then carry on in that until they went off at a tangent and into a new language that for some reason seemed better suited to it.

'I'm very fond of all of them,' he says. 'Especially Cecile. She was killed in an air crash in 1937.'

'What a tragedy,' Elizabeth says.

'Don, her husband, and my two nephews were with her. They were coming over here to a wedding. Cecile was heavily pregnant.' A muscle jerks in Philip's cheek. 'She gave birth on the flight, perhaps even during the crash. The baby died with her. It never had a chance to live.'

'I'm sorry.' Elizabeth's voice is so quiet that Philip barely hears her. He is remembering the sound of the gun carriages laden with coffins trundling over the cobbled streets of Darmstadt. He was sixteen. He flew to Germany from Gordonstoun and followed the coffins with his brothers-in-law in their Nazi uniforms, Uncle Dickie a row behind. Philip's memories are blurred but he remembers his uncle's hand on his shoulder during the funeral. He remembers the heavy tread of feet, the silent crowds watching. The sullen sky spitting sleety pellets of ice. The occasional stiff-armed salute and murmurs of 'Heil Hitler'.

The yawning disbelief and horror: that could not be Cecile with her dancing eyes and burble of laughter shut up in that box.

He swallows down the memories. What is the point of wallowing in them? What's done is done.

'Margarita, Dolla – that's Theodora – and Sophie – we call her Tiny – are still in Germany.' Philip's voice is even. All three were married to senior German officers. 'For obvious reasons, I haven't seen them for a while.'

'That must be difficult for you.'

Philip isn't going to admit to finding anything difficult. Isn't that what Gordonstoun and the war has taught him? You get on with what you have to do. You don't wring your hands and complain about your lot.

'The war is difficult for everyone,' he says almost curtly. 'We are not the only family divided by war.'

Elizabeth glances at him. 'I know,' she says coolly. 'My grandfather and Kaiser Wilhelm were cousins.'

The Great War had taught the British royal family to be chary of their German relations. They had changed their name to Windsor and insisted that the Battenbergs, descended from Queen Victoria and British to the back teeth, forfeit their princely title.

'Your sisters' German husbands will be your biggest handicap,' Uncle Dickie warned him. 'Distance yourself from them as far as possible.'

Why should he distance himself even further from his own sisters? God knows he has little enough family life to look back on, Philip thinks bitterly. His father is in Monte Carlo, his mother in Athens.

'I see now why you think I am lucky,' says Elizabeth.

The wind is slapping the ends of her scarf against her chin and she wrestles with the slippery material as she attempts to retie it. 'And I am. I have a family and a home.'

'I haven't had a home since I was nine,' Philip is appalled to hear himself say, and he scowls, hunching his shoulders against the cold. He can feel her clear eyes on his profile and cringes inwardly, sure she has heard the bitterness edging his voice.

'Is that when you were sent to school?'

'Yes,' he says stiffly, still ashamed of what he let slip. He is supposed to be charming Elizabeth, not telling her sob stories of his childhood. 'Until then, we were living in Paris but it was a somewhat hand-to-mouth existence. Pretty ramshackle, in fact.'

That was better. Make light of the whole business. Because he had been happy at Saint-Cloud. Why wouldn't he be? He'd been just a boy, oblivious to any undercurrents. His pretty mother's favourite, an adored autumn child. Indulged by his genial father and fussed over by his older sisters even as they accused him of being spoilt. Nanny Roose had been the only sensible figure in the household.

'Then ... my mother became ill,' he goes on. He doesn't want to brush his mother under the carpet. Elizabeth must surely be aware of the times Princess Alice spent in sanatoriums, in any case. Still, he has the sense of stepping onto quaking ground.

His adoring mother, who had grown vaguer and more

withdrawn, her eccentricities losing their charm as Philip was abandoned for spirituality and she declared herself a saint and a bride of Christ. There had been that miserable Christmas at Saint-Cloud when Alice took herself off to a hotel in Grasse, leaving his father, his sisters, and Philip to fend for themselves.

But it was fine, Philip reminds himself hastily. He was an energetic child, easily distracted. He had a bicycle he had saved up to buy for himself and there was plenty of fun to be had at school and mischief to be got into with his best friends the Koo brothers. He still winces at memories of steeplechases organised at the Chinese embassy where they lived, shouting and tussling between the precious china artefacts. No wonder Madame Koo had been glad to see the back of him when he went home!

'Everything happened about the same time,' he tells Elizabeth carefully. 'My mother was unwell, my father went to live in the South of France, and my sisters all married. So that was the end of family life, I suppose. I just had to get on with it. You do. One does.'

One thing about Elizabeth, he realises, is that she is not going to gush or probe or be excessively sympathetic. Her restraint is obscurely restful, and in a perverse way only makes him want to tell her more about his unsettled childhood.

'My parents wanted me to have a British education so I was sent to Cheam and my Mountbatten uncles stood as guardians while I was over here. Uncle Georgie – David's father – was the one who came to sports days and prizegivings. He and Nada had a pretty colourful and tempestuous life together,' he says, thinking wryly how that must be the understatement of the year. A Russian princess, Nada shrugged off scandal and her unconventional outlook is just one of the reasons Philip loves her.

'They were wonderful to me,' is all he tells Elizabeth, whose knowledge of sex is, he guesses, limited, to say the least. 'I spent most of my half-terms with them, which is why David and I are so close.'

'You still saw your family, though?'

'Oh, yes. I've got relatives all over Europe, so we'd have big family meet ups with my sisters and my father, and various uncles and aunts and cousins. I never knew where I'd be spending the holidays. Someone would write and tell me to get myself to Wolfsgarten or Panker or Bucharest or wherever and I'd pack my trunk and catch a train.'

'You must have been a very self-reliant child,' Elizabeth comments.

He shrugs. 'I thought it was normal, just like your childhood was normal for you. And those holidays were always fun, with everyone descending on a particular relative, and various cousins to play with. We had no shortage of places to stay and it's not as if there wasn't plenty of room. You know what those palaces and castles are like.'

'No, I don't.' The sleet has eased at last and Elizabeth knuckles the wet from her cheeks. 'I've never left the country. Balmoral is the furthest I've been.'

Philip is taken aback. He knew their experiences have been different, but not quite how different. 'Oh ... I suppose not,' he says. He might envy Elizabeth her family, but how stultifyingly decorous and boring her childhood must have been, shuttling between Windsor, Buckingham Palace, Balmoral, and Sandringham, always surrounded by deferential courtiers.

'So what *are* they like, these places?' she asks.

'Huge,' says Philip briefly. 'Most of them would make Buckingham Palace look cosy.'

'Really?' Elizabeth laughs in disbelief. 'We always used to joke that you need a bicycle to get around BP.'

'Wolfsgarten is the same. Some of the palaces are pretty dilapidated, too. I used to go and stay with my cousin Helen because Michael, her son, is more my age, and we had lots of good times there. He became King of Romania when he was five, though of course that didn't mean much to us then. He was just a playmate. They had a crumbling palace near Bucharest but when it was very hot in the summer we used to like going up to Peles Castle at Sinaia in the Carpathian Mountains. It's like something out of a fairy story, all turrets and towers and courtyards. Michael's grandmother told the most marvellous stories in her bedroom. I always called her Aunt Missie, and if we were naughty, we weren't allowed to go and say goodnight to her and hear a story. It was the worst punishment!'

He smiles at the memory and then breaks off, realising he has been running on. 'Sorry. There's nothing worse than someone rabbiting on about people and places you don't know.'

'I like hearing about your childhood,' Elizabeth says. 'It's so different from mine. Go on. Where else did you go?'

'Well, my sisters and I spent a few holidays near Le Touquet when I was younger with the Foufounis family. Like mine, they're Greek émigrés and I was great friends with their children, Ria, Ianni and Hélène. They had a terrifying Scottish nanny they called Aunty.' He smiles reminiscently. 'Ianni and I used to get into all kinds of trouble.'

His memories of Berck Plage are muddled now, he finds. Dusty tracks. Sand between his toes. The weight of Madame Foufounis's Persian rug on his shoulder when he and Ianni had the grand idea of pretending to be carpet salesmen like the Arabs on the beach. Poor Ria, up to her hips in plaster. The sinking feeling that followed the smash of a vase, knowing Aunty was rolling up her sleeves to deliver a sound spanking. Philip preferred his spankings from Nanny Roose, who was firm but fair.

'And then there was Panker, the Hesses's summer house on the Baltic Coast. There were always lots of us there too, a mass of children running around. We spent all day on the beach. I just remember miles of white sand and glittering water and a huge, windy sky and this marvellous light ...'

He trails off. Without warning, his throat has snapped shut, clogged with a hard, complicated knot of memories.

Chapter 11

Elizabeth glances at him. For a time, he had been relaxed talking about his childhood, but clearly some memory has proved too much. A muscle is working in his clenched jaw. He looks furious and she suspects that it is with himself for sharing so much with her.

She is glad that he has. She wants to know more about him. She needs to know more if she is going to suggest marriage.

The thought makes Elizabeth's heart thump once, painfully, against her ribs. She still isn't sure that she dares, but seeing him again, talking to him properly, has changed things for her. Before, she can admit that she was infatuated with the idea of Philip. He was young, handsome, a hero. How could she not have been?

But now, now she has a better sense of him. She likes his quickness and his humour, likes his impatience with protocol. He is brusque at times, and arrogant, but he has a presence that Elizabeth feels she herself still lacks.

It is her duty to marry and to have a family. She wants

that for herself, too, and why not Philip? He is a prince, after all, and he comes from a family used, like hers, to dynastic alliances. Mountbatten is keen on the idea, her parents less so, that is clear.

Elizabeth has the strong sense that if she wants him, she has to do something about it herself.

So she has decided to say something to Philip. She is desperately nervous about scaring him off altogether but she doesn't need to make a big production out of it, she has reassured herself. It is not as if he can't know that his uncle is pushing the idea of a marriage. Why else would he be here, after all?

But nothing has been said formally. Elizabeth is tired of being a dutiful girl, sitting at home in Windsor and waiting for something to happen. She wants to know what Philip thinks.

She is just going to mention the idea and see what he says.

Although ... that is easier said than done.

Elizabeth opens her mouth to say that she'd like to talk to him about something, but immediately changes her mind. She cannot spring a discussion like that on Philip without warning.

'You're lucky to have such happy memories,' she says instead, her voice trembling slightly with nerves. 'But then, I don't suppose it was all holidays and there must have been times when you would have liked a home of your own to go to.'

'Sometimes,' he admits with a grudging look. 'But the grass is always greener on the other side of the fence, isn't it? It's an alluring idea, but where would that home have been and what would have happened to it by now? And in any case, I'm a restless fellow. I'm like a dog that longs for a basket of its own but can't settle. There's a part of me that finds the idea of being tied to one place and one person utterly appalling.'

There's a tiny pause. For Elizabeth, it is a moment of complete clarity. Well, there is her question answered before she has asked it. Perhaps it was as well to wait.

'I see,' she says in what she hopes is an expressionless voice, but Philip stops and swears under his breath.

'I'm sorry,' he says, taking off his cap and dragging his hand through his hair. 'I've a tendency to speak without thinking sometimes. It's a bad habit of mine.'

'What would you have said if you *had* been thinking?'

'I don't know ... I hope I wouldn't have made the idea of commitment sound so ghastly, for a start.'

'Even if it is?'

'It isn't,' he insists. 'At least, not always. Of course I'd like to get married one day. It's just ... I'm not sure how good I would be at it. I haven't seen many examples of a successful marriage – your parents excepted.' He stares at Elizabeth. 'How do you do that?'

'Do what?'

'Say almost nothing and yet make me be more honest with you than I am with almost anyone else.'

'I'd like to think we can be honest with each other,' Elizabeth says, choosing her words with care. 'I know why you're here. I'm sure you had more exciting and enjoyable offers of where to spend Christmas.'

She holds up a hand as Philip opens his mouth to deny it. 'It's all right. We have a very quiet life here. It's how we like it. At least,' she amends with a wry smile, 'Mummy, Papa, and I do. Margaret would probably like more excitement.'

Calling the dogs, Elizabeth sets off once more. Now that they have started, she feels more composed and the conversation they need to have will likely be easier if they are walking. 'I know Uncle Dickie thinks a match between us would be good thing ... one day. You're a prince, I'm a princess. We would both expect to marry ... one day. Neither of us has a vast pool of potential partners to choose from.' She is rather proud of her steady voice. 'Things are different for us. We need to be pragmatic when it comes to marriage, so I perfectly understand why you'd want to come and ... look me over, as it were.'

'You make it sound as if I'm some horse trainer inspecting a prize filly!'

'It comes down to the same thing, doesn't it?' Elizabeth's cheeks are pink. 'Breeding, bloodlines, finding the right match.'

'You don't think it's about finding someone to love?'

The colour in her cheeks deepens at the thread of amusement in his voice.

'I think my options, frankly, are limited. Yours are much

wider. If you don't want to, you needn't marry at all. I, on the other hand, won't have a choice in the matter. But I do want to get married,' she adds honestly.

'One day?'

'Yes, one day.'

'If you can find the right prince.'

'Yes,' she agrees on a breath.

Philip is silent for a while, clearly thinking. Their footsteps make no sound on the wet grass but Elizabeth can hear the dogs trotting busily around them, a whirr of wings as one of them flushes a pheasant from cover. The slow, steady drip of damp from the trees.

'All right, I'll be honest,' he says eventually. 'I don't know what I want. Uncle Dickie does think I should try and sweep you off your feet, but you're not someone who can be swept away, are you?'

How little he knows about her, Elizabeth thinks. He has occupied her thoughts for two whole years. She is grateful for the stolid expression that makes her hard to read. Some things – many things, in fact – she prefers to keep to herself. She is only young, but she has her pride and she has no intention of letting Philip know how desperately she wants him.

Because what he says is only partly true. She can't be swept away by emotion, but only because she won't let herself. The strength of her own feelings frightens her at times, so she keeps them firmly locked down. She doesn't dare let them go, not when she has seen the effect her father's sudden outbursts of temper have on people around him. Not when she knows how her Uncle David was punished for giving in to his emotions.

'It's too hard to plan anything while we're still at war,' Philip goes on. 'I never know if a torpedo has got my name on it, and I want to *live*. If this damnable war has taught us anything, surely it's that we should make the most of our opportunities. There's so much I'd like to see and do, so much to be discovered; the thought of being tied down makes me itchy.'

Elizabeth keeps her hands in her pockets and her eyes down. They haven't all learnt the same thing from the war. It has taught *her* not about opportunity but the price of duty. The responsibility of leading a country at war has weighed heavily on her father. She has seen the hollow exhaustion in his eyes, the care carved into his face.

A lifetime of duty is not much to look forward to, but she has seen the cost of shirking duty too. Her Uncle David chose love over duty and was exiled not just from his country but from his family too. Elizabeth will not risk the same fate. She does not dare. Better by far to keep her feelings under tight control.

'But one day,' Philip says hesitantly, 'after the war ... if you're still looking for a prince ...'

'I could keep you in mind, perhaps?' she offers when he leaves the sentence dangling.

He looks at her seriously. 'I hope you will,' he says. 'I hope, if nothing else, we can be friends.'

Elizabeth's face relaxes into a smile. 'I hope so too.'

'Will you keep writing to me?'

'If you'd like me to.'

'I would. Real letters,' he says. 'Not polite ones. Let me know what you're thinking and feeling.'

'If you'll do the same.'

'I will,' says Philip. 'I'll be a better correspondent, I promise, and after the war ...'

'We'll see,' Elizabeth finishes for him, and he grins at her.

'Yes, let's see.'

Surreptitiously, Elizabeth lets a long breath leak out of her. In the end, the conversation has gone better than she has dared hope. Philip was never going to make a dramatic declaration of love. He is too honest for that, and no vows have been made, but they have made a proper connection. He has not ruled out a future together one day. And in the meantime, she has something to hope for and her pride is intact.

That evening is an enchanted one for Elizabeth. In contrast to the quiet Christmas gathering, the King and Queen have invited a number of guests for an informal party. Normally, her shyness makes such events an ordeal, but tonight Elizabeth is shining with happiness.

'You look very pretty, Lilibet,' her father says fondly, and Elizabeth realises with a start that for once she *feels* pretty. It is because Philip is there, because they are friends.

The King is not the only one who notices. 'You're the

belle of the ball tonight,' says Margaret, a little miffed as she is usually the one everyone looks at, the one who makes everyone smile. 'Is that a new dress?' she asks suspiciously.

'Of course not. Honestly, Margaret, where would I get a new dress?' Still, Elizabeth knows her eyes are sparkling, her cheeks becomingly flushed.

Even stern Tommy Lascelles unbends to compliment her on her looks, only to break off with a frown when he sees Philip and David moving furniture.

'Your Royal Highness,' he addresses Philip, tight-lipped. 'Is there a problem?'

Philip glances up at him. 'It's time the party got going. We're just rolling up the carpet so we can dance.'

'Have you asked the King?'

Philip actually rolls his eyes at Tommy. Elizabeth is both aghast and impressed at his daring. 'I asked the Queen, who thought it was a very jolly idea. Is that all right with you?' he asks, not even bothering to hide his sarcasm.

Clearly it is not all right with Tommy, who likes gatherings to be as decorous as possible, but he can hardly counter the Queen's agreement. His moustache bristles disapprovingly. 'In that case, get the footmen to do that.'

'For God's sake man, the footmen are all decrepit! David and I can deal with the carpet. Though if you want to help, you could ask if someone can bring down the gramophone from the Queen's sitting room.'

Margaret is standing beside Elizabeth. 'Golly, I can't

believe Philip dares to speak to Tommy like that,' she whispers as Tommy moves stiffly off. 'I suppose because he's a prince, he doesn't need to be deferential.'

'I think it's more about the kind of person he is,' says Elizabeth, but she worries. It's not a good idea, she thinks, to make an enemy out of someone like Tommy who is not only steadfast in his support of the monarchy but also a man of considerable power and influence.

But she forgets her concerns when one of the elderly footmen staggers in with the gramophone and another carries a box of records. Margaret claps her hands in delight and David drops the arm on the first record: 'That Old Black Magic'. The song could hardly be more appropriate, Elizabeth thinks as Philip grabs her hand to pull her out and start the dancing, swinging her round until she laughs giddily.

Their gaiety is infectious. In no time everyone seems to be dancing, apart from Tommy who glowers from the sidelines. David puts on all their favourite hit tunes from the year, and from 'Take a Chance on Love' to 'There Will Never Be Another You' it is as if every record has been specially written for Elizabeth. She dances with other men, but it is Philip she keeps coming back to, Philip who makes her fizz with happiness when he takes her hand in his. His clasp is warm and he holds her just a little too close.

Two years ago he asked her to dance, but then he was just being kind to a young girl. Now it feels different. Now he is dancing with her because he wants to and she lets herself relax, laughing up at him as they sing along to 'As Long As You're Not In Love With Anyone Else, Why Don't You Fall In Love With Me'?

When at the end of evening the King leads the traditional conga in and out of the rooms, Philip positions himself behind Elizabeth and takes firm hold of her waist. She can feel his hard hands burning through the satin of her dress, through her corset and onto her skin. The state apartments are all converted to offices, but they dance, feet stomping, the whole way along the Grand Corridor and back, and are all breathless and laughing by the time they have finished.

'That was a wonderful evening,' Philip says. 'I'll be sorry to go back to London tomorrow.'

Her happiness gives Elizabeth the confidence to say, 'Why don't you stay?'

'I can't, I'm afraid.' He is smiling still, but he doesn't meet her eyes. 'I've promised to spend New Year in London with good friends.'

Friends? Which friends? Elizabeth longs to ask but knows she can't.

'Oh, I see ...' She swallows her disappointment. It is a salutary reminder that Philip has another life, one he has already admitted he is reluctant to give up. She is a new friend, that is all.

'But I think Marina is inviting us all to a lunch at Coppins soon so I'll see you then, I hope?'

She summons a bright smile. 'Yes, of course.' What else can she say, after all? Hasn't she already decided not to embarrass him by making a fuss or demanding something he so clearly has no intention of giving? 'That will be lovely.'

Chapter 12

Cairo, April 1944

'Get out of the bloody way!' Philip leans on his horn as a street seller veers his cart directly into his path. He is hot and dusty and dying for a beer, and at this rate he'll never get to Shepheard's.

Whelp put in at Alexandria four days earlier and Philip has been summoned to meet his uncle in Cairo. When the Supreme Allied Commander of the South East Asia Command himself requested Philip's presence, his commanding officer could hardly refuse to let him go.

Glad of the excuse to borrow a natty little sports car and have some time to himself after the confines of the ship, Philip has enjoyed the drive through the Nile delta. There are advantages to being related to Mountbatten at times, he reflects, grinning at the thought that he has an afternoon off while his fellow officers are still sweltering on board *Whelp* overseeing repairs and restocking.

Enjoying the responsive feel of the steering wheel

beneath his hands, Philip zipped past fields of maize and cotton, past biblical scenes of men working in *jilbiyahs*, of water buffalo and thin donkeys trudging around wells. Several times he was tempted to stop and see how the irrigation systems worked, but with Uncle Dickie's telegram tucked in his shirt pocket he kept going. He tore through dusty villages, scattering chickens and followed by the barking of dogs and good-natured demands for *baksheesh* from the children who ran alongside the car as long as they could.

But now the car is nosing its way through the crowded streets of Cairo. The streets are jammed with bullock carts, cars, army jeeps, donkeys, camels, and pedestrians stepping on and off what passes for a pavement. After the tranquillity of the delta, the clamour of blaring horns and revved engines, of raised voices and braying donkeys and street hawkers' cries, assaults Philip's ears.

He makes it to Shepheard's Hotel just as the sun is setting and an amplified click and stutter announces that the *muezzin* is about to start the call to prayer. The light is unearthly, the sky flushed behind the date palms, and the sound creates a strange moment of stillness and silence in the raucous city before the *muezzin's* voice wavers out from the amplifier. '*Allahu Akbar!*'

Philip pauses to listen before tossing the car keys to a bellboy and taking the entrance steps two at a time. The lobby is vast and cool with tiled walls, massive pillars, and Moorish arches. Ceiling fans slap lazily at the air and guests cluster in wicker chairs between the potted palms. There are a fair number of men in uniform around but otherwise the scene can have changed little since the previous century.

The first person he sees is his cousin Alexandra. Sandra is the daughter of his cousin Alexander, one-time King of Greece. They are much the same age and shared many family holidays in Romania or at Panker so Philip is fond of her. She has her back to him and is leaning forward, apparently in the throes of an intense conversation with Frederika, Crown Princess of Greece, married to Paul, yet another of his innumerable cousins in the Greek royal family who have been forced into exile.

All except Philip's mother, Alice, who is still in Athens. 'God will protect me,' she said when the Germans invaded Greece in 1941. No one could persuade her to leave when the Greeks were enduring such hardship. 'People here need me,' she said simply. 'I must do what I can.'

It has felt at times as if his mother cares more for people in general than for her own family, but Philip is still proud of her.

Frederika catches sight of Philip over Sandra's shoulder and her eyes widen, but he puts a finger to his lips so he can creep up on Sandra and clap his hands over her eyes, making her shriek.

'Philip!' Squealing with delight, Sandra throws her arms around him when she jumps up to see who has startled her. 'What a lovely surprise! What are you doing here?'

'*Whelp*'s on her way to Ceylon to join the Eastern Fleet. We've put in to Alexandria to resupply and I thought I'd take the opportunity to run up and see you all.' Philip moves round to kiss Frederika. 'Hello Freddie, how are you?'

She lifts her cheek to be kissed. 'All the better for seeing you. Paul will be pleased – and the King, of course.'

'Is Uncle Georgie well?'

'Well enough. It's not much fun being a royal family in exile, and Georgie feels it particularly.'

'He must do,' says Philip. He is fond of George II, who is, in fact, his cousin rather than his uncle. The King is a short, dapper man with an extravagant charm when he chooses to use it and cosmopolitan tastes that Philip suspects would shock the domestic Windsors if they knew all of it.

'Sit down,' Freddie urges him. 'We've just had tea. Would you like some, or something stronger?'

'I've been thinking about a beer since I left Alexandria,' he confesses as he pulls up a chair.

'Let's all have a drink.'

'It was so clever of you to find us,' says Sandra when the waiter who materialises in response to the Crown Princess' lifted finger has gone.

'I was expecting to see you in Alexandria,' he agrees.

'We had to move south.' Freddie shudders. 'Those awful air raids!'

'But anyway, it's super to see you,' Sandra puts in quickly before Freddie gets upset. 'How long can you stay?'

'Not long, I'm afraid. I've had a summons to meet Uncle Dickie tomorrow.'

Freddie sat up. 'Dickie's here too? We heard he was in Karachi. Isn't he Commander in South East Asia now?'

'I believe he's on his way,' Philip says carefully. 'He's just flying in to Cairo for a few hours.'

'And he wants to talk to you?' Sandra quizzed him. 'What about?'

Philip would quite like to know that too. He flicks Sandra's nose. 'None of your business, brat.'

He waits until the drinks have been served. 'Anyway, it means I get to see you all so I intend to make the most of it.' Nodding thanks to the waiter, he picks up his glass gratefully and lets the cold beer slip down his parched throat. 'That's better,' he says at last, setting the glass back on the table with a sigh.

'There's so much to catch up.' Freddie leans forward eagerly. 'We hear you had Christmas at Windsor?'

'Yes, I did.'

'Well ...?' Sandra prompts.

'Well what?' says Philip, deliberately obtuse.

'How was it?'

'Very pleasant.'

Sandra and Freddie exchange a frustrated glance. Philip has a fair idea that Uncle Georgie will have dropped hints about the letter he wrote but he has no intention of indulging their curiosity. He is fond of his Greek relations but they are all the most appalling gossips. Mind you, Uncle Dickie isn't much better.

'And the little princess?'

'Margaret? She's a bright kid. Very spoilt and sulks if she's not the centre of attention, but when she drops all that, she can be charming.'

'I *meant* Elizabeth,' Freddie says. 'As you well know!'

'Elizabeth is not so little any more,' says Philip.

Elizabeth has been writing to him, as she promised she would. He likes to lie on his bunk and read her letters. Her image creates a pool of quiet that momentarily isolates him from the vibrating engines, the clanking of metal, the groaning of the propeller shafts and the sound of two-hundred-odd men barking orders, grumbling, joking, and farting. Elizabeth's quietness is obscurely restful. It is as if some quality in her absorbs some of his restlessness and smooths down his rough edges.

He writes back, better letters than before. He's aware that he has taken a misstep somewhere along the line. He's seen her only once since Christmas, at Coppins, when Marina invited him and the royal family to lunch in early January. Then, the tentative understanding he thought he had reached with Elizabeth seemed to have stalled. She was polite but her guard was up once more. Philip wishes he knew why.

All he knows is that he was relieved when her first letter came.

But he doesn't feel like confiding any of that to Freddie and Sandra.

He grins instead and picks up his glass once more. 'So, what's happening tonight?' he asks.

'We're all going to the Gezira Club.' Tacitly accepting the change of subject, Sandra inspects him over the rim of her cocktail glass. 'I hope you've got something to change into, Philip – you're absolutely covered in dust!'

The war has divided so many families that Philip is glad of the chance to catch up with some of his. The Greek royal family are close, perhaps because their exile leaves them rootless, dependent on each other for a sense of home. Greece isn't home, certainly not as far as Philip is concerned. He was little more than a baby when his parents packed him into an orange crate for a panicky flight from Crete.

In 1935 the Greeks voted for restoration of the monarchy and Uncle Georgie had returned to his throne after twelve years of exile. The following year, he had arranged for the remains of King Constantine, his father, his mother Queen Sophie, and his grandmother Queen Olga – all of whom had died in exile – to be brought from the Russian chapel in Florence for reburial in the family ground at Tatoï. Philip was given special leave from Gordonstoun to attend the ceremony.

It was a magnificent occasion, and the pomp and ceremony had struck a chord, bringing home as never before Philip's position as a prince, his membership of a royal family. He even toyed with the idea of staying in

Greece and joining the Greek navy. His father, though, vetoed the idea in no uncertain terms and Philip is glad now that he did. If he had a home at all, it was not Greece, but England.

Philip's arrival at the Gezira Club that night is met with cries of delight. Uncle Georgie greets him with an extravagant hug. No cool shaking of hands for the King of Greece. 'Philip! The very person I wanted to see! Now, come over here, my dear boy. I need to talk to you.'

Ignoring the pouts of the women, Georgie leads Philip out onto a quiet part of the terrace and offers him a cigarette. 'I had your letter,' he says.

Philip clicks his lighter to light first his uncle's cigarette and then his own. 'And?' he asks, blowing out smoke.

'I was very pleased to get it. I don't need to tell you that an alliance with the British royal family would be immeasurably useful to us as a family. I have hopes that I will be able to return to Athens one day, in which case the British would be powerful allies.

'I wrote to Bertie, of course, telling him that you had, as was proper, informed me as head of the family of your intentions towards Princess Elizabeth. I asked formally if he would consider you as a suitor.'

'What did he say?'

'He said she is too young for now. I understand he and the Queen think that she hasn't had much chance to meet any other young men yet.'

'That's rot,' Philip says hotly. 'Windsor Castle is stuffed

with Grenadier Guards. Elizabeth has the officers to lunch every week, for God's sake! If anything, she meets more young men than she does girls. Bloody Porchey is always hanging around.' He smokes moodily. 'The Queen wants to marry Elizabeth off to some tedious aristocrat in her hunting, fishing, and shooting set. She doesn't like me, that's the problem.'

'I suspect it's not you so much as your family. It would have been helpful if your aunts had been less forthright in their opinions about the Queen when she married Bertie but women ... what can you do?' Georgie shrugged and stubbed out his cigarette. 'I'm sorry, Philip, but the upshot is that I am to tell you not to think any more about Lilibet for the present.'

Philip scowls down at the cigarette in his hand, remembering that he had been in two minds after Christmas about whether to write to his uncle or not. He had decided definitely not to, in fact, until that lunch at Coppins when Elizabeth's smile had held a cooler edge for some reason. Perversely, that had made him want her, and he had changed his mind, dashing off a letter to Georgie. He'd regretted committing himself on more than one occasion since and wished he could recall his request that Elizabeth's father consider him as a suitor for his daughter. He should have been feeling relieved that the matter need go no further, but instead Philip finds himself outraged.

'Don't they think I'm good enough for them?' he demands. 'I'm descended from Queen Victoria. I've close family in practically every royal house in Europe. What more do they want?'

'Perhaps for your sisters not to be married to Nazis.'

Philip snorts and tosses his cigarette away.

'It might help if I could get back to Greece too, but there's no sign of that with the war on. It's not all bad,' Georgie tries to console him. 'You're only, what, twenty-three? Plenty of time to get married and in the meantime, you can sow your wild oats. Have a good time.'

That had been exactly Philip's plan, but the King's rejection has put him out of humour. Marriage to Elizabeth has become not a trap but a challenge, and Philip has never been one to back down from one of those.

'Then what does Uncle Dickie want to see me for?'

Georgie spreads his hands. 'You know Dickie. Always intriguing, the old devil.'

Which was rich coming from Uncle Georgie, Philip thinks. Both his uncles could give Machiavelli a run for his money.

'He'll have some plan for you,' Georgie is saying. 'He's been planning a match between you and Lilibet for a long time and he's not going to give up just because Bertie is digging in his heels. It's a pity he doesn't have a son of his own. It might be less pressure on you, dear boy. He thinks of himself as your father.'

Philip says nothing. Dickie is not his father. His father is not dead. He is in Monte Carlo. Perhaps Andrea's life has been a feckless one. Perhaps he is eking out a penniless existence far from the centres of power, and perhaps he did hand responsibility for his son over to the Mountbattens without much thought, but he is still Philip's father.

He is still the father who swung Philip up onto his shoulders, the genial, urbane man with twinkling eyes and a trademark monocle. Once he stood on trial for his life, but no one would ever guess from his amused air or the charm that makes everyone who meets him convinced they are the one person he has been waiting to see.

There is a part of Philip, a part he despises as childish, that wishes his father would keep that sense of pleasure and pride for his only son. He knows that when it comes down to it, for all his charm and fun, Andrea will always put himself first.

But Andrea is his father, and Philip loves him.

He is grateful, of course he is, to all the Mountbattens: to Georgie and Nada, and Dickie and Edwina. They were ones who came to pick him up from school, who turned up for sports day and cheered him on, and made room for a boisterous boy in their busy, glamorous lives.

How could he not be grateful? But Philip is obscurely resentful, too, for that sense of obligation that makes it impossible to walk away and refuse to be a part of any of Dickie's intrigues.

Suppressing a sigh, Philip turns back to his uncle. 'Come on,' he says, 'we'd better go back inside.'

Chapter 13

Standing next to Lord Killearn, the British Ambassador, Philip squints into the glaring sky until he sees a dot materialise. It grows bigger and bigger until it is a plane, lowering itself onto the runway. Philip watches it land with interest. He wishes he could learn how to fly. The idea of being up, up in the sky, the freedom and the light of it, tugs at him. He would have liked to join the RAF, but with Mountbattens in the family, it would have been seen as heresy to go outside the Senior Service.

He's feeling more than a little jaded after the night before. After his discussion with Uncle Georgie, he'd been in a rebellious mood, and he'd gone dancing and drinking into the small hours. It's safe to say that he is regretting it now, though.

Philip adjusts his collar. He's shaved and changed into his tropical uniform today; Uncle Dickie will expect him to look immaculate even if he doesn't feel it.

The heat wavers up from the tarmac as the plane taxies

to a halt, its propellers a blur. And then there he is, Supreme Allied Commander South East Asia, at the top of the steps, his uniform blindingly white and awash with gold braid. Urbane and smiling as always, he comes over, enveloping Philip and the ambassador in the charm he deploys like a weapon at times.

Philip salutes smartly.

'Very good of you to let us use the embassy, Killearn,' Mountbatten says as he shakes the ambassador's hand.

'Not at all, sir. We've laid on a light lunch for you.'

'Excellent.' He turns to his nephew. 'Philip, how good to see you.'

If Uncle Dickie is downcast by the way the King has knocked back Philip's request, he is hiding it well. He seems to be in high good humour. They exchange chit chat in the car and over lunch, and then he suggests that he and Philip have a stroll around the embassy garden. A sprinkler is hissing on the lawns and the date palms throw fractured shade over their white uniforms as they make their way along the gravel paths.

'All going well on *Whelp*?'

'Yes. What's all this about?'

'Philip, always so forthright,' Mountbatten sighs. 'You must learn a little more ... finesse.'

It was a common complaint from his uncle so Philip only grins. 'Well, what *is* it all about?'

'I've been giving some thought to the matter of your marriage.'

'What marriage? There isn't going to be a marriage. Uncle Georgie tells me the King says it's a no.'

'For now,' Mountbatten points out mildly. 'One needs to play a long game in these matters. Christmas at Windsor was obviously a success and writing to the King of Greece was the correct thing to do.'

'Much good it's done me,' says Philip, still miffed at George VI's flat rejection of him.

'That was just the first round.' Uncle Dickie studies his nails. 'I think it would be a good idea if you gave up your Greek nationality and became a British citizen. You need that in any case. The war is coming to an end and you won't be able to continue your naval career if you're not British.'

'I don't mind doing that. It's not as if I have any real connection to Greece. I feel British as it is.'

'That's what I thought. There's some understandable resistance to the idea of Princess Elizabeth marrying a foreign prince, particularly in view of the war, but you've been to a British school, and you only speak English now … That all counts in your favour. We will have to tread carefully, though, in view of Britain's relationship with Greece, but I see no reason not to set the wheels in motion – if you're agreeable?' Mountbatten adds as an obvious afterthought.

It is nice of Uncle Dickie to pretend he has a choice in the matter, Philip reflects a touch cynically. 'Fine by me,' he says.

'Good.' There is a delicate pause. 'Of course, it's probably better not to mention a possible marriage in connection with your naturalization. We'll tell your family it's purely a matter of your career. If they get a whiff of a wedding, there'll be no stopping them. Shocking gossips, the lot of them.'

Philip cocks a brow. 'That's rich coming from you, Uncle Dickie,' he says in a dry voice. Gossip is the stuff of life to his uncle.

'Don't be impertinent, boy,' Mountbatten says easily. They have stopped in the shade of a palm where they can look out over the Nile. 'How are you getting on with Lilibet?'

Philip is uneasily aware that he doesn't want to talk about Elizabeth with anyone. 'Fine.'

'There's no one else? What about that pretty girl? The one with the odd name?'

'Osla? She's just got engaged, as it happens.'

'Good. Don't take up with anyone else.'

'Dammit, Uncle Dickie, I'm not quite twenty-three!' Philip's hackles are rising in spite of himself. He doesn't like being pushed around. Doesn't like feeling that he's not his own man. The Mountbattens have been good to him and he hates the thought of disappointing them or, worse, being rejected by them, but still ...

'I'm sorry, Philip, but you need to think seriously about your options,' Mountbatten says, not ungently. 'You're a prince, and that comes with obligations. It's no use

pretending your life is your own. Nor do you have the
luxury of a private income. What are you going to do if
you don't marry Lilibet? Work in a bank? Or do you want
to end up like your father, living hand to mouth in some
backwater?'

Philip has to clamp down on the furious reply that
springs to his lips. The flicker of contempt in his uncle's
voice when he mentions Andrea stings all the more because
deep down, Philip feels the same. He loves his father, but
what has he done with his life? Philip *doesn't* want to be
like him.

He would like to defy his uncle and announce that he
can make his own way as a naval officer but he would still
need help to navigate the process of naturalization and, if
he is honest with himself, how far will he get in the Navy
without the powerful Mountbatten connection? If Philip
loses that, if he alienates his uncle, what will be left to
him? Can he afford to lose another family, another father,
another home?

Jaw tight, he stares out over the Nile at a man and his
son sailing their *felucca* together. They will have their own
problems, Philip knows, but how simple their choices must
be compared to his own!

Mountbatten lets him brood for a while. 'You don't
dislike her, do you?' he asks eventually.

'No, of course not.'

But it's a long step from not disliking a girl to being
forced into marriage with her. Philip is aware he is being

perverse. After all, only the night before he was feeling aggrieved at *not* being allowed to marry Elizabeth. It's not the idea that he objects to but the process, he reasons, trying to rationalise his reaction to himself. He has been self-reliant for so long that he instinctively digs in his heels at putting his future in anybody else's hands.

'She always seems a nice girl. Quiet. Steady.' There is a trace of wistfulness in Mountbatten's voice. Philip assumes he is thinking of his dazzling wife, Edwina, who, like his aunt Nada, is wonderful in many ways but could by no stretch of the imagination ever be called nice or quiet or steady. 'Pretty, too.'

Philip sighs. 'We're writing more regularly,' he admits. 'She's sent me a photograph and I've given her one of me.'

'Excellent. Exchanging photos is the first step in taking things further.' Dickie looks pleased. 'Think what it could mean, Philip,' he urges when Philip only rolls his eyes. 'Lilibet will be queen one day and you could be right there next to the throne. You're too talented to live your life as a nobody. Think of the influence you could have! It's a match that's suitable in every way.'

Philip's eyes go back to the tranquil *felucca*. 'I think you're taking a lot for granted.'

'Am I? I know how charming you can be when you feel like it. You must know perfectly well that you're a handsome devil, and more importantly, you're an intelligent young man – except when you're with your idiotic cousin David and try to drive around London in the blackout! If Lilibet isn't already in love with you, it wouldn't take much of a push for you to make it happen, you mark my words.'

'If it's all the same to you, Uncle Dickie, I'd prefer to manage my wooing without your advice!'

Mountbatten's eyes light up at the resigned acceptance in Philip's voice and he is quick to press the advantage. 'So we're agreed? We'll take the first steps in getting you naturalised?'

'Yes, I suppose so.'

'I'll speak to Georgie and Paul. There's little sign of the monarchy getting restored in Greece yet, but they'll both be keen to keep the British connection. I've already told Killearn I wanted to talk to you about naturalisation with the idea that you would be in a better position to help the King with royal functions.'

Philip's brows rise. 'And he bought that?'

'It doesn't matter if he didn't. The main thing is that we don't spook the horses by mentioning anything about a possible marriage. These diplomats are a worse lot of gossips than your aunts!'

His uncle claps a hand on Philip's shoulder. 'Don't look so glum! You don't have to commit to anything yet. Nobody's going to force you to the altar at gunpoint, Philip. I'm just asking you to think about what it would mean for you and for the family.' He pauses. 'The war's not over. We may have the Germans on the run, but there's still Japan to deal with, and that won't be easy. A lot can happen between now and you being in any position to marry at all.'

That's true, Philip thinks, his natural buoyancy of spirit returning. He watches the *felucca* drift out of sight. There is still action to be seen, fun to be had. He is still free.

'In the meantime,' Mountbatten goes on, as they turn back towards the embassy, 'it might be an idea if you keep on writing to Lilibet, without, obviously, mentioning our conversation today. Can you do that?'

Philips imagines Elizabeth, safe at Windsor. April: it will be spring there, with its fickle sunshine and gusty showers. He pictures her walking those ridiculous little dogs in the Great Park, sensibly dressed in stout shoes and an old coat, unaware – or is she? – of the plans everyone else is making for her future.

'Yes,' he tells his uncle. 'I can do that.'

Chapter 14

London, 8 May 1945

Outside the palace, a jubilant crowd is roaring and singing and cheering. 'We want the King! We want the King!' The chants rise and fall like waves.

Elizabeth smiles as she listens to the sound of a city euphoric that the long, bitter years of war are over.

Straightening her tie, she studies her reflection. 'What do you think, Susan?' she asks. 'Will I do?'

Susan cocks her ears and tips her head, recognising a question even if she is unable to answer. A year old now, Susan was a gift from Elizabeth's parents for her eighteenth birthday, a tiny bundle of the softest golden fur with bright black eyes and a long, pink tongue. Elizabeth picked her up that birthday morning, felt Susan's warm, wriggly weight in the palm of her hand, and fell in love. When everything else has been grim, Susan can always make her smile. She scampers ahead of Elizabeth on their walks and collapses, legs splayed, on their return. She rolls over and demands to have her tummy tickled and nips when she doesn't get enough attention. Susan is Elizabeth's utterly, her first dog, always alert to Elizabeth's voice.

Elizabeth adores her.

'You're right, it's not a flattering look,' she tells the dog now. She is in her ATS uniform: khaki jacket, khaki shirt, khaki skirt, khaki stockings, even khaki knickers, and for a change from khaki, heavy brown shoes. The belt around the jacket makes her look bulky.

Her mother looked appalled when she first saw Elizabeth in it. 'Oh, darling!' was all she could say in a faint voice.

But Elizabeth is proud of her uniform, prouder of it than of the crown and ermine robe she wore to her father's coronation. She polishes every button herself and on this day of victory, she wants to look not like a princess but like someone who, for a short time at least, shared in the war effort.

It took a lot of badgering to get the King to allow her to join the ATS at all. Or perhaps badgering is the wrong word. Elizabeth listens quietly, nods, and then asks again in a reasonable voice. She never gives up. She wore her father down eventually without a single voice being raised.

Joining the ATS was her first venture into the outside world. It hasn't given her quite as much freedom as she hoped. Every night after the training course she was driven back to Windsor and at lunchtimes she was ushered away from her fellow recruits to eat with the officers. Still, it was exciting to get out and meet some ordinary people after being secluded at Windsor for so long.

It meant she had something different to talk about in her letters to Philip, too.

Everyone is very bored of me talking about piston and cylinder heads. Only Susan never complains! The uniform is horrid but at least it means Margaret isn't jealous. She can get very sulky if she thinks I'm doing something she wants to do, but she says she has no desire to slide underneath a truck or get her hands filthy changing a tyre. I don't know why I enjoy it so much. I think it's because it's about doing *something and not just talking about it.*

It is over a year since she has seen Philip. Elizabeth knows her parents are quietly hoping she has forgotten him. They have organised little parties and dances to which they invite suitable young men. The men are all very nice and many have become friends but none of them have fierce blue eyes that drill into hers and demand she gives a proper account of herself. They are charming, but they treat her as a princess.

Philip treats her as an individual, as Elizabeth. He always calls her Elizabeth, too. Family members almost always refer to her as Lilibet but Philip is different. *Lilibet is sweet, but it's a little girl's name*, he said when she asked him why he never called her that. *I prefer to think of you as a young woman so Elizabeth seems more appropriate. You don't mind that, do you?*

Of course she doesn't mind.

Elizabeth wishes often that she had been warmer the last time she and Philip met. Marina invited the royal family to lunch soon after that Christmas, and Philip had been there. The trouble was that Elizabeth had found out by then that he had not been spending New Year with friends, as he had said. He had spent it with one friend, Hélène Foufounis.

David Milford Haven had told her all about it on Boxing Day when he had come to say goodbye. He had been drinking all evening and was swaying slightly, his eyes unfocused.

'Hélène is really special to Philip,' he had said, slurring his words. 'They've known each other since they were children. She's a great girl.'

It had been a salutary reminder to Elizabeth that there were other people in Philip's life, including 'great girls' who knew him really well. She was jealous of the unknown Hélène, she realised, testing out the feeling. She couldn't remember ever feeling jealous before – why would she? – but Elizabeth recognised its pinch straight away.

The fact that she knew that it was irrational and unfair only made the pinch sharper. Philip had not forsworn other friendships, other love affairs. They had agreed to write, that was all.

Once, when she and Margaret were quite small, before

Papa became King, Crawfie had taken them for swimming lessons with Miss Daly at the Bath Club. The first day they had both been apprehensive and had clung to Crawfie's hands. There had been a girl standing on the highest board, poised to dive. Elizabeth can still remember the echoing shouts, the mingled smell of chlorine and damp wood, remembers gasping as Miss Daly gave the word, and the girl bounced on the board and executed a perfect swan dive into the pool.

'I shall never be able to do that,' she had said, awed at the girl's bravery.

'Oh yes, you will,' Miss Daly had said with a laugh. 'That girl is blind, so if she can do it, you certainly can.'

Elizabeth often thought about what it must have been like for that girl to climb up the steps and walk along the board without being able to see what she was doing. Had imagined the bravery of taking the leap into the unknown. Meeting Philip again that Christmas felt in an obscure way as if she were walking carefully along a high board and getting ready to dive, but when she heard about Hélène, she lost her nerve. She crept back along the board to safety and climbed back down to the ground.

She hadn't given up, just as she hadn't stopped asking to join the ATS, but she had protected herself. She would not be too warm with Philip, she had decided. She would not make a fool of herself. She had her pride, after all.

It has been good to write, though. Elizabeth feels as if

she knows Philip better now and she longs to see him again.

And now the war is over.

Yesterday, Churchill announced victory from the balcony of the Ministry of Health in Whitehall. Elizabeth and Margaret leant close to the wireless to hear him speak to the crowd that had gathered in anticipation of the news they had been waiting for. 'This is your victory!' he declared and the crowd roared back as one: 'No, it's yours!'

Elizabeth's throat had snapped shut when she heard that. What would they all have done without Churchill?

'It is the victory of the cause of freedom in every land,' Churchill went on in his gravelly voice. In all our long history we have never seen a greater day than this. Everyone, man or woman, has done their best.'

Elizabeth can't help feeling as if her best has not been very much. It is barely a month since she joined the ATS. She has been hoping to join the headquarters as a junior officer to work on transportation, but Papa is already making noises about needing her at home to help him with royal duties.

Duty. The one word Elizabeth cannot turn her back on.

She holds the thought of Philip close to her, and she treasures his letters. He wrote and asked her to send him a photograph so that he could look at her while he was reading her letters to him. It felt almost like a declaration. A photograph means more than a letter. She spent ages choosing one to post out to him.

In return, as requested, he sent her a photo of himself looking coolly handsome in his naval uniform. Elizabeth put it on the mantelpiece in her sitting room where she could see it every day until Crawfie clucked and told her it was indiscreet.

Lately, Philip has grown a beard, he tells her. *Send me a photo so I can see what you look like now*, Elizabeth wrote, and when it arrived, she studied it carefully. She doesn't find him as handsome with a beard, but at least it would keep Crawfie quiet.

She put it on the mantelpiece in place of the photo her old governess thought so revealing.

'There, no one will recognise him now,' she said, but Crawfie only gave her one of her looks.

He is still in South East Asia but it cannot be long before the war is over there, too, and then surely, *surely*, he will be able to come home?

And what then? No promises have been made. Photo or no photo, Philip may have changed his mind. In all the joy of the war ending, Elizabeth is ashamed that she still has a wish left: that Philip will still want her.

'Lil, are you ready?' Margaret bounces in only to recoil at the sight of Elizabeth in her uniform. 'Why are you wearing that? It's awful!'

'It's my uniform,' Elizabeth says quietly. 'I want to.'

Margaret rolls her eyes at her sister's choice of outfit. 'They want us out on the balcony,' she says. 'Papa says we can't keep people waiting any longer.'

'I'm coming.'

Susan trots importantly along beside Elizabeth as she walks along the interminable palace corridors towards the room overlooking the forecourt where they always gather before appearances on the balcony.

This is the official day of celebration, although the jubilation has been going on since Churchill's announcement the day before. All night, fireworks streaked across the sky and the crowds surged through the streets.

The sense of relief is profound after six long years of war. They all feel it, a slackening of tension, a great unloosening, a collective exhalation, as if the country has been hunched in on itself, holding its breath and is now letting it go in an outpouring of emotion.

When she first heard the news, Elizabeth's heart had pounded so hard that she had had to press a hand to her chest to stop it breaking through her ribs. At last, *at last*! For a brief moment the relief had been so intense that it was painful.

Now poor, battered London has erupted in celebration. People who have lost everything but their lives are converging on the palace, clambering over the Victoria Monument and pressing up against the gates.

The room that overlooks the forecourt is full of people. Everybody is smiling and chatting and the noise both inside and out is deafening. Elizabeth is delighted to see her father's thin face relaxed for once. It lights up when he sees her.

'There you are,' he says as the chants of 'We want the King!' grow ever more insistent. 'Ready?'

Elizabeth nods, and waits for him to extricate the Queen from a conversation with her favourite brother, David Bowes-Lyon, and send his equerry, Group Captain Townsend, to gather up Margaret.

'It's worse than trying to herd the corgis,' the King pretends to grumble.

At last the four of them are all together. The King glances at the Queen, who smiles back at him in a wordless conversation. There is a bond between them that Elizabeth envies. She would like to be married to man who would look at her the way her father looks at her mother.

Philip is not like her father.

'Out we go,' the King says. 'Just be careful, though. The balcony is a bit shaky after that bomb.'

He and the Queen step out first and then Elizabeth and Margaret follow to stand on either side of their parents, Susan having been firmly commanded to stay inside. The cheer that goes up startles the pigeons pecking around the forecourt or hunched on the rooftops, oblivious to the drama. They flutter up and circle indignantly before returning, ruffled, to their perches. The sound hits the royal family like a great wave, a buffet of air that almost makes Elizabeth stagger back, such is its force. Overwhelmed, she lets out a shaky breath and smiles and lifts her hand to wave as her heart swells.

The balcony is draped in crimson and gold; beyond,

the seething mass of people stretches far back along the Mall. What would it be like to be down there? she wonders. To be part of the crowd, looking up instead of looking down? *Why are you cheering us?* Elizabeth wants to call down to them. *You are the ones who have stuck it out and survived. You are the ones who have taken every blow. I have just learnt to change a tyre.*

She wishes she could tell every single person down there how proud she is of them, and how desperately, desperately glad she is that the long war with Germany is over and that they can all start living rather than surviving.

For Elizabeth this is the beginning. She has spent the entire war cloistered at Windsor, but now she is eighteen and ready to become a woman.

Her only regret is that Philip is not there to share this incredible moment with her.

Chapter 15

'Isn't the crowd marvellous?' the Queen says when they step back inside, wrists aching from waving.

'It's going to be quite a night in London,' Peter Townsend says. 'I don't think anybody is planning on going home tonight.'

'I wish we could join in,' Elizabeth says wistfully. All at once the thought of sitting tamely in the palace having supper while outside the capital celebrates is unendurable. She looks at her father. 'Later, when it gets dark? We'd be perfectly safe. No one would hurt us, not tonight. There'll never be another night like this.'

'I don't think—' the King begins, but Margaret interrupts him, hanging around his neck as she used to when she was a little girl.

'Please say we can, Papa. *Please!*'

'But Margaret, what if someone recognises you?'

'They won't,' says Margaret confidently. 'We can slip out of the side exit. Lilibet's right, this is a special night. We've missed out on so much, Papa. Please let us have tonight, at least?'

'Poor darlings,' their father sighs, a sure sign he is relenting. He has never been any good at resisting Margaret. 'You've never had any fun. Very well, you can go – but not alone.'

'I'll go with them.' Her mother's brother steps forward as Margaret claps her hands in delight. 'They deserve to be part of this.'

'Thank you, David. That would make me feel much better. Take Miss Crawford as well – she's a sensible woman.' The King glances around. 'Major Phillips? Porchester? Would you go with them all and make sure no harm comes to them?'

They both salute smartly. 'It would be an honour, sir.'

Again and again, they are called back to balcony. At five o'clock, the King asks Mr Churchill to join them. There is a strange moment of silence when the Prime Minister steps out between the King and Queen, as if in the midst of the celebrations, everyone is struck, suddenly, by just how much is owed to one man. Unfazed by the eerie silence, Churchill bows to the crowd, an expression of acknowledgement and gratitude for their support, and Elizabeth's chest tightens at the roar of response.

As the light fades, she and Margaret and their escorts slip out of the side door of the palace. It's easier than Elizabeth thought to simply walk out. She and Margaret exchange thrilled glances as they mingle with the crowds and let themselves get swept up the Mall and into Piccadilly. They link arms with Crawfie, Porchey and Major Phillips acting as buffers at either end, but it's impossible to stay six abreast and their line soon breaks apart, much to Crawfie's distress.

Elizabeth doesn't care. They are all giddy with a sense of liberation. For almost everyone else, it is freedom from war and all the grief and destruction it has brought, but for Elizabeth it is liberation of a different kind. For this one night, she has been allowed to step out of the palace, out of a world where every day is planned with precision and her privileged life is hedged about with convention and duty.

It is as if walking through that gate has unlocked something inside her. Where usually she keeps herself tightly controlled, now she is free to shout, to open her mouth wide and sing, not caring what she sounds like. Her chest expands and she fills her lungs with air, feeling dizzy with the power of it.

'Run rabbit, run rabbit, run, run, run!' she sings, yelling along with everyone else. 'Don't give the farmer his fun, fun fun!' She can feel Crawfie's startled glance. Elizabeth is so quiet normally, so restrained. So guarded. No wonder her governess is puzzled at the change in her.

She will go back to the palace, Elizabeth knows. Her guard will go back up. But for now, for this one incredible night, she wants to let herself go.

Once or twice, she meets a stranger's eyes and they do

a double take, recognising her. Elizabeth just smiles brilliantly and dances on into the crowd.

The streets are jammed with people singing, cheering, banging dustbin lids together, anything to make a noise, as the light fades and searchlights sweep joyfully across the sky above London. Broken chairs and tables are dragged out of bombsites and tossed onto bonfires. The crowd is a living thing, surging up and pausing to warm itself at a fire before circling and swirling on. Elizabeth finds herself at a bonfire and holds her hands out to the flames. She isn't cold, but the fire has a mythic power to which she cannot help but respond. The city has been dark for six years, and now they are allowed to make light and warmth once more.

It is a carnival where all the rules about being the restrained, polite, stoical British are abandoned. Strangers hug and kiss each other. At first, it is true, Elizabeth stiffens at finding herself clapped on the back or swept against some khaki jacket in an embrace so brief she barely has time to register a face. She is not used to being manhandled. But then, nor is anyone else, she remembers. Theirs is not a society where anyone touches easily. Tonight, though, it is a different world, with different rules. In this world, she is not a princess, just an ordinary young woman celebrating the end of a time of terrible tension.

So she lets her hand be grabbed, lets an intoxicated young soldier pull her into a circle so they can jitterbug.

Breathless and laughing, she exchanges caps with a sailor and thinks fleetingly of Philip, but there is no time for sadness, not tonight. Before the sailor's hat is securely on her head, she is swept into a conga line and singing 'Roll out the Barrel' at the top of her voice.

The noise and the energy in the streets is extraordinary. Porchey and Major Phillips struggle to keep their little party together. Even Crawfie is letting her hair down and singing along with everyone else. 'We've got the blues on the run,' she joins in with Elizabeth, laughing, while David Bowes-Lyon keeps a firm hold on an exhilarated Margaret's belt.

'We should try and stick together,' Porchey shouts in Elizabeth's ear.

He's worried, she can see. Normally she would do her best to stop him worrying. Normally she would be sensible and agree to go back. She knows Porchey can't relax and enjoy himself as he deserves to. It's not fair on him. She should suggest they all return to the palace.

But she doesn't want to.

This is her one chance to be ordinary, to be invisible. It will end, of course it will, but surely she can be allowed a little longer?

'Let's dance,' she shouts back, tipping the sailor's hat to a rakish angle. 'We'll stick together that way.'

People are climbing up lamp posts and onto the dignified lions in Trafalgar Square, splashing into fountains and pulling each other up onto cars as makeshift stages to dance and kiss. Elizabeth watches one couple who have made it onto the plinth of a statue exchange a lascivious kiss, their hands roaming frantically over each other, and her eyes widen.

Porchey follows her gaze. 'Oh I say,' he says as he pulls her away. 'We'd better leave them to it.'

Elizabeth nods, but as they romp onwards she can't stop thinking about that uninhibited embrace. It's like an itch behind her eyelids. What would it be like to be kissed like that? Her blood booms at the thought, and she thinks about Philip, still so far away.

The movement of the crowd is taking them back towards the palace. Elizabeth would like to go the other way, but the people around her have other ideas. Whooping and cheering, they surge back down the Mall, bearing Elizabeth, Margaret and the others with them.

'We want the King! We want the King!' the crowd shouts, and Elizabeth links arms with her sister as they look up at the palace. It is a view she has never seen before. The balcony looks so small, so far away. It is empty now, but inside her parents will be exchanging glances and getting to their feet. Her mother will be putting on her hat and gloves, making sure her lipstick is in place.

'Isn't this amazing?' Margaret yells into Elizabeth's ear, and Elizabeth nods and squeezes her sister's arm.

By unspoken agreement, they join in with the calls for the King and Queen to appear, and when their parents do step onto the balcony, the sisters cheer themselves hoarse.

I will never forget this night, Elizabeth thinks. She can't wait to write and tell Philip what it has been like. She can't wait for the war with Japan to be over.

She can't wait for him to come home and for the future to start.

Chapter 16

Buckingham Palace, January 1946

Elizabeth picks up Philip's photograph as she has done so many times over the past two years. It is so long since she has seen him and tonight, at last, he is coming to supper.

Her heart is jerking high in her throat. Who is this man with a beard? What does she know of him, really? She has spent so long thinking about him. She has read and reread his letters, so she knows his father has died. She knows that while she has been waiting for him to come home, Philip has been to Ceylon and New Guinea. She knows he has rescued pilots from the shark-infested Java Sea, seen action again in Japanese islands, and has had nearly three months of shore leave in Australia while *Whelp* was refitted. He was on board the US flagship *Missouri* to witness the formal surrender by the Japanese.

She knows where he has been and how he has been

and how he thinks, but she knows nothing of what he actually *feels*.

The letters that have arrived, boldly addressed to her at Buckingham Palace, are not love letters. They are friendly and chatty and entertaining, but Philip has always held himself back from committing feelings to paper.

But then, she has done the same, hasn't she? She has had so little to hold on to. She has his photograph, and the memory of how he made her feel, of the blueness of his eyes, the direct gaze and the restless energy. It is not enough for her to make any assumptions.

Still, he is coming. In a few minutes she will know if her feelings for Philip are real or not

Elizabeth isn't even sure which she wants to be true. Restlessly, she puts down the photo and goes over to the window to pull back the floral curtains and peer outside.

Surely he will be here soon?

What if he doesn't come?

Outside, a fog has crept through the palace gates and is pressing against the windows. It is like a living thing, poking into crevices, probing for a way in. It smothers the yellow light from the lampposts and muffles sound. She stands at the window and rests a hand against the pane. The blank, silent world is the opposite of the joyous celebration of VE Day and, three months later, VJ Day, when she and Margaret once again slipped out into the streets to join in the fun.

Since then, there has been little fun. The country is in

survival mode. Rationing is more severe than ever, and the winter has been brutal. There is no more of the rugged defiance that got them through the war. Now it is about endurance and the long slog back to prosperity.

For Elizabeth it has been about waiting. Oh, she has been taking on some new duties to help the King, and there have been visits to Balmoral and Sandringham and parties and dances to attend, but she has been going through the motions until Philip comes home.

Now he is here. He wrote to her from Portsmouth ten days ago. Elizabeth went straight to her parents and asked if she could invite Philip to a private supper. She could tell her mother was displeased and her father unenthusiastic. They have been hoping she would forget Philip.

'He can come as long as Margaret is there too,' the Queen said. 'We don't want to give the wrong impression.'

Elizabeth sighs and turns back to the room. She has her own sitting room now, with pink and cream armchairs and a selection of pastoral paintings on the walls. The mantelpiece holds Philip's photograph and one of the palace's vast collection of clocks. There's an electric fire in the grate and Susan is curled in a basket nearby.

Margaret rushes into the room making Susan lift her head. 'Lil, I think he's here!'

'How can you tell?' Elizabeth asks. Her heart is beating very fast. 'I can't hear anything.'

'Well, there's a commotion downstairs,' says Margaret. She studies her sister, head on one side. 'Are you excited?'

'I'm nervous,' Elizabeth confesses with a shaky smile as she smooths down her dress.

'You look very nice. That blue suits you.'

Blue becomes you, ma'am.

'Thank you, Margaret.'

'It's freezing in here, though.' Margaret hugs her arms together. 'Can't we have another bar on the fire?'

'You know we're supposed to be saving energy. I'm lucky to have an electric fire in my sitting room at all.'

'Susan would like it warmer, wouldn't you, Sue?' Margaret asks the dog, who has rested her nose back on her paws and ignores her.

'Margaret, no.'

'Lilibet, don't you ever get tired of being good and dutiful?' Exasperation threads Margaret's voice. 'An extra bar for an hour or two to make the room more welcoming won't bring the country to its knees!'

'It's a matter of principle. Besides, I'm not cold.'

Which was true. She was too nervous to feel anything except the churning in her belly.

Elizabeth had been inclined to be resentful when her parents had insisted that Margaret be present at her first meeting with Philip. Margaret is livelier and prettier and funnier than she is, and she is not good at sharing the limelight.

But now Elizabeth is glad. There will be no shortage of conversation if Margaret is there, and it will give Elizabeth a chance to observe Philip and decide if she really does like him or whether she has built him up to be something he is not. She doesn't think so, but how can she be sure? People can change, although she doesn't feel that she ever does. She never has a reason to change, while Philip has done so much more and seen so much more than she has. He might be different.

Both sisters swing round as the door to Elizabeth's sitting room opens. 'His Royal Highness Prince Philip of Greece,' Cyril says in fatherly tones. He has been the princesses' footman since their nursery days at Windsor and is a comfortingly familiar figure at Buckingham Palace.

And there Philip is, striding into the room, bringing with him an energy that stirs up the air and makes the cream-papered walls seem to shrink inwards. Elizabeth feels the breath leak out of her lungs, almost as if his presence has sucked up all the spare oxygen.

Her first thought is that he is taller than she remembered. Taller and more ... more immediate somehow. She is instantly paralysed with shyness.

'Philip.' Somehow she summons enough breath to speak and she smiles, a little shakily, as she holds out her hand. 'How nice to see you again.'

'Elizabeth.' Philip seems amused more than anything by her formality. His bow is cursory, but his blue eyes gleam in a swift upward look as he bends to kiss her hand. His lips are warm where they graze her knuckles and she has to stop herself touching them when he lifts his head.

Turning to Margaret, he makes a big production of

bowing and Margaret peeps at him from under her lashes and giggles. 'We thought you were never coming to see us,' she complains. 'You've been back for *ages*.'

Elizabeth is mortified. 'Hardly ages, Margaret,' she says sharply. 'And I'm sure Philip has had things to do.'

She sounds prim and priggish, in contrast to Margaret's easy flirtation. This has all been a mistake, she thinks wildly. She has waited so long for Philip to come back and now she is too stiff and nervous to enjoy it.

'We thought we'd have a casual supper,' she says, gesturing towards the round table that has been set up in front of the fireplace. 'Just the three of us.'

'Splendid.'

If Philip is disappointed not to have a chance to be alone with her, he doesn't show it. Elizabeth doesn't know whether to be glad or sorry about it.

'It's just nursery food, I'm afraid,' she ploughs on. 'Fish and jam roly-poly.'

'Sounds delicious,' says Philip.

'You won't think that if it's coley again,' says Margaret, sitting at the table. 'I am *so* sick of it. I wish rationing would end!'

'Coley's a lot better than some of the things I ate in New Guinea.' Philip pulls out a chair for Elizabeth and then sits down himself. 'Believe me, if you're offered a choice between porcupine and coley, go for the coley!' He winks at Elizabeth. 'Coley's fine by me. I might have had a problem if you'd offered me lobster, though.'

'Lobster? We should be so lucky!' says Margaret, talking over Elizabeth's quiet question.

'Why not lobster?'

'It's too embarrassing to tell you.'

'Oh, go on!'

'Well, I must have been about fifteen and I was in Greece for the reburial of King Constantine, Queen Sophie, and Queen Olga, all of whom had died in exile. It was supposed to be a solemn occasion but of course it was a big family reunion too and there were all sorts of get-togethers planned. The night before the funeral service, there was a formal dinner and I wore my first dinner jacket. They served lobster and because I was a greedy schoolboy, I ate a lot of it.

'I don't know if one of the lobsters was off, or if I was just being punished for my greediness, but the next morning I felt sick as a dog. There was no way I could stay in bed: this was the culmination of the whole week and I was expected to wear a morning coat and top hat to the service. The ceremony felt endless and I was so sure I was going to be sick.'

'Oh, you poor thing,' Margaret says with an exaggerated grimace.

'It gets worse,' Philip warns. 'I made it through the ceremony, but then we had to get into the cars for a procession back to the palace and ... well, that was it. I couldn't keep it in any longer.'

'Oh dear,' says Elizabeth faintly. 'How did you, er ...?'

'I had my new top hat,' he confesses with a grin. 'Probably not intended for the purpose, but it made for a very handy sick-bowl.'

'Eeeuwww,' says Margaret.

'Then, of course, there was the problem of what to do with it,' Philip goes on. 'I should have just left it in the car, but I didn't think of that. When we stopped and got out, I just pushed the hat and contents into the hands of an unfortunate aide-de-camp with an apologetic look and walked into the palace. I still feel bad about it,' he adds as Margaret starts to giggle.

'Poor man,' says Elizabeth, but she is smiling too. She remembers Philip as a boy, with his white-blond hair and boisterous manner. She can imagine him bluffing it out.

The ice has been broken and her shyness fades as Philip chats easily about his experiences in South East Asia. He treats her just as he treats Margaret – if anything, he has more fun with Margaret who shows off outrageously and laughs when he teases her. He seems completely relaxed but there is nothing in his manner to suggest that he is doing anything other than having a casual supper with friends.

Not even friends, Elizabeth thinks despondently. He is treating them almost as if they are his younger sisters or cousins.

'What are you doing now?' she asks when Philip pauses.

'Nothing very interesting.' He makes a face. 'I've got my

first command, but it's just overseeing the decommissioning of *Whelp*. After that, it looks as if I'm being sent to naval training,' he says without enthusiasm.

'Where will that be?'

'I'm not sure. Possibly Wales, possibly Corsham.'

'But you'll be in the country at least?'

Philip nods. 'There's that. And I should be able to get up to London at weekends. Uncle Dickie says I can use the house in Chester Street.'

'Then perhaps we'll see you again?' Elizabeth says, although if she had the choice she would spend her weekends in the country, not in town.

He looks straight at her and smiles in a way that makes her heart lurch alarmingly. 'I hope so,' he says.

Chapter 17

That went pretty well, Philip congratulates himself, as he runs down the palace steps and out to the car he has parked in the forecourt. Not the most exciting evening he's ever had, and he'd been momentarily dismayed by the nursery set up, but on the other hand, there was something restful about not having to be witty or sophisticated. Without thinking, he had reverted back to being a teenage boy, showing off and basking in their admiration.

In Margaret's admiration, anyway. He wasn't so sure of what Elizabeth thought. She's harder to read.

The two princesses are such innocents, almost childlike still. Philip thinks of the girls he met on shore leave in Australia, in Sydney and Melbourne: smart, funny, clever girls out to have a good time. There is something almost touching about the princesses' lack of sophistication, although Margaret has all the makings of a minx. She's only sixteen and has the potential to be a beauty, but she is obviously spoilt and determined to be the centre of attention.

Elizabeth allows herself to be overshadowed, but there's a restraint about her that he approves of, a refreshing quietness in contrast to the frantic rush of so many of his contemporaries who have survived the war and now don't know what to do with themselves.

It's a feeling he shares. After the first giddy rush of the war being over, he's been left with a hollow sense of 'now what?' The truth is that he is going to miss the buzz of action. Training petty officers or whatever they have in mind for him is not going to offer the same satisfaction, but what else can he do? He has no inheritance to fall back on. He isn't cut out for university, even if he could afford to go, and to stay in the Navy requires him to be a British citizen, something that is now looking uncertain.

The truth is that *everything* looks uncertain now that his father is dead. It is just over a year since Philip heard the news and he is still surprised by how much of a shock it has been, by how the painful jab of memory can still catch him unawares.

A heart attack after a party, in bed with his mistress: somehow it seemed a fitting death for Prince Andrea. Philip didn't get those details until later, though. He was on board *Whelp* in the middle of the Indian Ocean when the news reached him. Mountbatten sent a naval message, meticulously deciphered by the rating on radio watch.

So shocked and grieved to hear of the death of your
father and send you all my heartfelt sympathy. Following
has been received from your mother: "Embrace you
tenderly in our joint sorrow."

Philip gets into his car but he doesn't start the engine immediately. He is back on the bridge, taking the message with a brusque nod of acknowledgement. His mind is on the ominously purple clouds boiling up on the horizon and the way the ship is pitching from side to side. He's thinking about whether they will be able to outrun the storm or whether they should just batten down and ride it out so when he opens the message, he doesn't immediately register the words. Then he looks again and the pitching is inside him.

Death of your father.

Death of your father.

Death of your father.

He is looking blindly out at the clouds and remembering his father's laugh, the warm weight of his father's arm around his shoulder.

Pushing the memory aside, Philip puts the car into gear. There has been no time to grieve, either during the war or since, and anyway, he is not the type to weep and wail. He hadn't seen his father for several years, and no one could say he had been an attentive parent.

But still, he was Philip's father, and it is too late now for Philip to tell him that he understood the choices he had made, that he didn't blame him for any of it. That he is grateful to have been his son. His father's death means that one of the pillars holding up his world has now been knocked askew in a way Philip hasn't expected, tipping everything to one side.

When they were at war, they all knew what they had to do. Now it is not so easy. Between Andrea's death and the situation in Greece and the question mark over whether he will be able to continue as a naval officer, is it any wonder Philip feels edgy and uncertain about everything?

Mountbatten has explained that his application for British citizenship is on hold while civil war rages in Greece. 'I have been informed, delicately but in no uncertain terms, that the situation there is so unsettled that the British naturalization of a member of the Greek royal house is likely to be misinterpreted,' he wrote. 'I fear we will have to wait until the situation has stabilised.'

So Philip is in limbo.

Marriage to Elizabeth could still be his best bet. He's had time over the past couple of years to think about what he wants and he's still none the wiser, so why not marry her?

He remembers how pragmatic she was when they discussed the matter at Windsor that Christmas but she is very young still. If he has changed his mind several times, why shouldn't she? She invited him to supper, but perhaps she wanted to see how he had changed? Philip has the sense that he needs to tread carefully. It would be a mistake to take Elizabeth for granted. She is not someone who can be rushed into letting down her guard.

Fine, he thinks. That suits him too. Far better to take things slowly. He will play jolly brother for a while if that makes her feel more comfortable and then, well, then they can see. He would rather not commit himself either.

In the meantime ... Philip looks at his watch as he drives out of the palace gates. It's still early. He runs his tongue round his teeth. Orangeade was the only drink on offer and he was longing for a beer. Might as well ring David when he gets back to Chester Street and see if his cousin wants to make a night of it.

Some ten days later, Philip receives another invitation to supper at Buckingham Palace with the princesses. This time he is prepared for the nursery atmosphere and dresses down in an open-necked shirt and tweed jacket. They eat sausages and mash served by the avuncular footman, Cyril, and drink orangeade again. It's awful stuff, but after a heavy night with David the previous evening, Philip is quite glad to give his system a rest.

Margaret's presence keeps the conversation light. She likes to be teased, although not too much, and is inclined to get huffy if she feels he has gone too far. Not that Philip takes any notice of that. Margaret is tough, as only the truly self-centred can be. She can take it, he reckons.

He is gentler with Elizabeth but he's not going to treat her like glass. He has a shrewd notion that she is surrounded by deference and that, if nothing else, his breezy attitude will make a refreshing change. So he teases her too and enjoys seeing her face bloom into a smile. It transforms her into a warm and pretty young woman. She will never be a beauty, he thinks, but she is very appealing when she laughs.

Privately, Philip makes it his mission to make Elizabeth laugh more often. She needs more fun in her life, he decides.

'Let's have a race,' he says.

They look at him blankly. 'A race?'

'It's raining and it's dark,' Margaret points out, as if to a child. 'Where are you thinking of holding this race?'

'We don't have to go outside. How many miles of corridors have you got here?'

'We can't run inside,' Elizabeth says, shocked.

'Why not? We used to get the crew running round the deck to keep them amused and fit. There must be more room here.'

'Well, yes, but—'

Margaret jumps to her feet. 'I'll race you, Philip. I bet I can beat you too.'

'Is that a challenge, brat?'

'Down to the end of the corridor and back,' she suggests but he shakes his head with a grin as he gets lazily to his feet.

'That's not far enough. I vote down the corridor, along to the staircase, down to the entrance, up the Grand Staircase and back here.'

'All right,' says Margaret, brightening at the thought of a challenge.

'Elizabeth, you're in this race too.'

'Oh, no, I don't think ...'

'No excuses.' Philip stands over her, holding out a hand, until she takes it and lets him pull her to her feet.

'I'm not sure we should be doing this,' Elizabeth says nervously but Philip isn't having any of it.

'You're a princess,' he reminds her. 'You can do what you like in your own home. We're all racing.'

Ignoring her feeble protests, he chivvies her into a starting position next to Margaret who is already crouched and ready to go. 'Look, even Susan is up for it,' he points out as the corgi heaves herself out of her basket and follows them out into the corridor. 'I'll even give you a head start,' he offers.

'We don't need your charity,' says Margaret, giggling.

'I'll count to ten, then I'm coming after you.'

'Oh, Cyril—' Elizabeth begins in relief, spotting the footman coming down the corridor to clear the plates.

'Cyril's not going to save you,' Philip interrupts her briskly. 'Cyril, out of the way, that's a good man. The princesses have a race to run. Are you ready?' Encouraged to see that Elizabeth is starting to laugh helplessly, he holds out his fingers as an imaginary starting gun. 'On your marks ... get set ... go!'

Shrieking, Margaret sets off, followed by Elizabeth, the puzzled corgi yapping at her heels.

'Stop it, Susan,' Elizabeth tries to shush her through her giggles as she runs after her sister.

The corridor is ringing with the sound of Margaret's laughter, pounding feet, and barking.

'... Seven, eight, nine, ten!' Philip finishes quickly. 'I'm coming to get you!'

Looking over their shoulders, the girls squeal with laughter at his mock growl. He pounds after them down the long palace corridors, past blank-faced footmen who flatten themselves against the walls as they pass, past priceless paintings and fragile porcelain vases, up and down the elaborately gilded staircases, and they are all breathless and laughing by the time they make it back to Elizabeth's sitting room and flop into the pink and cream chintz armchairs.

'I declare myself the winner,' says Philip. 'And Susan,' he adds, pointing at the panting corgi, '*you* are the loser.'

'Not fair!' says Elizabeth, who has come in third. She is breathing hard and fanning her pink face with her hand, but she is going to stand up for her dog, who has flopped at her feet, stubby paws stretched out back and front, panting cheerfully. 'Her legs are shorter than ours.'

'I can't help that. Susan knew the rules – and I did give you all a handicap.'

It was childish fun, but there was nothing wrong with a bit of nonsense now and then, and increasingly Philip finds himself looking forward to the cosy suppers at the palace.

Chapter 18

As February blows itself into March, it feels to Philip as if he is leading a strange kind of double life ... actually, a triple life, when he comes to think about it. There are those innocent evenings at the palace, drinking orangeade and larking around in the corridors, and then there are the evenings he spends in London with David Milford Haven and other friends, drinking in smoky clubs, all of them struggling to adjust to the dull grind of peace-time life.

Then there is another world again, at HMS *Arthur* in Corsham, where he is training petty officers and sleeps in a chilly and sparsely furnished munitions hut with a tin roof. He spends his evenings in the Methuen Arms, drinking mild and bitter and playing darts or skittles and discussing the possibility of cricket in the summer. It is a long way from Buckingham Palace. The work is frankly dull after the excitement of the war, but he needs his first lieutenant's salary, especially as his application for naturalisation is still stalled until the situation in Greece resolves itself. His future, it seems, is bound up with the British government's Balkan diplomacy, with everyone waiting to see what the results of a plebiscite on the restoration of the Greek monarchy will be. Approving Philip's application might make it seem that the British don't hold out much hope for his uncle Georgie's future, and until that is clear, Philip is stuck.

Philip can adapt to all three worlds – he's good at adapting – but he feels at home in none of them.

'How are things going with Elizabeth?' Uncle Dickie asks whenever Philip sees him in Chester Street, and Philip always answers the same way.

'Fine.'

'Any sign of being able to move matters forward?' his uncle asks hopefully at the beginning of March when Philip encounters him at the breakfast table.

Waving away the butler's attempt to serve him, Philip pours himself a cup of tea and tries to ignore the pounding in his head. Definitely one too many martinis last night.

'I'm taking it slowly.'

'Well, don't take it too slowly, or she'll think you're not interested. We don't want anyone else to swoop in and bowl her over.'

Philip bites down on the impulse to tell his uncle to butt out and let him manage his affair with Elizabeth in his own way.

'There isn't anyone else,' he says.

'That you know of,' says Mountbatten darkly. 'What about Henry Porchester?'

'He's just a friend.'

But there had been that one weekend when Philip was invited to Windsor and he saw Elizabeth in the stables. She was a different girl with horses: easy, confident, affectionate. Philip watched her stroking a horse's nose and laughing as it nuzzled her hair and found himself wishing she was that comfortable about touching him. It had come to something when he was jealous of a horse!

Of course Porchey was there, too, looking good in the saddle and chatting easily to Elizabeth about bloodlines or hocks or something horsey that Philip knew nothing about. Philip watched closely but he couldn't detect anything other than friendliness in the way Elizabeth treated Porchester.

She prefers him, he is sure of it.

At least, he thinks he is.

In spite of all the cosy evenings at the palace, he has barely got beyond occasionally touching Elizabeth's back. Sometimes he offers a hand to help her up, or takes her elbow to steer her round a puddle, and very occasionally he is able to manoeuvre his chair so his knee can brush against hers, but she hasn't given any indication that she wants any more from him.

It doesn't help that Margaret is usually there. This is deliberate on the Queen's part, Philip suspects. Her brother, David Bowes-Lyon, has taken against Philip and the feeling is mutual. In Philip's book, Bowes-Lyon is a slimy, vicious gossip. He is damned if he is going to ingratiate himself with the man, but it has cost him an ally in the Queen.

Still, the estimable Miss Crawford does try and draw Margaret away when Philip is around so he can be alone with Elizabeth sometimes. The best times are when his cousin Marina, Duchess of Kent, invites him and Elizabeth to lunch at Coppins. Philip suspects this may be at Mountbatten's instigation but he doesn't protest. Elizabeth is always more relaxed in the country and Philip enjoys driving her down in his sports car. At least Marina is subtler about pushing them together than his uncle.

'Darlings, would you mind awfully amusing yourself for a bit before lunch?' she says languidly. 'I'm having a disaster with the cook. Philip, take Lilibet round the garden and pretend you know the difference between a flower and a weed.'

So Philip and Elizabeth stroll around the Coppins garden; they talk easily and he makes her laugh and blush ... so why then is he hesitating?

He tells himself that he doesn't want to spook her but the truth is that he can't be sure *how* Elizabeth feels. There is an untouchable, unreachable quality about her, as if she is isolated behind a glass wall and it both intrigues and frustrates Philip.

Perhaps that restraint is a good thing, he tries to persuade himself. There is nothing wrong with guarding your emotions. He does it himself. The last thing he wants is someone who would push and probe and want him to talk about his feelings. Elizabeth understands that, Philip thinks.

And she is kind. He has observed that about her. She notices if the footman winces or the dog limps. She imagines what it must be like for families notified that a son or a father is missing, presumed dead. She worries about the staff who may be blamed if they knock over a vase as they run around the corridors.

She asks him about his father, and he finds himself telling her how strange it was to hear about his death while he was so far away. 'There isn't any time to grieve when you're at war and now that the war is over ... it seems too late somehow. I still haven't had time to go and collect his belongings.'

For the first time, Elizabeth reaches out and touches him voluntarily. She rests her hand on his. 'I'm so sorry,' is all she says and when he turns his palm up, she lets their fingers link together.

A clasp of hands may not be much to base a proposal on, Philip realises. But just because Elizabeth isn't passionately in love with him doesn't mean they can't have a successful marriage. In fact, it might work better without messy emotions, he reasons. He only has to look at his own parents whose love match couldn't survive exile and illness. And look at Dickie and Edwina's tumultuous marriage! Two passionate, larger-than-life personalities endlessly clashing, constantly having affairs and furious arguments, forever separating and making up. All emotions conducted at fever pitch, for every belly laugh shared, a cutting comment. Every interaction a drama. It is hard sometimes to tell whether they love or hate each other. Philip shudders inwardly at the very thought of being trapped in such a volatile, emotional relationship.

There would be no emotional dramas with Elizabeth. No expectations or demands. And it's not as if he isn't fond of her. He is. Perhaps it might not be the most exciting marriage, but he could do worse, he knows. A lot worse.

Chapter 19

Elizabeth tips her head back against the rim of the bath while Bobo bustles around in the bedroom, laying out an evening dress and finding shoes and a bag. *What ghastly weather we're having.* She could try that. Or, *I do like your dress.* But then what if she's trying to make conversation with a man? The dress opening won't work then. *Isn't it crowded?* That's always a reliable opener, even if it is dull.

Sighing, she gropes around under the water for the sliver of soap, contemplating it glumly when she draws it out. Once, a new bar of soap was a pleasure: the smooth pristine weight of it, the creamy suds, the heady fragrance of lavender or rose or lily-of-the-valley. Nowadays, with rationing still in place, they must eke out every last piece until it is like this one: cracked and almost transparent, riven with brown lines, grudgingly producing a meagre lather, barely more than a smear.

Rather like her attempts at conversation. Everyone else seems to find talking so easy. She has observed them at parties, laughing and chattering and flirting, but she just

145

can't do it. She knows she comes across as stiff and stilted but she is shy, and her position only makes things worse. Nobody knows what to say to the future Queen and she doesn't know what to say to them, so the whole business is wretchedly uncomfortable.

She usually ends up making a beeline for Porchey, who is always happy to talk horses.

But now there's Philip, of course.

She hopes he'll be there tonight. He can always make her laugh. He doesn't make her feel boring or standoffish. Under his intent gaze she becomes intriguing instead of uptight, and the muscles of her face relax into a natural smile.

He won't monopolise her. Elizabeth half wishes he would, but he is careful not to give rise to any gossip. If he talks to her, it is never for too long and if there's dancing, he only dances with her once.

Elizabeth has to watch him charming another woman as they dance past, and that woman is always, *always* beautiful and sophisticated. The other woman knows how to make Philip laugh. She knows just what to say and how to say it, how to tilt her head and smile and slide a glance under her lashes.

Whenever Elizabeth watches that other woman, she has to remind herself to smile at her own partner. It didn't take long before someone told her how 'very close' Philip had been with Osla Benning, who is exactly as beautiful and assured as the other women Philip asks to dance. Osla is married now, Elizabeth is glad to know. She has met Philip's old friend Hélène, too. Bright, bubbly, pretty, friendly ... Hélène is everything Elizabeth is not, and although she is also married with children, she inevitably makes Elizabeth feel gauche in comparison.

With another sigh, Elizabeth gets out of the bath and wraps herself in the towel Bobo has warmed for her. The Scotswoman has been with her since she was a tiny girl, so long that Elizabeth cannot remember Bobo's real name.

Used to being dressed, she lets Bobo fuss around her, zipping her into the dress and twitching the skirt so it hangs properly.

'It's a lovely dress,' Bobo says approvingly. 'The blue is very nice on you.' She bends to pick up a pair of shoes and move them close to Elizabeth's stockinged feet. 'What do you think of these shoes with it?'

'I'm sure they'll be fine.' Elizabeth wiggles first one foot then the other into the shoes while Bobo clicks her tongue.

'You should take a little more interest in what you look like!'

'Honestly, Bobo, I'd rather be in jodhpurs.' Elizabeth studies her reflection glumly.

'Och, come now,' Bobo scolds, handing her a pair of evening gloves. 'You look very pretty. Or you would do if you would only smile,' she adds sternly and Elizabeth blows out a breath.

'I wish Philip was coming here. It's so much more comfortable not to have to go out and make conversation.'

Bobo snorts at Philip's name. 'Don't you like him, Bobo?'

'It's not my place to like or dislike him,' Bobo says stiffly.

'But ...?'

'But he treats you a mite too free and easy, if you ask me.'

Elizabeth smiles and pulls on the gloves, pressing down between the fingers. 'I like that. I like that he doesn't treat me as if I'm made of glass.'

'There's nothing to stop him putting on a tie when he comes to the palace, is there?' Bobo counters. 'But I like the way your eyes always sparkle when he's been,' she concedes.

To her relief, Philip is one of the first people Elizabeth sees when she enters the party that night. He's across the room, looking dashing in evening dress. The room is crowded and the chatter of conversation deafening, competing with music from a gramophone in the corner. Almost everyone is smoking and her eyes sting as she threads her way through the throng, trying to get over to him as subtly as possible.

'Bobo thinks you should dress like that when you come to the palace for supper,' Elizabeth tells him when she gets there, nodding at his dinner jacket and tie. She has to raise her voice above the sound of the party.

Philip raises his brows. 'And who exactly is Bobo?'

'My dresser.'

'Oho,' he says, his eyes gleaming with amusement. 'It's

a good sign if you're talking about me with your dresser. What else does Bobo say?'

Elizabeth laughs and shakes her head. 'I've said too much already!' She mimes zipping her mouth shut. 'Bobo would never tell my secrets, and I would never tell hers.'

'I wish I could say the same about Uncle Dickie's butler who looks after me when I'm staying in Chester Street,' Philip leans closer to make himself heard. 'The man never stops talking! He's a marvel, though, I have to say. I turn up with a razor and a pair of spare shirts, and John shakes his head and whisks everything way. He washes and irons – and even darns my socks.'

His voice is swallowed up by a new record blaring out from the gramophone and Elizabeth cups a hand to her ear. 'He does what?'

'It doesn't matter. It's too noisy to talk. Let's dance instead.'

Elizabeth lets him take her hand and lead her into the middle of room where a small space has been cleared and a few couples are dancing, although there isn't room to do much more than sway together. They have to do the same. She is very conscious of Philip's solid body and the firm clasp of his hand. He's holding her close, but then, he doesn't have much choice, she reasons. It might not be because he wants to ... but he might.

He still hasn't said anything of his feelings. Elizabeth just doesn't know. Gossip has started about his frequent visits to Buckingham Palace. *It's inevitable*, her mother says. Someone has noticed his car coming and going, or perhaps one of servants has been indiscreet. It could even be someone within their social circle.

Ignore it, is her mother's advice but the Queen doesn't want there to be a story. She wants it to be a rumour that can just be dismissed.

It's different for Elizabeth. It might be easier if she were sure of what Philip felt, but as it is, she feels exposed and raw. Only a week earlier, she was asked to open a factory. As soon as she got out of the car, she could see the public lined up to watch her walk to the entrance, their faces alight with avid curiosity.

'Where's Philip?' they yelled.

Elizabeth was horrified. Her feelings for Philip are her own. She kept her expression blank with an effort but inside she was shaking with a mixture of horror, outrage, and disgust. How dare they ask her something so personal? How *dared* they?

'Crawfie, it was *horrible*!' Nearly in tears, she had told her governess what had happened when she got back to the palace.

Crawfie tried to convince her that the crowd wasn't aggressive or rude or as threatening as they appeared. 'I know it seems intrusive, but they don't mean any harm,' she said. 'They're just cheerful and interested.'

It didn't feel like that to Elizabeth. It felt as if the people leaning over the barriers and asking about Philip had pushed into her mind and smeared grubby hands all over her most private thoughts.

Her feelings for Philip are *hers*. They don't belong to anyone else. Those insensitive questions about him have tarnished something precious to her. Now Elizabeth can't bear the thought of going out and being exposed to similar questions.

She isn't a fool. She suspects the reason she found the calls about Philip's whereabouts so offensive is that she didn't know the answer. She didn't know where Philip was. She doesn't know what he feels. He comes to supper at the palace. He is charming. He makes her feel happy.

But what does *he* feel?

Determinedly, Elizabeth pushes the memory of that disastrous factory visit from her mind. She is not at the factory now and there are no crowds shouting questions at her. She is with Philip and he is holding her close and that is all that matters. His cheek is almost, *almost*, resting on her hair and she can see the pulse beating steadily beneath his ear, where his jaw meets his throat. Elizabeth lets herself relax against him. The party has receded and it is as if the two of them are quite alone, dancing in a bubble of air.

When the music ends, Philip doesn't let her go immediately. Slowly she lifts her eyes and they look at each other, still mid sway.

She is sure Philip is going to say something but someone catches his eye and she turns her head to see David Milford

Haven, his eyebrows raised in amusement and a knowing smirk on his face. Philip returns his cousin's look

All at once, Elizabeth sees herself as he must do, a lovestruck nineteen-year-old mooning over a handsome man. Humiliation stabs at her. Is that what the factory crowd see too? Are they all laughing at her?

Snatching her hand out of Philip's, she steps back as if slapped. 'Thank you,' she says with a brittle smile, and ignores his puzzled look as she turns away.

'I'm ready to go home,' she tells the policeman assigned to accompany her out in the evenings.

Chapter 20

Philip curses under his breath as he watches Elizabeth leave. What just happened? She is upset, obviously, but he has no idea why. Everything seemed to be going so well, too, he thinks in frustration. One minute they were dancing, and she was warm and supple in his arms, the next she was rigid and her face was closed.

The coolness in her eyes has hurt him more than he expected. He has grown used to the warmth of her smile when she is with him. Perhaps he has become complacent, Philip thinks with a flicker of anxiety. He has been enjoying the knowledge that Elizabeth prefers him to other men. He's not even worried about Porchey anymore. He is the one, Philip is sure of it. Princess Elizabeth, surely the most sought-after young woman in the world, is his for the taking. It is impossible not to feel an arrogant sense of satisfaction.

Unless she is not for the taking at all. The thought slides uneasily into Philip's mind.

For all her warmth when she looks at him, there is an

unreachable quality to Elizabeth, as if she is detached from the rest of the world. Even at a party like this, where almost everyone comes from an aristocratic or privileged background, she is alone.

And it's true that he has been hesitating to declare himself. She is only nineteen. There is plenty of time and plenty of life to be lived, surely, before he has to settle down and toe the line.

Still, he doesn't like the fact that Elizabeth is upset.

David wanders over and offers Philip a cigarette. 'Lilibet gone already?'

'Yes.'

David raises a brow at the curtness of Philip's reply. 'Had a row?'

'Of course not,' Philip says, bending his head over the lighter and taking a long drag of the cigarette.

'Then why are you looking like thunder?'

'God, David, I don't know,' Philip admits, exasperated with himself more than with his cousin. 'What am I doing? I'm fond of Elizabeth but do I really want to tie myself down for life?'

'Only you know the answer to that, but you'd better make up your mind soon,' warns David. 'I don't know if you really believe you've been discreet, but the gossip columns are linking your name with hers and all sorts of rumours are doing the rounds. If you don't want to go ahead, you should back off now,' he says, adding for good measure, 'and good luck telling Uncle Dickie that!'

Uncle Dickie. Philip needs no reminding of Mountbatten's interest in the affair. He doesn't want to alienate his uncle who would be furious if Philip backed off now. He has already lost one father. He cannot afford to lose another.

It is time to commit himself. The thought leaves Philip depressed. He has to be back at Corsham the next day which at least gives him a chance to postpone the need to make things up with Elizabeth. She'll get over it, whatever it is, he tells himself, but the stricken look in her eyes niggles at him and he is snappy all week. An attempt to distract himself with a darts competition at the Methuen Arms ends in humiliation when he can barely hit the board, to the jeers of the local team.

On Thursday, Philip rings Elizabeth. 'Can I take you out for a drive this weekend?'

There is a slight hesitation at the other end of the line. 'I think it's better if you come here,' she says. 'We'll have supper.'

He misses the joyful lift in her voice, Philip realises as he hangs up. He will have to try harder.

Her dresser's criticism of his wardrobe lingers and he even finds his hand hovering over a tie as he gets ready to go to the palace, but why the hell should he follow convention? He is not going to change. Elizabeth will have to take him as he is.

It's a relief to be shown into her sitting room and discover that Elizabeth is alone, apart from her precious corgi which bustles over to sniff at his ankles.

'No Margaret?'

'Crawfie's taken her to a ballet. I thought it would be better if we were alone.'

'I'm glad.' Philip hesitates. Her hands are folded at her waist as if holding herself in. 'Did I do something wrong last weekend, Elizabeth?' he asks gently. 'You left the party so abruptly.'

Her eyes slide away from his. 'It wasn't anything you did,' she says with difficulty. 'I was ... embarrassed.'

'Embarrassed?' It is the last thing Philip has been expecting.

'People are gossiping.' Elizabeth takes a breath. 'About you and me.'

'I'm afraid they will,' he says. 'Do you want me not to come and see you so often?'

'No ... oh, I don't know what I want!' she bursts out. 'I hate knowing that my private life, my *feelings*, are being talked about in pubs and shops and parties.' She struggles to contain herself before she goes on. 'I went to open a factory the other day and everyone was calling out "Where's Philip?" as if you and I were ... were ...'

'Lovers?' Philip suggests when she trails off.

Colour stains her cheeks and she doesn't answer.

'Is that what you want, Elizabeth?' he asks after a moment.

She turns away to the long window that looks out over the Mall, lit in the darkness by car headlights. A fretful spring day has thrown showers against the windows and the glass is still gleaming with raindrops, tiny silvery circles against the darkness.

Behind her, Philip studies her shimmering reflection in the glass. She looks mysterious, unknowable.

'Do you remember the conversation we had that Christmas at Windsor?' Elizabeth asks at last, still without looking at him.

'Of course. We talked about marriage.'

'We said we would see how things were after the war,' she ploughs on, 'but now the war is over, and I suppose :… I suppose I'd like to know what you think now.'

'About marriage?'

'Yes.'

'To you?'

She lets out a little breath. 'Yes.'

'It wouldn't be straightforward,' Philip says carefully, talking to her reflection. 'It's not just about what we want. I'm still seen as a foreign prince, and you need your father's permission to marry. He's not in favour of the match, you know that.'

'But in principle?'

It's now or never. He can practically hear Uncle Dickie's voice in his ear.

Philip lays his hands on her shoulders and turns her gently to face him. 'In principle, I think I'd like that very much,' he says, 'if you would.'

She swallows. 'I would too.'

'That's settled then.' Ignoring the sinking feeling in the

pit of his stomach as the door to a gilded cage yawns ahead of him, he smiles down at her.

'So what should we do now?' Elizabeth asks.

'I think I should talk to Uncle Dickie and to Uncle Georgie in Greece before I talk to the King.'

'All right.' Her shoulders have relaxed and she looks happier. Philip is conscious of a pang of contrition. It must be hard for her.

'But before that ...' he begins, and she looks up enquiringly when he trails off.

'Yes?'

'There's something else we should do. Something more important.'

Elizabeth looks faintly alarmed. 'What?'

'I think we should kiss, don't you?'

His arms slide down her arms as her eyes widen and an adorably uncertain smile trembles on her lips.

'Maybe we should,' she says.

Chapter 21

Germany, Schloss Salem, April 1946

The driver pulls up outside the arcaded entrance to the Schloss and hauls on the brake. 'This it?' he asks dubiously.

Philip looks up at the familiar façade, pockmarked with artillery fire, its white paint peeling and stained with God knows what. At the decorative brickwork around cracked windows and the red roof tiles patched here and there. An image of the castle as it was before the war shimmers in his head and he tries to superimpose it over the bleak reality.

'Yep,' he says, twisting round to get his kitbag. 'This is it.'

The Canadian studies the array of windows stretching to either side of the crumbling entrance. 'Guess they'll have room for you, anyway,' he says and Philip grins as he drops his kitbag onto the gravel and swings down from the cab.

'They should be able to squeeze me in.' Thumping the door with the flat of his hand, he calls a farewell through the window. 'Thanks for the lift!'

He watches the truck trundle away down the avenue before turning back to face the *schloss*. It is not a place of particularly happy memories for him. The year he spent at school here was not one he enjoyed and it was a relief to be sent back to England.

An even greater relief not to have to visit his mother sitting blank-faced in the sanatorium nearby.

Still, it's sad to see the state the once great palace is in now. If Windsor Castle is looking tired and Buckingham Palace battered by the war, their dilapidation is nothing compared to the *schloss*.

It was an impulse decision to come to Germany. He is on his way to Monte Carlo to collect his father's few effects. That journey is going to be hard enough without complicating matters with a side trip to Germany. But it is nine years since he has seen any of his sisters, and they are all gathered at Schloss Salem for Sophie's wedding to Freddie's brother, Georg, Prince of Hanover. How could he *not* make the effort to come?

Hoisting his kitbag onto his shoulder, he runs up the steps and into the great hallway. An ancient butler with watery eyes starts to confront him in distress at the intrusion, but Philip jerks his head to dismiss him.

'Don't worry, I'm family,' he says, his German coming back without thinking. 'Where are they all? In the salon?

Don't worry,' he says without giving the butler a chance to answer, 'I'll find them myself.'

Dumping his bag unceremoniously on a fragile chair, Philip strides down the long hallway. The sound of chattering leads him unerringly to the right doors, which he throws open so he can step inside. At first glance, the room seems full of women, but as his gaze sweeps over them, he finds just his three sisters. Margarita, Theodora, Sophie.

Only Cecile is missing.

They are all looking older and thinner, but there's plenty of the old dash about them, too, Philip thinks.

All three are sitting on uncomfortable-looking sofas but have turned their heads at the sound of the door opening and, as their eyes alight on him in incredulous disbelief, he grins.

'Hullo.'

There is a moment of absolute silence. Unconsciously, the three women are in the same pose, hands pressed to the base of their throats in shock. They stare at him as if he is a ghost.

'Philip?' Sophie whispers at last. She puts a hand on the arm of the sofa and pushes herself to her feet as if unsure her legs will hold her. 'Philip, is it really you?'

'You didn't think I'd miss your wedding, did you, Tiny?'

'Philip ...'

Sophie stumbles towards him and Margarita and

Theodora are up too and the next moment they have enfolded him in a warm, scented embrace. They are all crying and babbling in a mixture of German, French, and English, kissing and hugging and patting him as if to convince themselves he is real.

Philip endures it for as long as he can before disentangling himself. 'Come on, now, let me breathe!'

Margarita wipes her cheeks. 'Oh, Philip, I can't believe it! What are you doing here? How did you get here?'

'I hitched a lift with the Canadian army.' Philip has spent the past two days in the back of a truck with a platoon of friendly gum-chewing Canadian soldiers. He only made it to the cab to give directions to Schloss Salem. He makes a show of rubbing his backside. 'Not the most comfortable journey I've ever had!'

Far worse than the hard seat was seeing the terrible destruction as the truck jolted across a continent ravaged by war. Almost a year after the Allied victory, Germany is in chaos still, so many of its buildings reduced to rubble, its roads pot-holed, its people bowed under the weight of defeat. After years of patriotic bombast and anti-German propaganda, it is sobering to see the other side of the war. The struggle to rebuild Britain is hard enough, but to Philip the task facing the Germans seems insuperable. Nobody, surely, wanted victory to look like this.

'I am sorry you had an uncomfortable journey,' Sophie says, lifting his hand to her cheek, 'but thank you! Thank you so much for coming, Philip.'

Her eyes fill with tears again and he shifts, uncomfortable with her gratitude. His war has been so much easier than theirs.

Seeing him squirm, Margarita interrupts. 'Oh my God, when he came in, I thought for a moment it was Papa standing the doorway, didn't you, Dolla?'

Theodora nods vigorously. 'I thought the same thing! They look exactly the same. The same way of standing even!'

'I haven't got a monocle,' Philip protests. 'Or a moustache.'

'But everything else ... your features, the way you hold yourself ... it is incredible.' Theodora pats her chest in remembered shock. 'It was like seeing a ghost.'

'Poor Papa, how proud he would have been to see you looking so strong and handsome!'

Three pairs of eyes well up at the thought of their father.

'Here,' Philip says bracingly. 'If you're all going to snivel, you'll make me sorry I came! Weddings are supposed to be happy affairs.'

'Oh, I know,' sniffs Sophie. 'It's just so wonderful to see you and to realise that our little brother has grown up. You've changed so much!'

'So I should hope,' he says. 'I was only sixteen when—' He breaks off, remembering that the last time they had all seen each other was that desperate day in Darmstadt when they had buried Cecile with her husband and two sons and the baby that had never been named.

They are all silent, remembering. 'That terrible day,' Margarita says softly at last. 'The worst of days.' She lets out a long sigh. 'Things have been very bad lately but I often think nothing could be as bad as that day.'

'I wish Cecile could be here now,' Sophie adds. 'She loved it when we were all together. Remember how much fun she was? And you were her favourite, Philip, you know that.'

Cecile had been his favourite sister, too, but Philip keeps that to himself. The memory of Cecile is like a boulder sitting on his chest, crushing his ribs, but somehow he finds a smile.

'I thought I was the favourite of all of you?'

'So you are,' says Margarita, bravely following his lead in trying to lighten the atmosphere. 'That's why you were always the spoilt little prince!'

Philip spreads his hands and affects an air of humility. 'Is it my fault Mama and Papa were so pleased to have a son after all you girls?'

'Hah! We never got a look in after you were born, did we?' Margarita says. 'Do you remember that day, Dolla? Poor Mama had to give birth on the dining room table!' She shudders at the thought.

'Like yesterday,' Theodora says. She claps her hands onto her thighs. 'But before we start on the do-you-remembers, Philip must want a wash.'

'No, I don't,' he says, to tease her, but Dolla is not to be overruled.

'After two days in an army truck, Philip, you certainly do! I'll sort out a room for you,' she says as she stands up. 'Tiny, why don't you ring the bell for some tea?'

'Or something stronger,' says Sophie, getting obediently to her feet and winking at Philip.

Philip stands up too. It never was any use trying to resist Theodora, who was always the practical member of the family, but there's something comforting about how quickly they are able to fall into their old roles. 'Still a bossy boots, I see, Dolla,' he says with a grin and she laughs and makes shooing motions with her hands.

'Still cheeky, *I* see!'

He is glad to have banished some of the sadness in the room. After the first joy of meeting again, he is shocked at what his sisters have been through. He has heard some but not all of it. Sophie's first husband, Christoph, was killed when his plane crashed in 1943. There are rumours that he was murdered on Hitler's orders, but when Philip raises the question, his sisters are evasive.

'We have learned to keep quiet,' Sophie explains later when they are walking in the neglected gardens alone, her hand tucked into the crook of his arm. 'Anyone who spoke out ...' She sighs a little. 'Do you remember Princess Mafalda? They sent her to the camp at Büchenwald. She may have died because of an American bomb, but it was that devil Hitler who killed her.'

Her voice shakes with emotion. Philip isn't sure if it is anger or grief; maybe it is both.

'I have been looking after her children ever since. Poor things, it has been hard for them, with Mafalda in that dreadful camp and their father in prison. We were all staying with Christoph's mother at Friedrichshof, but when the Americans came, they wanted the castle as a rest home for their soldiers.'

She lifts her shoulders in a gesture of resignation. 'Well, we are defeated, we have no choice. We had two hours to pack up and get out. There was no time to retrieve all the family jewels that Christoph hid in the cellars. We thought they would be safe. They were well hidden. And what else could we do? We were all jammed into a tiny house, but it was unendurable. In the end, I took all the children to Wolfsgarten where they gave us refuge.'

Philip frowns. He has heard of how dangerous it was in Germany in those first lawless days after the Allies moved in. Nobody was safe. 'How did you get there?'

'By cart. The children hid under the straw.' Sophie smiles faintly at his expression. 'I know, a princess reduced to travelling in a smelly farmer's cart! That's just how things were, Philip. There were no buses, no trains, no fuel for cars, even if there were any that hadn't been requisitioned. It was frightening, though,' she admits. 'I was terrified that someone would spot the children and rip the clothes from their backs. Or worse. I tell you, in those days, people were starving. Their cities were obliterated. They were feral, like animals. It was every man for himself.'

Philip thinks about his war, those moments of terror

interspersed with, frankly, some bloody good times. He remembers reading Elizabeth's letter about the euphoria on VE Day. The British have suffered during the war, undoubtedly, but not like Germany.

'Come, enough of that.' Reading his expression, Sophie smiles and pats his arm. 'Let us talk of more cheerful things. Tell me about you, Philip. What are you going to do now the war is over?'

He hesitates. 'I'm thinking of getting engaged,' he says slowly.

'We've heard the rumours, of course, but it's hard to know how much to believe.' She cocks her head on one side, studying him. 'It would be a great match.'

'Oh, I know, I know ...' Philip kicks moodily at the weedy gravel. 'Uncle Dickie is being very helpful,' he says, but not as if he is glad about it.

'I can imagine,' says Sophie in a dry voice. 'You don't sound very keen,' she ventures after a while as they turn and walk up the shallow stone steps to the terrace. 'What is Elizabeth like?'

'She's decent,' he says. 'One of the most decent people I've ever met, in fact,' he adds, almost in surprise, realising it as if for the first time. 'There's no side to her. She's shy, and she's kind, and she thinks about other people, which is not something that can be said about the rest of that family,' he adds humorously. 'The Queen can be charming when she wants, but she never considers anyone but herself. Same for the King, but without the charm, and as for

Margaret, she has to be the centre of attention. But Elizabeth ... perhaps it's because she doesn't have to try to be the centre of anything. She just is.'

'Your voice softens when you talk about her,' Sophie observes.

Philip nods. 'I like her.'

'Not love?'

'Come on, Tiny, you know the ropes. For the likes of us, marriage isn't about love.'

'I loved Chri,' she says quietly.

Chastened, he squeezes the hand on his arm. 'I know. I'm sorry, Tiny. Mama wrote to me about what a hard time you've had.'

'Thank you.' Sophie musters a smile. 'But now I am to marry again,' she says, determinedly cheerful. 'I will be happy with Georg. I like him.'

'Not love?'

'Ah, touché ...' She lets go of his arm to lean against the stone balustrade and look out over the neglected gardens. In the distance, Lake Constance gleams in the late afternoon sun. 'Georg is a gentle man, a good man. I will be safe with him. I can make a home with him. I want that more than anything. After all the upheavals, I want to stop moving around and making do and finding my way. And I want the children to have somewhere to belong.' She slides him a glance. 'I suppose you think that's very dull?'

'I don't, actually.' Philip knows exactly what a tantalising idea a home is.

'So now we can stay here at Salem with Dolla and Berthold. Georg is going to be headmaster of the school here. Did you hear that?'

'No, I didn't.'

She glances at him, detecting reserve in his voice. 'A come down for a Prince of Hanover, you think?'

'I'm a Prince of Greece and I barely own what I stand up in,' Philip says. 'I'm in no position to talk about come downs to anyone, Tiny!'

'But that would change if you married. You would leap-frog over them all.'

He lets out a half-laugh. 'Perhaps.'

'So you could marry someone kind who you like and snub your nose at anyone who's ever looked down at you?'

'Has Uncle Dickie been talking to you?' Philip gives her a quizzical look and she laughs.

'Of course not. Come, what is the problem? You have a girl who is decent and kind – and let me tell you, kindness is the most underrated of qualities – on top of which, she is a great heiress, possibly the greatest in the world today.'

'Because she is heir to the throne of England,' he agrees. 'Which I know is the point. If she weren't, Uncle Dickie wouldn't be pushing so hard for me to marry her. But with the throne goes the court,' he says. 'God, Tiny, if you knew what they were like! It's bristling with moustachioed old men who fought in the trenches. Very honourably, no doubt, but their ideas haven't moved on since. Things at Buckingham Palace have hardly changed since George V.

The whole place needs a good boot up its backside, if you ask me.'

He scowls out at the lake, remembering. 'They're all living in the last century with their protocols and God knows what. Half of them are having conniptions because sometimes I turn up to a nursery supper without a tie! It'd be like wading through mud trying to change anything, and it needs to change,' he insists. 'We've just been through a war. *Everything* needs to change.'

'If you were married to Elizabeth you could be part of that change,' Sophie suggests mildly.

His mouth turns down at the corners. 'I don't see that lot letting anything change without a fight and honestly haven't we all had enough of fighting for now?'

'Well, all I can say is that I was happy with Chri and I hope to be happy with Georg too. Perhaps as women we don't ask for so much. That might be true of Princess Elizabeth too. But you must do what feels right for you,' she says, straightening. She takes his hands and squeezes them. 'I'm just *so* glad to see you. I can't tell you how much it means to me that you came, Philip.'

'I'm glad I did.'

Chapter 22

In spite of the tears that make him squirm, it's true. They have been divided by war, but now they are sitting around a table, a family once more. Philip remembers kindly Berthold, Theodora's husband, and Prince Gottfried of Hohenlohe-Langenburg, married to Margarita, from before the war. It is surreal to think that until the year before, they were the enemy, high ranking SS officers. Now they are just Berthold and Friedel again.

How he has missed this, Philip realises. The teasing and the reminiscences, the jokes and the laughter. Thinking about his mother usually leaves him seething with conflicting emotions but here with his sisters, he is at last able to see the funny side.

Remember how she used to bless her teacups?

What about the time she climbed out of the window with a bundle of laundry?

Don't forget when she decided she was a saint and bride of Christ. That creepy smile she had!

'Oh, it's not funny really,' Dolla says as one story follows another and they are all laughing helplessly.

No, not funny, Philip thinks, but this is the first time he has been able to listen to stories of his mother told with affection. The first time he has been able to laugh about her with people who loved her as much as he did.

He belongs here in a way he never has anywhere else, except perhaps on the deck of a warship.

'It's a shame Mama couldn't be here,' Margarita says as Theodora sends Berthold to find another bottle of the wine secreted in the cellars.

'I did ask her,' says Sophie. 'But how would she have got here from Athens? It's impossible trying to move around at the moment.'

'Philip managed it,' Berthold points out.

'Philip is resourceful, and a young man. I can't see Mama hitching a lift in an army truck, can you?'

'Oh, I don't know. Your mother has no sense of grandeur. I've never met anyone who behaves less like a princess. She would be quite happy in the back of a truck.'

'That's true,' says Theodora with a sigh. 'I think she is safer in Athens, in any case. Although she would probably approve of how dull we are going to look at the wedding tomorrow. Didn't Tiny tell you?' she asks when Philip looks enquiring.

'Tell me what?'

Sophie's hand flies to her mouth. 'Can you believe I forgot? That is the good thing about you coming, Philip.

We were all in shock about the jewels, but you arriving quite knocked all that out of our heads.'

'What jewels?' he asks.

'All the Hesse family jewels! Diamonds, rubies, emeralds ... necklaces, tiaras ... even some letters from Queen Victoria ... everything of value we had.' Sophie sighs. 'Remember I told you that we didn't have time to take them when we left Friedrichshof? Well, we asked permission to go back and retrieve them and Dolla, Margarita, and I went there yesterday.'

'We wanted to put on a show for the wedding,' Margarita puts in.

'But when we got there, they'd been stolen!'

'Stolen?'

'We've taken the matter up with the American authorities,' Friedel says grimly. 'It looks as if someone there has been poking around in the cellars. When it was obvious that we were going to end up at war, Christoph built a secret chamber and it made sense at the time to put all the princesses' jewels safely together in a box which he hid under the flagstones and then bricked in. But someone must have noticed the new brickwork. They'd broken down the wall, lifted the flagstones and helped themselves to the jewels.'

'It was such a shock!' Margarita's voice trembles at the memory. 'That empty box! It was as if they had taken all our dignity away.'

'We will have to rely on the Americans to get the jewels back,' says Berthold.

'Well, anyway, even before you arrived, Philip, we had decided not to be downcast about it,' Dolla tells him. 'We have endured worse than losing our jewels. It would have been nice to have put on a show for Sophie's wedding, but we don't need tiaras to hold our heads high.'

'Good for you,' Philip says, smiling at her. His sisters were tougher than he remembered.

'And it means more to have you here than to have diamonds to wear,' Margarita tells him fondly.

Sophie marries Georg in the chapel the next day. Her dress is old, even to Philip's inexpert eye, and for a royal wedding, it is a quiet affair. But bride and groom look happy, which Philip supposes is the main thing, and Dolla and Berthold do their best to provide a wedding breakfast, helped along by another of Berthold's secret visits to his cellar for champagne.

'Your turn next, I hear?' Berthold says to Philip when they are sitting over the remains of the meal.

Philip suppresses a sigh. 'Nothing is settled yet. It may never happen, Berthold. Plenty of people don't like the idea of Elizabeth marrying me.'

'Because of us?' Berthold glances around the room.

'Partly. The German connection is never going to be helpful,' Philip says honestly. 'It's unfair but there it is. Nothing is settled in Greece either, and until it is, it seems I can't be naturalised as a British citizen. The King and Queen aren't keen on me.' He shrugs. 'Meanwhile the gossip mills are going into overdrive. It was a relief to get away for a while,' he admits. 'And the truth is that I haven't yet asked Elizabeth to marry me – or she hasn't asked me, which I gather she has to do, technically.'

'And what will you say if she does?'

Philip meets his brother-in-law's eyes and smiles a little crookedly. 'I have absolutely no idea,' he says.

Chapter 23

Café de Paris, Monte Carlo, April 1946

The white-jacketed waiter sets two martinis on the table in front of them and fades discreetly away. Philip picks his glass up and throws half the martini down his throat.

'Steady on,' says Mike. 'You'll be blotto before she gets here.'

'That was the idea. It's not every day you meet your father's mistress for polite chit chat.'

The gin is a welcome burn at the back of his throat but Philip puts his glass down. After all the hugging and kissing and tears when he said goodbye to his sisters, he was glad to meet up with Mike Parker. A fellow naval officer, the Australian has been his friend and rival since their days based at Rosyth, escorting merchant navy ships down E-boat Alley. Mike can be counted on to offer undemanding company on Philip's trip to Monaco. Philip is grateful for the moral support and the knowledge that Mike won't weep on him or ask him how he feels about his father or anything else.

He is here in Monte Carlo to pick up Prince Andrea's effects, but first he has to make the acquaintance of Comtesse Andrée de la Bigne. They have arranged to meet at the Café de Paris, which in other circumstances Philip would have enjoyed. The café is decorated in the *belle époque* style, with its elaborate light fittings and ornate décor, although its glory is faded like so much else after the war, and there is an air of faint desperation to its customers. Their once-fashionable clothes are shiny with use and threadbare beneath the women's furs.

Of course, he is not one to talk, Philip thinks, wiggling his big toe under its latest darn.

He's not sure why he feels so nervous. He can hardly remember his parents living together and although Princess Alice still thinks of herself as Andrea's wife, his mother has been serenely accepting of the comtesse's role in his father's life. It is not as if the comtesse has been a secret either. The war might have made communication difficult, but letters have been going backwards and forwards via neutral countries. Even his grandmother, frosty-eyed in her apartment at Kensington Palace, had shown herself remarkably well-informed about his father's affairs and had issued dire warnings when Philip had told her he was going to Monaco.

'Don't expect an inheritance,' she said. 'That woman will have sucked him dry. Such women generally do.' She waved cigarette smoke from her face with a harsh, wheezing cough. 'Be careful she doesn't get her claws into *you*, Philip. You don't want any association with that kind of woman getting back to the palace. If you take my advice – which I know you won't because you never do – you'll leave well alone. Your father was a wastrel.'

Philip and Mike have barely finished their martinis when there is a stir at the door. They look up and Mike's jaw drops. Philip rather suspects he looks equally dazzled. A woman of a certain age is standing there, accepting the attention as her due. She is striking rather than beautiful, svelte and superbly elegant in a tight-waisted pale blue suit and a chic hat set at precisely the right angle. She has a presence that cannot be ignored: having cast a dazzling smile around the room, she gives a gracious nod of acknowledgement and her gaze settles on Philip who without thinking gets to his feet. The smile warms and she glides over to their table.

'Oh, how like your father you are, dear boy,' she greets him in a husky voice. 'I would have known you anywhere.'

'Comtesse ...'

'No, no, you must call me Andrée,' she insists. 'We are practically family, are we not?' Her gaze turns to Mike, who actually blushes. 'And who is this handsome fellow?'

Before Philip quite knows what has happened, she has settled them on either side of her, summoned a waiter without appearing to lift so much as an eyebrow and ordered a bottle of champagne.

'Because your papa would want us to celebrate meeting at last. There will be time to be sad later.'

Her charm was a tangible thing. It was impossible not to like her. Philip was mesmerised by the husky laugh, the humorous lilt in her voice. She *was* beautiful, he decided. In her fifties, perhaps, but aging so gracefully that the faint lines only added to the character of her face.

After joining them in a glass of champagne, Mike made his excuses and discreetly left them to it.

'What a good friend he is,' the comtesse comments before she turns back to Philip. 'But I confess, I am glad to be alone with you so we can get to know each other properly. I have heard so much of you from Andrea. He was so very proud of you.'

Halfway through the bottle, she and Philip are getting on like the proverbial house on fire, and Philip is feeling decidedly tipsy. 'I understand now why my father was so happy to stay here in Monte Carlo,' he says. He has a feeling he might be looking a bit owlish but doesn't care. 'If he had you for company, Comtesse, he must have been a happy man.'

'Ah, Philip ...' She pats his cheek. 'You have his charm! But you know, your father was *not* a happy man.'

'I remember him as happy,' Philip says stubbornly. 'He was always joking and making everyone laugh. He had a real ability to see the funny side of life.'

'That, yes.' The comtesse shrugs in the way only a Frenchwoman can. 'But he wasn't happy. He was in exile.

How could he be completely happy when he could not go home?'

'But it had been years since he was in Greece!'

'It was still his home, and no one can be truly happy if they cannot go home.'

'That rather depends on whether you have a home to go to, doesn't it?' Philip asks and she looks at him closely. 'Where is home to you?'

'I don't have one,' he says. 'I haven't had a home since my parents fled Crete and I was barely more than a baby.'

The Comtesse shakes her head. 'Then you must find a home, Philip. Find a place you can belong and be happy.'

Later, she takes him to the villa where she is staying and shows him into a room where his father's effects are laid out on a bed. 'I will leave you alone,' she says with a glance at his face.

Philip walks over to the bed. Andrea's gold signet ring is there. He slides it onto his little finger where it sits, a cool, unfamiliar weight, a part of his father that is now a part of him.

There is an ivory shaving brush, some books, some pictures. Clothes, mostly motheaten and heavily darned. It is not much to show for a life, let alone for a life as the son of a king. Philip's chest aches as he touches the items gently and remembers his father, the chuckle in his voice, the kindness and the genial charm.

Had he been unhappy? Now that the Comtesse has pointed it out, Philip knows it was true. Andrea had had a wife, admittedly eccentric, and a large and happy family, but they were never enough. Oh, he had loved them, but perhaps none of them could make up for the loss of his home.

You must find a home, Philip. Find a place you can belong and be happy.

Andrea had loved his son, but the truth was that he had handed over responsibility to the Mountbattens, Georgie and Dickie. Could he do any better as a father? Philip wonders.

What would that be like, to have a son? To have a family of his own? A home?

If he marries Elizabeth, he could have all of that.

His son, if he has one, could be King of England.

He has to ask Elizabeth to marry him first.

Enough drifting, Philip decides abruptly. His sisters are getting on with their lives. It is time he knuckles down and does the same.

Chapter 24

Buckingham Palace, May 1946

'We haven't seen much of Philip lately.' The Queen pours another cup of coffee and glances with studied casualness at Elizabeth who is gazing abstractedly out of the window.

Sunshine is pouring into the breakfast room, striping the mahogany table and making the silver lids on the jam pots flash. Outside, the sky is a soft clear blue. After a disappointingly cool start to spring, the air has warmed over the past few days and the last leaves on the trees in the palace garden have unfurled in a fresh flourish of green. Elizabeth is wishing that she were at Windsor. It is a perfect day for a ride.

Or to spend with Philip. He might drive her down to Coppins where Marina is always so relaxed and welcoming and you're allowed to curl up on a sofa with your feet tucked up beneath you. Elizabeth likes being there, with Philip lounging in an armchair and the dogs' paws twitching as they sleep. It feels as if that is what a home should be like.

But Philip isn't here.

'Lilibet.' Margaret nudges her beneath the table with her foot. 'You're daydreaming again.'

'What? Oh, sorry.' Elizabeth picks up her knife and resumes buttering her toast. 'What was that, Mummy?'

'I was just saying that Philip hasn't been around as much.'

Elizabeth doesn't miss the hopeful note in the Queen's voice. Her parents would like it if she lost interest in Philip.

'He's in France at the moment.'

Philip has written to her about his visit to his sisters in Germany, but Elizabeth decides not to share that with her mother. His German relatives are a sore point with the Queen. He has told her about his meeting with the Comtesse de la Bigne, too, and the villa where his father died. He described the bougainvillaea scrambling over the terrace and the heady smell of mimosa. He has told her that Prince Andrea left debts of over £17,000, *seven-tenths of which is mine*, he added wryly. *I am afraid it is not much of an inheritance.*

Elizabeth does not care about his inheritance, but she understands that Philip might. Niggling at the back of her mind is the fear that he might use his poverty as an excuse to back away.

'Still?' The Queen sniffs. 'It can't take that long to sort

out his father's affairs, surely? It's not as if Andrea had
anything to leave.'

'Yes, still,' Elizabeth says shortly. 'Margaret, please could
you pass the marmalade?'

Philip's latest letter was from Paris. He stopped there
on his way home and arranged to meet Hélène Foufounis
or whatever she was called now. For reasons Elizabeth
does not understand, Hélène, now divorced, has left her
two children with her mother in London and is living on
her own and working as a shop girl in Paris. Philip has
told Elizabeth of the fun they are having, how they raced
across Paris, he on a ridiculously small bicycle, while
Hélène took the metro. Hélène won, of course, and was
helpless with laughter at the sight of him pedalling frantically down the Champs Elysées, his knees practically
up to his ears.

Hélène had actually dared walk into the Travellers Club
where he was staying.

*No women are allowed across its hallowed portals, so
you can imagine the horror! I bundled her out pretty
quickly and gave her a lecture on not intruding into
an all-male sanctuary, though she didn't seem to understand in the least.*

He and Hélène lunch or dine together almost every
day, delicious meals in marvellously cheap bistros where
Hélène knows the owner, of course. They have taken a

horse-drawn carriage across Paris. They have strolled over the Pont Neuf and under the lime trees in the Tuileries.

Elizabeth knows none of these places. All she knows is that Philip is having a good time without her and seems in no hurry to come home.

He kissed her, Elizabeth reminds herself again and again. It was her first kiss, and he would not have done it if he hadn't been serious, would he?

She thought it was all settled, bar some complications to do with Greek politics, but then Philip disappeared. He told her he was going to collect his father's effects, but he has extended his trip again and again, first to Germany and now to Paris. Elizabeth doesn't mind him enjoying himself, of course she doesn't. He probably needs some light-hearted fun after the emotion of going through his father's things. And she isn't jealous of Hélène, not really. She understands that Hélène is one of Philip's oldest friends.

It's just hard to convince herself that Philip is missing her as much as she is missing him.

'He'll be home soon,' she tells her mother, praying that it will be true. She takes a bite of toast and waits until she has swallowed before adding, 'I thought it would be nice to invite him to Balmoral this August.'

She is tired of waiting, Elizabeth realises. She wants things to be settled. There are too many distractions for Philip here in London. She longs to get away and take him with her, where they can think. The image of Balmoral rises before her: golden hills, clear air, the quiet broken only by the wind and the gentle rush of the Dee.

Across the table, her comment is met with an unenthusiastic silence. The Queen has been stirring her coffee and now puts the teaspoon into the saucer with a chink. 'Do you think that's a good idea?'

'I wouldn't have suggested it if I didn't.'

The Queen looks taken aback at the sharpness in her daughter's voice. 'I just meant that Philip isn't ... well, he's not exactly ...'

'Not exactly what?'

'Well ... he's not at home in the country, is he? Does he even shoot?'

'He can learn.'

'I just feel that he might not ... *fit in* at Balmoral.' The Queen is floundering under Elizabeth's cool stare. 'It might be uncomfortable for him.'

Elizabeth sets her knife neatly on the plate. Her face is calm, her movements precisely controlled as she folds up the napkin on her lap and puts it to one side. 'What are you trying to say, Mummy?'

'I know you like Philip, Lilibet, but Papa and I really don't feel it would be a good match for you. I mean, he's very handsome, I can see that, but you want more than good looks in a husband. You want someone who understands you, someone who belongs, and Philip doesn't. He's not *one of us*,' she finishes with a helpless shrug.

'She means he didn't go to Eton,' Margaret puts in from the other side of the table.

'He's a prince,' Elizabeth points out. 'I would have thought being royal would trump going to Eton.'

The Queen's lips tighten. She is not royal by birth, and it rankles.

'He's a foreign prince. That's not the same thing at all.'

'He won't be foreign when he has British citizenship.'

'Attlee thinks the timing isn't right for that. The situation in Greece is very precarious at the moment. George may be back as king but the communists are still strong. British troops are there supporting the royalists, but if a Greek prince suddenly becomes a British citizen, it won't look good politically – or diplomatically,' the Queen points out. 'We can't afford to look too involved in Greek affairs.

'As far as the public is concerned, he'll still be foreign,' she goes on. 'Most of his family are Germans, not to mention that ghastly old grandmother of his in Kensington Palace. His brothers-in-law were part of the Nazi regime. Philipp of Hesse could be facing a war crimes trial. It may be unfair but the people won't like it, not after the war.'

'Isn't it more a question of what *I* would like?' Elizabeth asks.

'Papa and I only want what's best for you,' the Queen says irritably. 'You're very young still and you've barely met any other men.'

'Mummy, that's ridiculous,' Margaret says. 'Lilibet's met bags of men.'

'Thank you, Margaret.' Elizabeth offers her sister a faint smile.

'Well, if you'll take my advice, Lilibet, you'll be careful about encouraging Philip too much.' The Queen pushes back her chair. 'Fitting in might seem boring to you, but we all know what happened the last time a member of the royal family chose someone who wasn't one of us!'

Margaret rolls her eyes after their mother. 'The dreaded spectre of Uncle David and Mrs Simpson! I wondered how long it would be before she brought them up.' She pours herself more coffee and glances at Elizabeth's set face. 'Don't take it to heart, Lil. They'll come around to Philip, if he is who you really want?'

'Yes, it is. It's him or no one.'

It's a relief to own it to her sister. Philip is the only man for her. Elizabeth feels it deep in her core, an unwavering certainty that she doesn't even understand herself. Sometimes Philip can be distant, at others warm and friendly. The mixture of boisterous fun and arrogant reserve is intriguing. She likes the unpredictability of it. It's invigorating, never knowing what he will say or do. It keeps the blood fizzing along her veins.

Everybody else behaves to her in exactly the same way: they are often charming, always polite and deferential. At social occasions, the onus is on her to put people at their ease, but there is never anyone to put *her* at her ease. They treat her like a princess.

Philip treats her as Elizabeth.

It is not just that he is handsome. It is more that his vitality seems to suck the oxygen greedily from the room, leaving her short of breath. The very air seems to crisp when he walks through it. The light is sharper, smells are more intense. In his presence, Elizabeth is aware of her own body in a way she never has been before. She can feel the slow pulse of blood along her veins, the tiny fizz of awareness underneath her skin.

She meets Margaret's gaze. 'I won't give him up,' she says.

'I shouldn't worry,' Margaret says. 'They won't let you do an Uncle David. If you refuse to be Papa's heir, then they would be left with me, and we all know what a disaster *that* would be.'

Elizabeth can hardly miss the thread of bitterness in her sister's voice. 'You'd be bored as Queen,' she says lightly. 'You'd have to behave yourself.'

If she wasn't going to be Queen, would Philip even think of marrying her?

'That's true.' Margaret threw herself carelessly back in her chair in a way she would never have dared if her mother had still been there. 'It doesn't sound any fun at all. You can keep the top job, Lil. You can always wait until you're twenty-five and then you can marry who you want without Papa's permission.'

Five years is a long time to wait. Elizabeth can't see Philip having the patience for that.

She is going to have to do something.

Chapter 25

Balmoral Castle, August 1946

'I'm perfectly capable of unpacking my own bag, dammit.' Philip jerks an irritable shoulder as he stands at the window.

Behind him, the footman who has been assigned to act as his valet is laying out the meagre and much-patched contents of his solitary naval valise on the bed. Philip has driven himself to Balmoral, a long but exhilarating drive, and he hasn't brought a valet with him. What does he need with a valet? True, John Dean, the Mountbattens' butler, often ensures that he looks presentable in London, but he can hardly drag his uncle's servant to Scotland without so much as a by-your-leave.

But it seems that he has miscalculated. The King, a stickler for convention, has insisted that he have a valet for his visit, and the dour Ewan, at least twice Philip's age, is evidently under instructions not to be sent away.

Watching Ewan lay out his father's threadbare dinner

jacket without comment makes Philip more uncomfortable than he wants to admit. Next come the worn socks, all of them badly in need of a darn, and the scuffed walking shoes with an unmistakable hole in the sole.

Ewan studies the shoes for a moment. 'Would you like these to be sent to the cobbler in the village, sir?'

Philip's mouth twists with a mixture of embarrassment and impatience. 'That would be helpful, yes,' he manages to grind out.

Ewan pokes around in the valise. 'And your spare shoes ...?'

'I've got what's there. That's it.'

The unpacking continues in disapproving silence. When everything is laid out on the bed, Ewan studies Philip's wardrobe.

'I see you have no kilt, sir.'

'Do I look like a man who'd wear a bloody skirt?'

The footman's expression is carefully blank but the atmosphere is frosty.

'And pyjamas?'

'Never wear the things. Can't stand 'em.'

Nor does Philip possess plus fours for shooting or a gun of his own. He is wearing flannel trousers and an open-necked shirt but in spite of being in the middle of bloody nowhere, it appears something more formal is expected.

It's too late now, Philip tells himself, shrugging off Ewan's unspoken contempt. The man will get no kudos in the servants' hall for looking after the penniless prince, that is obvious.

The main thing is that he is here. Invitations to Balmoral are an honour and he wonders how Elizabeth managed it. Reading between the lines, Philip gathers that neither the King nor the Queen were keen to invite him and although Elizabeth hasn't said as much, he understands that the visit is something of a test, a chance for him to prove himself.

Well, he is ready for that. Uncle Dickie has warned that there are still problems with his naturalisation, largely thanks to his cousin George's inability to deal with the communists in Greece, and there is no sign that the King is ready to give his daughter permission to marry, but Philip is determined to sort matters out with Elizabeth once and for all. There has been too much shilly-shallying.

Turning his back on Ewan's carefully blank expression, Philip contemplates the view, such as it is. Heavy grey clouds slump over the landscape, obscuring the hills he drove through earlier, and the trees themselves seem to be sagging beneath the weight of the rain that has evidently been falling in sheets but has now slowed to a dreary mizzle. Scotland's summer seems every bit as damp and dreich as its reputation.

His room is on the ground floor and about as far away from the bathroom as it is possible to get. Although apparently he is lucky that there is a bathroom at all. Modern conveniences are evidently an afterthought at Balmoral.

Like the rest of the house – or at least what he has glimpsed of it so far – the room is decorated in a riot of tartan: tartan curtains, tartan carpet, tartan rug on the bed. There's even a tartan soap dish on the old-fashioned washstand. Ewan has already informed him that hot water will be brought in a jug. A jug! Perhaps he's lucky not to have been issued with a chamber pot.

Philip allows himself a wistful memory of the Mountbattens' house, so comfortably equipped and convenient. What is it about the Windsors that makes them embrace frugality so eagerly? It's almost as if they're embarrassed by their own royalty.

Nothing appears to have changed at Balmoral since Queen Victoria's day. On the way to his room, he was led down corridors crowded with gloomy landscapes – all too accurate judging by the view from Philip's window – and moth-eaten antlers. The flocked wallpaper in his room is still marked with the old queen's cypher, VRI. Philip traces it with his finger. Victoria Regina Imperatrix. Victoria, Queen and Empress.

And his great-grandmother, Philip reminds himself.

He may not be able to afford a new suit or plus fours, but he is as royal as Elizabeth. He has stayed at some of great palaces of Europe. He shouldn't care what a footman thinks of his wardrobe.

But he still wishes the fellow would stop fussing around and go.

It is all worth it, though, when he goes along to the

drawing room as commanded and Elizabeth comes towards him, holding out her hands. Her smile is so dazzling that Philip actually blinks. Recovering, he smiles back as he takes her hands and gives her fingers a meaningful squeeze. He even begins to lean down to kiss her on the cheek before he catches the King's eye over her shoulder. The royal gaze is thunderous, and Philip, in a rare burst of discretion, straightens and steps back.

Still, he is glad that Elizabeth stays by his side as he goes to make his bow to the King, who is correctly dressed, unlike Philip. The buttons on his short jacket and waistcoat are bright, his kilt and sporran neat, his ghillie brogues polished to a shine. In person, though, the King is thin and prematurely stooped, and a muscle twitches under his eye.

'What do you think you're wearing?' he barks. He can't bear incorrect dress.

Philip looks down at his dinner jacket and trousers, annoyed to find he is glad Ewan polished up his old shoes without asking so at least they look respectable. 'Sir?'

'Papa, you can hardly expect Philip to have a kilt,' Elizabeth puts in calmly.

'I can expect him to be properly dressed,' says the King, eying the bagginess around Philip's shoulders with disfavour. 'Where did you get that jacket from?'

'I borrowed it from Uncle Dickie,' Philip says cheerfully. He might as well be upfront about his lack of wardrobe. 'He's much broader than me, as you know, so it's not a great fit.' He plucks at the front of the jacket to demon-strate. 'But it seemed a better option than my father's old dinner jacket, which fits better but which is distinctly threadbare.'

The King snorts.

Elizabeth lays a hand on her father's arm. 'Papa, do you think we should tell Philip what the routine is at Balmoral?'

'Haven't you told him yet?' The King is clearly still in a bad mood although Elizabeth's touch seems to be calming.

'I was afraid it might put him off.' She sends Philip a glimmering smile. 'There's walking, fishing, shooting, stalking ...'

'A sportsman's paradise,' the King adds.

'I'm afraid my sport is cricket,' says Philip. 'Although I'm not bad at darts either.'

The King is unamused. 'You don't shoot?' he asks incred-ulously.

'Sadly not, sir.' He notices the temperature dropping and encounters a clear look from Elizabeth. 'But I'm very willing to learn,' he recovers himself and is rewarded by a lessening of the black look on the King's face.

'Good, good. We'll send you out with a ghillie tomorrow. Get you a feel for stalking,' the King says. 'It's a sport that demands fitness, cunning, and endurance, isn't that so, Lilibet?'

'It is.' She exchanges a warm smile with her father but when she turns to Philip, her eyes hold more than a hint of mischief. 'You'll love it, Philip. Wait until you bag your first deer.'

Somehow Philip doubts that. There's cricket, of course, but generally his tastes run to activities that will make his adrenalin surge: waterskiing or driving fast along a winding road or clinging to the mast, the salt spray stiff on his face, as a boat ploughs into a ten-foot wave.

The thought of spending a day trudging over a boggy hillside in the rain leaves him cold, but the message is clear.

He must learn to shoot to please Elizabeth and the King.

He forces a smile. 'I'll look forward to it.'

When he is woken early the next morning to the sound of rain slashing against the window, Philip is strongly tempted to turn over and tell Ewan to bugger off and let him sleep. But the memory of that bad-tempered twitch under the King's eye has him dragging himself out of bed. He will need to make up for the lack of proper wardrobe somehow.

Still yawning, he stumbles along to the breakfast room, only to be met by an appalled silence as the King and the other assembled men, all of them dressed in the regulation plus fours, regard his flannel trousers in horror.

'For God's sake, man!' The King glares at him. 'Didn't they send you a clothing list? You're not seriously proposing to go out on the hill in those trousers, are you?'

'It's these or nothing, I'm afraid, sir.'

Determined not to be cowed, Philip helps himself to

bacon and eggs from the large chafing dishes set out on the sideboard. The faces around the breakfast table are mostly familiar from the evening before: a mixture of local landowners with beefy faces and the stalwarts of the moustachioed courtiers, all of whom seem to have perfected that long-faced, well-bred English look which enables them to convey contempt with the slight lift of an eyebrow.

Apart from Elizabeth, and Margaret who is as pert as ever, his welcome at Balmoral has been distinctly chilly. How quickly the war has been forgotten, Philip thinks to himself, remembering how much warmer the King and Queen had been when he had tales from the frontline to amuse them.

Or perhaps it had been when he was just a distant relative instead of a penniless and determined suitor to their daughter's hand?

Chapter 26

Philip doesn't care. He is here because Elizabeth wants him here, and if the rest of them don't like it, they can go hang. Standing next to her last night, he had met the assembled disapproval with a challenging gaze.

'I keep expecting you to nip Lilibet's neck,' Margaret said to him at one point when they found themselves alone. She was sitting on the arm of a sofa; he was watching Elizabeth who was talking to a stout young man who doubtless had acres of grouse moor to his name.

Philip stared down at Margaret, unsure if he had heard correctly. 'To do *what*?'

'Nip her neck. You know, like a stallion.' Margaret sipped at her glass before registering his blank expression. 'Oh, I keep forgetting you're not a horsey type. A stallion nips at a mare's neck to cut her out of the herd. That's exactly what you look like when you're standing next to Lilibet, like you've cut her out and staked your claim and are daring anyone else to have her. It's quite ... arousing.'

Philip was betrayed into a laugh. 'How old are you now, Margaret?'

'Sixteen. Almost,' she added.

'Pretty and precocious, that's a dangerous mixture. You're going to be a handful.'

'Oh, I do hope so,' she said. 'There's nothing else for me to be, is there?'

After breakfast, Philip finds himself with others milling around outside the entrance in the rain with dogs and lugubrious-looking ghillies while the King barks orders about who is to go where and with whom. It is the only time Philip has ever seen him look truly confident. Here, on this isolated estate, Bertie can be king indeed.

There is a near disaster when the King discovers that not only does Philip not own plus fours, he hasn't brought his own gun.

'He can borrow mine, Papa,' Elizabeth says quickly, spotting that the King is on the verge of one of his notorious 'gnashes'. 'I'm riding today anyway.'

'Thank you,' Philip says sincerely as Elizabeth hands him her gun, and her quick smile warms him. He lowers his voice. 'The King isn't really planning to go out in this, is he?' he says, turning his collar up against the rain. 'I thought he would have cancelled by now'

Elizabeth looks surprised. 'Why would he do that?'

'It's raining.'

'This isn't *rain*.' She pats his arm and he observes darkly that there is a glint of amusement in her eyes. 'This is just a bit of drizzle. It'll clear up, don't worry.'

The King is in such a bad mood by the time everyone is sorted out that Philip is glad to be sent off on his own for the day, accompanied by a monosyllabic ghillie introduced as Murdoch. It is apparently Murdoch's task to find him a deer and show him how to kill it.

For miles and miles, Philip trudges behind Murdoch into the hills. He has had to borrow some boots until his shoes come back from the cobblers and as most of the time they seem to be walking through a bog, his socks are quickly sodden and a mammoth blister is developing on his heel.

Elizabeth is right, it does clear up. Or at least the sullen clouds haul themselves sufficiently off the mountain tops to enable him to see the bleak hillsides stretching into the distance. At which point the misery of the rain seeping down his collar is replaced by the torment of midges swarming around his head.

You'll love it. Wasn't that what Elizabeth had said? She must have known what it would be like.

Suspecting some kind of test, Philip grits his teeth and soldiers on.

Meanwhile Murdoch walks ahead with a steady, untiring tread, apparently unbothered by midges or rain or anything else. His weathered face is unreadable beneath his tweed cap. Every now and then he stops and takes out binoculars to scan the hillside, which at least gives Philp a chance to try and ease the agonising rub of the rough sock on his blister.

It is a huge relief when Murdoch indicates that they should stop for lunch. Sitting with their backs to a massive boulder, they share a venison pie and a flask of tea. Murdoch is evidently not much of a one for conversation and Philip is so tired he is happy to sit silently and study the majestic sweep of the mountains, where subtle shades of gold and brown blend seamlessly with grey rocks and purple heather.

There is a kind of beauty to it, he grudgingly admits to himself, though frankly he would have preferred to admire it from his bedroom window.

'It doesn't look as if we're going to see any deer today,' Philip suggests at last, slapping at his neck where a crowd of midges are dive-bombing like a plague of Messerschmitts. He is hoping Murdoch will suggest they go back but the ghillie only finishes his mouthful of pastry before answering.

'It's a wee bit early to give up yet,' he says. 'Unless you want to, sir?'

'No, no, of course not,' says Philip hastily. 'Let's go on.'

'Terrific,' he says when Elizabeth asks him how he got on. 'Any luck?'

For Philip the luckiest part had been the moment when Murdoch had finally decided there were no deer to be had that day. And then being met at the foot of the hill by a comfortably upholstered car to be driven back to Balmoral. Stripping off his sodden clothes and limping along the endless corridors to find tea laid out on a table in the drawing room: shrimps and scones, bannock cakes and hot sausage rolls. *That* had felt like luck.

'Afraid not,' he says.

'Oh, poor you. Better luck tomorrow.'

About to take a bite of sausage roll, Philip pauses and looks at her more closely. 'You knew what it would be like on the hill today.' He pretends to scowl. 'You're enjoying this, aren't you?'

Elizabeth gives in and laughs. 'A little bit, maybe. Usually I'm the one who feels out of place,' she confesses. 'Now you know how I feel at parties. Was it awful?'

'What, you mean apart from the incessant rain and the midges and a blister the size of Paris on my heel?'

She grimaces with sympathy. 'A blister? Ouch. Try padding it with some fleece, Philip. You'll find bits on the hillside wherever the sheep have been. But you don't have to go again. Stalking isn't for everyone.'

'Oh yes I do,' Philip says grimly. 'There is no way I'm going to tell your father I gave up after one day. I'm going to bag a deer if it kills me. I'm thinking of it as my quest,' he adds, only half joking. 'I need to slay a deer to win my princess.'

So day after day he slogs up the hillsides with Murdoch. The ghillie teaches him how to scan the landscape for the deer that are so perfectly camouflaged against the moorland. He shows Philip how to drop onto his stomach and wriggle through the heather inch by inch, ignoring the black boggy water and the flies and the sheep droppings. For most of the time Philip is wet and cold and uncomfortable but the challenge of stalking a wild beast across the hillside has captured his imagination. There is something primordial about what he is doing. It reminds Philip of sailing at Gordonstoun, struggling to keep control of the cutter as it bucked over the waves and the wind screamed and threw spray viciously at his face. Stalking may not feel as dangerous, but it is man against nature again, and nature definitely has the upper hand.

Sometimes Murdoch gestures to Philip to freeze and drop to the ground. He passes him the binoculars and points, and when Philip brings them into focus, he sees a herd in the distance. But they always scatter before they are close enough to take aim.

'I had a stag in my sights today,' he tells Elizabeth at tea one day. 'He must have got a whiff of us or something because he took off before I could pull the trigger.'

'Oh, what a shame!'

'Ye-es.' Philip chews a fish-paste sandwich thoughtfully. He is oddly torn. 'Part of me wanted to take the shot and prove I could do it. But another part of me was glad he got away. He was such a magnificent beast. I didn't want to kill him. It's a pity we can't have the challenge of stalking and the reward of taking a photograph at the end.'

'We need to shoot them to manage numbers,' Elizabeth says. 'I understand what you mean: to see an animal like that in the wild is a thrill, but if we let them breed unchecked, half of the herd will starve or succumb to diseases and that is a much grimmer death than a clean shot. It's not just shooting for the sake of it: we manage the deer and the habitat, we eat the venison ... it's part of the natural order of things.'

She loves Balmoral, that is obvious to Philip. She is out all day, whatever the weather, and returns as wet and wind-blown as everyone else, her eyes shining and her skin glowing. It is frustrating not to be able to spend time alone with her, but the days at Balmoral are organised with military precision. At breakfast, everyone is assigned to join a group activity of some kind. The notion that you might want to spend a wet day lying on a sofa reading a book appears not to have occurred to the King. No, they are all dispatched outside to hike up mountains, shoot grouse, catch fish or, like Philip, to stalk deer.

Philip's favourite time is the tea, which is usually his first chance of the day to talk to Elizabeth, but even their conversation has to take place under the disparaging eyes of the other guests, most of whom have evidently decided that Philip is not 'one of us'. The Queen's brother, David Bowes-Lyon, is particularly bloody to him, but Philip hasn't survived Gordonstoun and the war without being able to tough out snide references to his lack of wardrobe or his German relatives.

His sisters might be married to Germans but they are a damned sight more fun than the Balmoral crowd, Philip tells himself.

The dismal weather tends to clear into soft, golden evenings, but by then there is barely time for a bath in the frigidly old-fashioned bathroom at the end of the corridor and to change for pre-dinner drinks in the drawing room, decorated in the ubiquitous tartan and hung with the dreary landscapes favoured by Queen Victoria. They eat roast grouse every bloody night, as far as Philip can tell, and when dinner is finished a ghastly caterwauling starts up as the King's seven pipers march through the hall and twice around the dining table. Philip feels his jaw tense and makes an effort to look as if he is appreciating the ritual as much as anyone else, but it is hard. He keeps his eyes on Elizabeth, always seated as far away from him as possible, and tells himself she will be worth it.

The bagpipes aren't the end of the evening either. Nobody is allowed to slope off for a quiet cigarette or a stroll. No, they have to gather back in the drawing room and play charades or sardines. At least sardines gives Philip the chance to grab Elizabeth's hand. 'Let's hide together,' he says.

'Philip, we're supposed to be looking, not hiding!'

'All right, let's look together,' he concedes. There must be plenty of rooms where they won't be disturbed. 'I never get a chance to see you,' he grumbles.

'You're seeing me now.'

'You know what I mean. We're never alone.'

'I know,' Elizabeth acknowledges. 'I think a lot of people are going on Saturday so things should be quieter after that. Maybe we could go for a walk one day?'

'Good.' Philip smiles and takes her hand to pull her closer. 'I'm in need of some reassurance,' he tells her and she laughs softly but before he can kiss her, the door opens and to Philip's frustration, the King's equerry, Group Captain Townsend, puts his head in.

'Oh, sorry,' he says as Elizabeth quickly pulls her hands away.

'Anyone in there?' David Bowes-Lyon pushes past Townsend and smiles maliciously when he sees Elizabeth with pink cheeks and a scowling Philip. 'Oh, I say, are you two lost? You don't seem to have mastered the rules of the game, Philip, old boy.'

Two days later, Philip is lying in the heather beside Murdoch. They have been following a group of red deer for two hours. One animal seems to have an injured leg.

'She'll no last the winter,' Murdoch says, studying the deer through his binoculars. 'You'll be doing her a favour.'

Wriggling back out of sight of the deer, he takes the gun, loads it, and hands it up to Philip, who lifts it to his shoulder and puts his eye to the scope. The deer springs into focus. He can see the redness of her coat, the twitching ears, the wary expression in her eyes as she stops and looks around. She is beginning to fall behind the others.

For a moment she seems to look directly at him and Philip almost hesitates, but then she turns her head and stands, almost as if she is inviting him to end it for her. Very carefully, he fixes the sights and pulls the trigger. The deer drops, the rest of the herd take off, and Philip lowers the gun with a strange sigh that is part exultation, part regret.

'A good, clean shot, sir,' says Murdoch approvingly. 'Now all we have to do is carry her down to the road.'

That turns out to be the hardest part of the exercise, but Philip is triumphant when he finally gets back to Balmoral. His success is met with congratulations all round. Shooting a wild animal has, it seems, ensured his temporary acceptance. The King shakes his hand and tells him that Murdoch is impressed by how quickly Philip has taken to stalking.

Philip seizes his chance. 'Could I have a word with you in your study, sir?'

The King looks wary but agrees to give Philip a few minutes after dinner. Philip has prepared what he will say: he talks eloquently about his regard for Elizabeth and asks permission to tell her how he feels so that if his feelings are reciprocated, which he believes they are, they could become engaged. All this round-about-the-houses is because Uncle Dickie has impressed on him that Elizabeth must do the proposing. Nothing can happen until the King agrees in any case. The Royal Marriages Act of 1772, which Uncle Dickie knows inside out, of course, requires the

King's consent for Elizabeth to be married before she is twenty-five.

But the King is not inclined to give his consent. Lilibet is only twenty, he says. She is too young to be married and there are serious matters still to straighten out on the diplomatic front.

'My advice is to wait,' he tells Philip.

Philip bows, because what else can he do? You don't argue with the King. But when he leaves the King's study, the set of his jaw is uncompromising.

Wait? *To hell with that*, he decides.

Chapter 27

'Not shooting today?' The King registers Elizabeth's tweed skirt and pale blue blouse with concern.

'No, I thought Philip and I might go for a walk.'

'A walk?' Her father looks suspicious. 'With Philip?'

'Yes.'

Elizabeth has heard all about Philip's visit to her father's study. 'Damned impertinence,' the King had grumbled. 'Things are far too precarious in Greece at the moment, as Philip must very well know. Besides, I'm not ready to lose you, darling Lilibet. It's so comfortable with just the four of us, isn't it? I don't want that to change. There's plenty of time for you to think about marriage. I told Philip the time's not right and that he should wait.'

Her father hasn't told *her* to wait.

Elizabeth has been patient. She has been dutiful. She has been careful not to rock the boat. But now she is ready to act. She is ready to change her life.

'It's a beautiful day,' is the only explanation she offers her father.

And it is. It can be like this in Scotland. Day after dreich day of relentless rain or blustery showers until you wake up one morning without warning to find the sky a brilliant blue and the mountains serene in the crystalline air.

'Where are we going?' Philip asks as they set off. Elizabeth has a cardigan slung around her shoulders; he is in flannels and an open necked shirt. Susan snuffles ahead, her fat bottom waggling with pleasure. The air is fresh and well rinsed after a week of rain. The warmth of the sunshine draws out the coconutty smell of the gorse and the peaty tang of the earth while linnets twitter busily in the birches and beady-eyed blackbirds hop along the ground in search of worms.

'There's a small loch, more of a lochan really, up there,' she says, pointing. 'It's a little way, but worth the walk, I think.'

'Sounds good to me,' says Philip. 'Especially if it's in the other direction from your father. He wasn't in the best of moods when I left him last night.'

'No,' Elizabeth agrees in a dry voice.

'Did he tell you?'

She nods. Loyalty makes her find an excuse for her father. 'He does get very tired and irritable. There's no let up from the red boxes, even here at Balmoral. It's a lonely job, and it's not one he ever wanted. It's ... hard for him.'

'And the last thing he needs is some pushy young fellow badgering him about the daughter he doesn't want to lose?'

She smiles faintly. 'Something like that.' She isn't quite

ready to talk about what her father's objections might mean to them. 'How's your blister?'

'Much better since your tip about the fleece,' says Philip, tacitly accepting the change of subject. 'I got my own shoes back from the cobbler, too, so I'll go as far as you want.' He takes a deep breath of the sweet air and looks around him. 'All those days plodding after Murdoch through the rain,' he remembers. 'You wouldn't think this was the same place at all.'

'I don't mind the rain,' Elizabeth says. 'It just means we appreciate days like this all the more when we get them.'

'That's true.' He takes her hand. 'But not as much as I appreciate being alone with you at last.'

Philip's fingers are warm around hers, setting Elizabeth's senses trembling with awareness. It is as if she has never seen the river before, not properly. As if she has never noticed how it tumbles a glossy brown around the boulders, how it glitters as it swirls into the patches of sunlight between the trees in a dazzling display of light and shade, bright and dark. A fish leaps, showering an arc of diamond drops in the air, while a dipper bobs up and down in search of flies and the burble and rush of the water over the stones provides a tranquil soundtrack as they walk in companionable silence.

Turning away from the Dee, they start to climb, pushing through coarse bracken until they emerge onto a hillside scattered with great granite boulders, as if tossed there by some petulant giant. A loch lies half hidden in the curve of a hill. The brilliant light turns its still surface into an enchanted mirror, reflecting back the rugged golden sweep of the hills. A cluster of birch trees fringes the far shore, their leaves a silvery trembling in the slight breeze.

Philip stops as they round the shoulder of the hill. He is silent for a moment, looking at the view. 'Nice,' is all he says, but Elizabeth is satisfied that the loch has had the right effect on him.

'This is my favourite place,' she says as she leads the way over to where a flattish boulder lies abandoned close to the shore of the loch. Hoisting herself up, she leans back on her hands. The rock is smooth and so warm beneath her palms that it feels like a living thing. 'I like to come here on my own, if I can. It's one of the few places where I'm not a princess. I'm just me.'

Philip levers himself up beside her. 'It must be lonely. There can't be many people who can think of you as anything other than a princess and a future queen.'

'There's no one,' she says, matter-of-factly. She doesn't want him to feel sorry for her. It's just the way it is.

'What about your family?'

'Margaret, perhaps,' she allows. 'But even then, everything in her life is defined by the fact that I was born first. I'm the one who will be queen, not her, and that's always there between us. It's hard for her.'

'Harder for you,' Philip comments. 'The rest of us can mess up but you don't have that luxury. Aren't you ever tempted to behave badly, just once?'

She thinks about that. 'No, but then, I'm not a natural rebel, so perhaps it's just as well I'm the one who will have to behave.'

He stretches out on the rock beside her and turns to lie on his side, propped up on one elbow so he can look at her face. 'You don't ever resent having a life of behaving well mapped out for you?'

Elizabeth doesn't look at him. She looks at the shining surface of the loch, feels the breeze caress her cheek and lift her hair. 'Sometimes I think what life would have been like if Uncle David hadn't abdicated,' she admits at last. 'But there's not much point in wishing that things were different. I don't want to waste my life feeling resentful. I can't change things and ... and it seems cowardly to want to avoid responsibility and duty,' she goes on, struggling to put her thoughts into words. 'I think of it as God's will. It's my destiny to be Queen one day and I will always, always have to do the right thing because that is what I am now and I can't change it. It just is.'

'I understand that,' Philip says. 'We have to accept the way things are. That's what I felt when my family broke up and I was sent to school. I could have wept and wailed but it was clear to me even at nine that nothing I did was going to change the situation, so I just had to accept it.'

She turns to look at him then. He does understand. 'I wasn't right about what I said earlier.'

'What was that?'

'About no one seeing me for myself. There *is* someone,' she says. 'There's you.'

There's you. Her words seem to echo in the quiet air: *you ... you ... you.*

Elizabeth's gaze is tangled up in Philip's blue eyes and she can't seem to look away. His body is long and astonishingly solid beside her. Close enough to touch if she chooses to. If she dares. But she can't move. She is held in place as surely as if the boulder has slid invisible bonds around her wrists and ankles. All she can do is breathe while the silence stretches until the sound of Susan lapping noisily at the edge of the loch breaks the tension at last and they both laugh.

'That's why I wanted you to come here,' she says easily enough after all.

Strange how sharp and clear everything suddenly seems, Elizabeth thinks as she lies right back and looks up at the sky. The intense blue is broken by the occasional puff of cloud drifting on the breeze that carries with it the smell of heather and peat and bracken. Somewhere a curlew is calling. The space and the stillness of the mountains seem to pulse, as if the earth's heart is beating and as she stares into the blue she can almost swear she can feel the world turning. Instinctively, she spreads her hands out on the rock beside her to anchor herself.

Now is the time to say it. *Will you marry me?* It will sound too bald just on its own, Elizabeth realises. She should lead up to it but the carefully prepared speech that she rehearsed to herself over and over again has gone out of her head.

Perhaps she doesn't need a lead up? It's not as if her proposal will come out of the blue. Surely, if Philip has spoken to her father about it, he must want to marry her? She should just come out and say it.

But when she opens her mouth, the words crumble on her tongue. It's not fair that she is the only woman in the world who has to propose marriage, Elizabeth thinks in an uncharacteristic flash of resentment. Is this what it is like for poor Papa whenever he has to speak publicly? Feeling the words strangle in your throat? It is awful.

Well, hasn't she just been telling Philip that she accepts her role? Get on with, she tells herself.

'Philip,' she blurts out, before she can change her mind. If she can just start, maybe the words will come.

But he is speaking at the same time. 'Elizabeth—'

They both stop awkwardly.

'You first,' Philip says.

Elizabeth sits up, biting her lip. But she has to do this now. 'All right.' She takes a breath. 'I've been thinking about marriage,' she says, agonisingly aware that her voice sounds thin and high. 'I know we've skirted around the idea a couple of times and talked in generalities about what it might be like.'

This isn't anything like the persuasive speech she prepared! Swallowing, she clears her throat and ploughs on because if she stops she will never finish. 'There wasn't any rush before, and there isn't any now. It's just ... just ... well, I've been feeling that I'm ready to move into the next stage of life and I ... I'd like someone to share that life with me. Someone who understands what it means to be royal.'

'Someone like me?' Philip asks. His voice is grave but his eyes are smiling.

'Yes.' Elizabeth rushes on before he misunderstands. 'I'm not asking you for anything you can't give, Philip. I don't have any expectations that ... well, it wouldn't be a marriage like others can have. Obviously.'

She sighs, tries again. 'There's no need for you to pretend to have feelings for me, or vice versa. We both understand what's involved in a royal marriage and that's not what it would be about. Neither of us is silly or sentimental. But I ... I think we'd make a good team, so I was wondering if you'd mind ... if I could ask you what you thought ...'

'About marriage?' he finishes for her as she flounders to a halt.

'Yes.'

'Are you proposing to me, Elizabeth?'

'Yes,' she says again on a shaky breath. There, it was done. The proposal was made. Now all she can do is wait for Philip's reply.

He doesn't answer immediately. A flock of oyster catchers fly squabbling over the loch and she watches them disappear up the valley before Philip speaks.

'Can I be honest?'

Her heart sinks. It doesn't sound very promising. 'Of course,' she says with a brittle smile. 'I hope you will be.'

'I do have one small problem,' he confides.

'Oh. I see.'

Philip picks up her hand. 'The thing is, I know that it's protocol for you to propose to me, but I really, really wanted to propose to you.'

'Oh ...' A smile, a real one, trembles into life as she turns to him. 'I thought Papa told you to wait?'

'He did, but we've done enough waiting, don't you think?'

Elizabeth nods vehemently. 'I do.'

'Well then, as we're here alone, and this is the place where you're just Elizabeth, I say we forget about protocol,' Philip says. 'Let's agree that we want to get married because it suits us and because we think we can make it work, and to hell with everybody else. We may not be lovers, but we're friends and we can be partners.'

'Exactly,' Elizabeth says, wishing she could have put it that clearly. Perhaps it would have been nice to have been lovers as well as friends and partners, but there is no use in longing for the impossible and at least this way she will be with Philip. That is what matters.

'In that case, let's forget about what your father thinks and what the government thinks and what the public thinks,' he goes on. 'Let's decide what *we* want.' His hand tightens around hers. 'Will you marry me, Elizabeth, and be my wife so that we can face whatever the future brings side by side?'

Relief and happiness are making Elizabeth feel giddy. 'Yes,' she says, smiling, curling her fingers to tangle with his. 'Yes, I will, Philip.'

He throws back his head and laughs. 'Well, that went better than I thought!'

'You must have known I would say yes.'

Philip sobers at that. 'I wasn't sure. I know you don't want to disappoint your father. They're not going to like it,' he warns.

'This is all I'm asking for myself,' Elizabeth says. 'I don't think it's too much.'

'I don't either,' he says. He eases her down onto the boulder. 'And now all that's agreed, can I kiss you?'

Laughing shakily, she slides her hands up to his shoulders. 'I was hoping you would.'

Chapter 28

It is an enchanted morning, one Elizabeth tells herself she will remember for ever. When things are hard, as they will be, this is the memory she will turn to: the breeze, just enough to keep the midges at bay, ruffling their hair tenderly; the curlew calling in the distance; the mountains standing guard.

And Philip beside her. The warmth of his hand around hers, the way his eyes crease when he smiles. His mouth. That, especially. Thinking about the way it feels when he kisses her, when he touches her, sets a fine tremor going in the pit of her belly. It is a strange feeling, half thrilled, half languid, as if she is drenched in the sunshine that pours down and through her, seeping into every last inch of her and bringing a warm throb of happiness.

They won't like it, Philip warned and Elizabeth knows he is right, but she doesn't want to think about the difficulties ahead, not yet.

They sit by the loch, leaning against each other, talking

in a way they have never been able to before. Because now everything has changed.

I want to marry you.

Philip wants to marry her, Elizabeth.

By mutual consent, they don't talk about the future. It is too uncertain for now, so they talk about the past instead. About the time they met at the Royal Naval College before the war.

'I thought you were a show-off,' Elizabeth tells Philip, tucking her tongue into her cheek.

'I can't help it if I beat you at croquet,' he says. 'Admit it, you were impressed by me.'

'Only by how greedy you were,' she says.

Philip grins and links his hands behind his head so he can lie back. 'When did you first realise that your life was going to be different from everybody else's?' he asks, wriggling his shoulders into a more comfortable position. 'Was it at your father's coronation?'

Elizabeth rests her cheek on her bent knees and thinks about it for a while. 'Before that,' she decides. 'I was taken to Westminster Hall to see my grandfather lying in state. It was a horrible night. Dark, wet, bitterly cold.'

She wore a black coat and a new black velvet tammy. She remembers stroking the beret and thinking how soft it was before she had to put it on. Bobo instantly tutted at the unconsciously jaunty tilt she achieved and straightened it to a more sober angle.

'I remember driving past all those people, standing in

silence, a long queue that went on and on and on, like a great snake,' she tells Philip. 'I asked Mummy what they were doing and she said they were waiting to pay their respects to Grandpa England.'

The huge medieval hall yawned before Elizabeth as they paused at the entrance and let their eyes adjust to the gloom. It was very dark, lit only by the candles on a raised platform where her grandfather's coffin was draped in the Royal Standard, and the silence pressed around them like a blanket. She was glad to hold her mother's hand, Elizabeth remembers that. She remembers other things, too: their footsteps on the stone floor; the damp, suffocating smell of the flowers piled up around the platform.

'The coffin was on a dais,' she goes on. 'Papa was standing at one corner, Uncle David, Uncle George and Uncle Henry at the others.'

'Keeping vigil?'

She nods. 'I remember how completely still and silent they were. It was so strange. I looked at Uncle David and I couldn't believe it. He was normally so restless. Always shrugging or frowning or smiling or lighting a cigarette ... Margaret and I used to love it when he played with us. He was funny and kind to us.' Elizabeth swallows, reminding herself that her uncle is persona non grata with her parents now. 'Anyway, it seemed extraordinary to me that he could stand so still. He didn't move so much as an eyelid. I was looking straight at him, too.'

'Were you sad?' Philip asks after a moment.

'I don't think I really realised that it was Grandpapa in the coffin so I didn't cry.' She wouldn't have been allowed to cry in any case. 'I was sad when he died, though. He was a wonderful grandfather. He used to get down on all fours and play with me.' A reminiscent smile curves her mouth. 'He had a parrot called Charlotte, and he gave me Peggy, my first pony. I know Papa used to find him daunting, but he wasn't like that with me.'

'I'm sure I would have found him daunting too.'

'You?' She turns to him. 'I doubt it. I can't imagine you being daunted by anybody. You're so sure of yourself. You're not frightened of anything.'

'You haven't seen me quaking in front of Queen Mary,' Philip says.

Elizabeth laughs. 'Granny's bark is worse than her bite. She's a bit stiff but very kind really.'

'A bit stiff?' Sitting up, he pulls an expression of exaggerated incredulity. 'In the same way that the South Pole is a bit chilly?'

She laughs again and bumps her shoulder against his. 'Your turn. When did you realise you were a prince and not like everyone else?'

He doesn't answer immediately. 'It wasn't the same for me,' he says eventually. 'I didn't have a surname at school, but apart from that … I suppose the truth is, I *am* like everyone else.'

Elizabeth's happy mood dims a little. 'You know that will change, Philip?'

'I know,' he says. He takes her chin and turns her gently to force her to look at him. 'Elizabeth, are you sure want to do this?'

'I'm sure.'

There is something reckless in the smile that blazes in Philip's face as he jumps off the boulder. 'Then let's go back and face the music!' He holds up a hand to help her down. 'We're going to come under a lot of pressure, but if we can hold firm, we'll make it through.'

She is brushing off the odd bits of lichen clinging to her skirt, but at that she looks up at him and smiles. 'We will,' she promises him. 'We're in this together.'

Elizabeth is standing at the window in the drawing room, gazing unseeingly at the hills and twisting her pearls.

Philip requested an interview with the King as soon as they got back and he is in with her father now.

'Perhaps I should come with you?' Elizabeth said when the message came that the King would see Philip. 'He's not going to be pleased that you've gone directly against his wishes.'

Her father's violent outbursts of temper are familiar to all of them, but Philip didn't appear at all nervous about the interview.

'I should see your father alone,' he said. 'It's the right thing to do, and he'll think even less of me if I go in hiding behind your skirts.'

She bit her lip. 'He can get so angry.'

'Let him be angry,' was all Philip said before he left. 'He can't eat me, no matter how much he might want to.' He cast a quick glance to check they were alone and then pulled her close for a quick, fierce kiss. 'We're holding firm, remember?'

Now a discreet cough behind her makes Elizabeth start and swing round. Group Captain Townsend is in the doorway. 'Your Royal Highness? The King has asked if you would join him in his study.'

'Thank you, Peter.' Outwardly calm, Elizabeth follows her father's equerry along the corridor and waits for him to open the door for her.

'Her Royal Highness, Your Majesty,' he says before stepping back and closing the door.

The King is sitting behind his desk, his face thunderous, while Philip has got to his feet at her entrance. He sends her a faint smile and a wink.

'S-Sit down, Lilibet,' her father says, the stammer a sure sign of his agitation. 'You too,' he adds with a scowl in Philip's direction.

'Philip has t-told me that in d-defiance of my *express wishes*, you have decided to become engaged.'

'Yes, Papa.'

'I'm d-disappointed in you, Lilibet. I thought you understood the situation! I thought you *both* understood that a betrothal is not possible at the moment,' the King goes on with another glare in Philip's direction. 'You are not just

226

any girl. You can't m-marry whenever you feel like it. Your marriage is a matter of *state*, of diplomacy, politics.'

Elizabeth has her hands tightly folded in her lap. 'I do understand that, Papa,' she manages, 'but I hope there will also be room for personal feelings.'

Her father's only answer to that is an exasperated snort.

'I ... I hope to have a marriage as happy as yours and Mummy's,' she ploughs on.

'Your mother was twenty-three before she married,' the King snaps. 'You're only twenty. And she took a good, hard look at some other chaps before she said yes to me. That's how I knew she wasn't just interested in a royal title.'

Philip shifts in his chair but the King ignores him.

'Yes, yes, you want Philip now, I can see that, but how many young women know their minds at twenty? If I give permission for this marriage to go ahead and then you change your mind, there won't be a way out of it.'

Elizabeth steals a glance at Philip. His face is expressionless, but a muscle is jumping in his jaw. She is just glad that he is hanging on to his own temper. Her father may be in a vile mood now, but he won't have held back when Philip was alone. Philip must have endured much worse.

'I know my mind,' she says quietly. She is trying not to show that she is shaking inside. She adores her father and she has spent her whole life trying to please him. She is the good girl, his trusty squire, the one he can rely on. He tells her so all the time. He is never angry with her.

But he is now.

Why isn't her mother there to support her? Elizabeth wonders. She must know what is happening.

It seems that if she wants to marry Philip, she will have to stand on her own. But not alone, she thinks, with another glance at Philip.

We're in this together. She was the one who had said that.

She lifts her chin. 'I won't change my mind,' she says. 'I want to marry Philip. Please, Papa, give us your blessing.'

'My *b-blessing?*' the King bellows, outraged. 'When you have both defied me?'

'Sir—' Philip starts through gritted teeth, but her father turns on him.

'I've heard enough from you, young man. How dare you s-saunter in here and tell me you want to get engaged to my daughter when I f-forbade you to mention the matter only yesterday?'

'Papa,' Elizabeth interrupts before Philip can speak. 'I was the one who asked Philip to marry me.'

'Then he should have said no!'

'I didn't want to say no.' Philip's cool voice cuts through her father's fury and abruptly the King subsides. He sinks back into his leather chair, still glowering, but Elizabeth is glad to see the red light of rage has left his face.

'You should both have waited.'

'We have waited, Papa,' she says gently.

'Then wait longer!'

Elizabeth and Philip exchange a look. 'Papa, we're not going to undo this,' she says. 'We want to get married.'

The King sighs and shakes his head, pinching the bridge of his nose.

'Please, Papa.' She doesn't want to plead, but she knows that for all his fury, her father loves her. He won't want her to be unhappy.

Sure enough, his shoulders slump. 'It doesn't sound as if either of you are going to listen to sense,' he grumbles, but Elizabeth can hear the resignation in his voice.

Wisely, she and Philip stay silent.

'Very well,' the King says heavily at last. 'I'll allow the betrothal *but*—' He holds up a hand as Elizabeth opens her mouth to thank him. '*But*,' he repeats, 'the engagement is to remain secret for now. No announcement will be made for at least six months.'

'Six months!' Philip echoes in dismay.

'Think yourself lucky I'm allowing it at all,' the King says. 'I'll have to talk to the Prime Minister; he's not going to be happy about this either. It will complicate the diplomatic situation considerably. So there'll be no announcement, no ring, no wedding plans until I say so. Is that clear?'

Elizabeth meets Philip's rueful gaze, and he nods. It is disappointing to have to wait, but this is clearly the best they are going to get. And the first hurdle has been cleared. They are committed to each other now.

'Yes, sir,' Philip says. 'Thank you.'

'Yes, Papa. Thank you, Papa.'

The King throws himself back in his chair. 'We'll have a small celebration with your mother and sister tonight, but that's it.' He points at Philip. 'You'd better leave tomorrow before all the gossips get wind of this.'

'Oh, Papa!' Elizabeth protests.

'Tomorrow,' he says firmly. 'You and Lilibet may meet in London, but you are not to even consider making the relationship public for six months and until I have discussed your marriage with the Prime Minister. Not a word to anyone, do you hear me?'

'May I at least tell my immediate family?' Philip says with studied restraint.

The King sighs irritably before giving a jerky nod. 'No one else,' he warns. 'I mean it. Not a word, do you hear me?'

'Yes, sir.'

Philip looks at Elizabeth who mouths *sorry*. What else can they do?

'Lilibet?'

'Yes, Papa. I understand. We'll keep our engagement a secret for now.'

Chapter 29

London, October 1946

'*S*outh Africa? For how long?'

Scowling, Philip paces around Elizabeth's sitting room. Outside, as if mirroring his mood, a blustery, bad-tempered wind is swirling autumn leaves in eddies across the Mall.

'We'd be away three months. The plan is to sail at the end of January.' Elizabeth has her head down, petting Susan. 'I'd be there for my twenty-first birthday in April. Papa says we'll be able to announce the engagement once we get home.'

'He said we'd have to wait six months. It'll be nine months before you get home!'

'I know.' Elizabeth is clearly upset but Philip is too angry to comfort her.

He left Balmoral in high spirits. The King's lack of enthusiasm for the engagement had galled, but on the whole Philip was pleased with the way things had gone.

Elizabeth's proposal had been a bonus, and her practical approach to the marriage frankly a relief. She made it clear that she isn't going to expect any nauseating displays of emotion but at the same time, there is a sweetness and an innocence to her that Philip finds touching.

True, his own enthusiasm for the marriage has wavered at times, but now that he has committed to it, Philip sees no reason why they shouldn't have a successful marriage. But he's frustrated at not being able to enjoy his triumph to the full. First there was the King's grudging acceptance of the engagement and then the demand for secrecy. Philip doesn't buy the alleged concern about the political situation in Athens. When has Britain ever cared what is going on in Greece? No, they're just hoping Elizabeth will change her mind about marrying him.

In the meantime, instead of shouting the news from the rooftops, he has to continue the absurd charade of pretending that he and Elizabeth mean nothing to each other. It's not that he wants to hang over her and make a fool of himself, Philip reassures himself, but nonetheless she belongs to him now and it grates that he's not allowed to show it. Oh, he is permitted to take her to the theatre occasionally and sometimes he takes her for a drive to Richmond Park but chances are that on any given evening he will have to stand by and watch one of her faithful Guards officers escort her to restaurants or out to one of the fashionable clubs.

'I'd much rather be with you,' Elizabeth assured him

when she got back from Balmoral at the beginning of October. 'I wish you'd been able to stay in Scotland,' she added wistfully. 'It wasn't the same without you.'

'Has your father forgiven you yet?' Philip asked and she pulled a face.

'Not really. He was livid when that Greek newspaper claimed that the announcement of our engagement was imminent.'

'That was nothing to do with me.' Philip has already been hauled over the coals by the King about that. 'I told my mother and Uncle Dickie. He can be a gossip but he knows how important it is to stay on the side of the King right now, and as for my mother ... she's really more interested in the religious order she's joined. If you ask me, it was Uncle Georgie indulging in some wishful thinking.'

The King had told Tommy Lascelles to issue a sharp denial of the story.

And now they're proposing taking Elizabeth away to South Africa for three months!

'He's still hoping it won't happen,' Philip says bitterly and Elizabeth looks up.

'It will happen, Philip. We just need to hold our nerve.'

'Do you have to go to Africa?'

'I asked Papa that, but he wants all four of us to go. With the war we've never had a chance to do a royal tour as a family, and Papa is keen for us to be together.'

'More likely he's keen to separate us,' Philip says with a morose look.

It's obvious what the King is planning. Elizabeth is to be taken away, entertained royally and given all sorts of new and exciting experiences. He is hoping distance will give her a chance to forget about Philip.

'They want you to change your mind.'

Giving Susan a final pat, Elizabeth gets up. She is not a demonstrative person, but now she lays a hand on his arm.

'I won't change my mind, Philip, I promise you.'

He covers her hand with his own. 'It's going to be a long three months,' he says.

There is nothing for it but to grit his teeth and do as he is told. Elizabeth's father is the King and until she is twenty-five she needs his permission to marry. If they're not careful, they'll find themselves waiting five years, Philip thinks savagely. He's sure her father would be perfectly happy to keep them waiting forever.

Indeed, the King seizes any opportunity to keep them apart. After being snapped looking into each other's eyes at Patricia Mountbatten's wedding to John Brabourne, Elizabeth and Philip find themselves plastered over the papers, and the king is incandescent.

'I'd have thought as a serving naval officer you'd have understood the meaning of *secret*,' he snarls, stabbing the offending photograph with his finger. 'You might as well have sent an open invitation to the press to tittle-tattle about a possible betrothal.' He scowls at Philip.

'We were just looking at each other,' Philip says, jaw clenched with the effort of not losing his temper.

The King had no such inhibitions. 'Well, stop looking! I've told Tommy to deny everything and you're not to see each other again until all these rumours have died down. Is that understood?'

So Philip is confined to a freezing Nissen hut in Corsham during the week and at the weekends he is allowed to stay at his grandmother's dilapidated apartments in Kensington Palace, but no longer is he permitted to go to Buckingham Palace for cosy suppers, nor is he to escort Elizabeth anywhere.

It is humiliating. The unfairness of it chafes at Philip all through that long, grindingly cold winter.

The King relents enough to allow Philip to spend Christmas at Sandringham with Elizabeth and the rest of the royal family. It is a concession, but at times it feels as if he has been invited to underscore how much of an outsider he is. Oh, he gets on well enough with Margaret, although she is inclined to play silly games of precedence that make him roll his eyes. The King is wary of him and though the Queen is charming on the face of it, in private she refers to him as *the Hun*. Philip learns this courtesy of her brother, David Bowes-Lyon, who makes it his business to ensure Philip feels unwelcome. If Philip had been wavering before, the royal family's evident lack of enthusiasm for the marriage only makes him dig in his heels.

But at least there is Elizabeth.

Philip sets his jaw and refuses to care. Elizabeth wants to marry *him*. He will have the last laugh. They can keep their court with its arcane rituals and oppressive deference. Sometimes it feels as if nothing has changed since George V's time: at least Edward VII had some jolliness about him. None of the courtiers bowing and scraping around the King appear aware that not only are they no longer in the nineteenth century, they are almost halfway through the twentieth and things are changing. The King may want to return to the pre-war years, but the rest of the country is looking forward. Labour's victory in the general election the previous year was surely a sign of that, but no one at court seems to want to realise it. They are all harking back to the past, Philip thinks impatiently, when they should be looking to the future.

The King is adamant that Elizabeth is to go to South Africa. Clearly, her parents have calculated that they can indulge her by inviting Philip for Christmas, but only if she agrees to the visit. Philip thinks sourly that he wouldn't be surprised if the entire tour has been arranged with the sole purpose of separating them for as long as possible.

The date of departure is set for 1st February. On 23rd January, snow begins to fall out of an iron-grey sky. It is pretty at first, but as the temperature drops and the snow keeps falling, swirling relentlessly down and blown into great drifts by bitter winds, the novelty of a landscape blanketed in white soon wears off. Trains burrow into snow tunnels, cars skid over icy roads. Electricity cuts plunge cities into darkness; fuel shortages shut down factories and workers are laid off. In his Nissen hut in Corsham, Philip wears his greatcoat and a balaclava to bed. The pipes are frozen so no one can have a bath and when everyone is huddled together the smell is soon ripe enough to make his eyes water.

As the big freeze tightens its grip, the King himself begins to have doubts about whether the tour should take place. Elizabeth writes to Philip that she is secretly hoping it will be cancelled. It can't look good for the royal family to be heading off to the sunshine when the country is enduring the worst winter anyone can remember.

But the tour is intended as a celebration of the Commonwealth and to thank the South Africans for their service during the war. It cannot be cancelled, the King is reluctantly persuaded, while Elizabeth even more reluctantly allows herself to be measured for summer dresses.

The final blow is the King's refusal to allow Philip on board HMS *Vanguard* to say goodbye to the royal party. 'It'll only give the gossips more to chatter about,' he says brusquely, hardening his heart to Elizabeth's protests. 'You'll have to say your goodbyes before then.'

Philip can hardly force his way onto the ship, but his pride, already bruised by the King's attitude, takes another kicking. He may be down, but he is not out, he vows, not by a long chalk. He is not giving up on Elizabeth now.

Chapter 30

The sleet drives needles into Elizabeth's face and she has to screw her eyes up against its sting as HMS *Vanguard* pulls away from the quayside. The world is monochrome: grey sea, grey sky, grey ship, with a frosting of white over the metal. The only colour comes from the Royal Standard snapping high on the central mast, with its familiar red, gold, and blue. The lions passant and rampant, the gold harp. Elizabeth's smile is fixed, her teeth aching in the icy wind that drills through her coat but she refuses to shiver. If she is cold, how much colder must the sailors be, standing to attention, or the crowd that has braved the bitter weather to wave them on their way without gloves or fur collars?

'I'll miss you,' Philip said when Papa gave permission for him to come to the palace for a last farewell. But he sounded almost surprised when he said it, as if he hadn't meant to at all.

'Will you write to me?' she asked almost fiercely and he had taken her hands and shaken them to settle her.

'Of course, Elizabeth. Of course I will.'

So now there was nothing more she could do. But it is hard to share Margaret's enthusiasm when they are finally able to go below deck to explore the admiral's quarters which have been made over for them.

'We've got our own cabins,' Margaret said, delighted. 'And look at the day cabin!' It was furnished with comfortable sofas and chairs, satinwood tables and prints of London scenes on the walls. 'It's almost like being at home,' she said, twirling excitedly.

'Apart from the fact that this cabin would fit into a quarter of Mummy's sitting room at the palace?'

'Well, I think it's cosy.' Margaret led the way down to their sleeping cabins and pushed into Elizabeth's, peering through the porthole before throwing herself onto the bed. 'This is going to be such fun! I can't wait to get away from this awful winter.'

Restless, Elizabeth wanders around the cabin, touching things. Bobo is travelling with them and has already unpacked for her. She has left Philip's photo on top of the small chest. Elizabeth picks it up and studies it: the cool angles of his face, the cool eyes, the cool mouth. She can hear the ship's engines, feel the throbbing through her feet. Combined with the smell of fresh paint, it is making her queasy.

'I'm not sure we should be going.'

240

'Why on earth not?' Margaret demands.

'Haven't you been reading the news?' Elizabeth lifts her eyes from the photo to stare at her sister. 'They're saying this winter is worse than the war. The fuel shortages haven't affected you, Margaret, but millions of people are going to bed without a hot meal because they can't cook anything. There's no fuel so they can't keep warm. The coal can't get to the factories either so they're closing down and their employees are out of work. Everybody is cold and tired and hungry and frustrated at not being able to get around. Meanwhile, *we* are off to the sun for three months. Doesn't that make you feel even a little uncomfortable?'

Margaret pouts a little. 'Don't you *ever* get tired of being dutiful, Lil? I'm sure it's very terrible, but how would it change anything if we stayed in Buckingham Palace shivering along with everyone else? Besides, Papa says the government *wants* us to go to South Africa and bolster the Empire or whatever, so we're just doing what we're asked to do. And if we have to go, we might as well enjoy ourselves.'

She settles herself more comfortably against Elizabeth's pillows. 'You're just sulking because you won't see Philip for a while.'

'More than a while. We'll be gone three months!'

'It's not that long.'

'It is when you're in love,' Elizabeth says.

Margaret raises her brows. '*Are* you in love with Philip?'

'Of course I am!'

'It's just that it's hard to tell sometimes. You seem so cool about him.'

Cool? Elizabeth thinks about the heat that trembles and flares inside her whenever she looks at Philip's mouth, about the way the merest brush of his hand leaves warmth simmering long after his touch.

Margaret wants her to swing around lamp posts and scatter rose petals as she runs singing through a meadow. She wants her to hang around Philip's neck and shower him with kisses to prove her love.

But Elizabeth can't do that. Her feelings for Philip are so strong that the only way she can control them is to bank them down, to bury them beneath a layer of cool composure. As it is, she is afraid they will spill over and leave her vulnerable to embarrassment and jeering.

To prurient speculation and avid public interest.

To Philip's rejection.

That would be worst of all. She has been so careful not to make him feel awkward. Elizabeth fears that if he knew just how deeply she feels about him, he would regret asking her to marry him. When it comes down to it, they have made an arrangement. They have been clear with each other. It is not a love match. She saw the relief in Philip's face when she told him she would make no messy emotional demands of him.

Very carefully, she sets Philip's photo on the chest of drawers where a raised ridge has been added to stop items falling off when the ship tilts. The sleet is rattling against the porthole in a blur of white.

'Philip and I don't need to make a big show of how we feel,' she tells her sister.

'Well, as long as you know,' Margaret says doubtfully. 'I like Philip, but he can be a bit off-hand with you, I think. I'm not the only one who has noticed either. He's not exactly devoted, is he? I can't imagine him whispering sweet nothings in your ear.'

Nor can Elizabeth.

'I like that he doesn't paw me in public,' she says. 'I would hate it if he hung over me. It would be embarrassing.'

'I just hope he's more attentive behind closed doors, that's all.'

Elizabeth doesn't meet her sister's gaze. She straightens the photo and lets her gaze rest on Philip's face, on his mouth. How could she possibly explain to Margaret the dark knot of emotions that tangle around her whenever Philip is near? Desire and anticipation, nervousness and fear, guilt and exultation, all tumbling together to leave her edgy and unsure of everything but the fact that she loves him.

She is holding on to that.

She knows Philip can come across as arrogant. He is quick-tempered and impatient of pretentiousness and deference. Sometimes, yes, he is off-hand with her. He isn't attentive but he teases her and disagrees with her and tells her exactly what he thinks. He doesn't love her, but he likes her and he treats her like a woman instead of a princess. That is enough for Elizabeth.

'We're happy,' she tells Margaret, uncomfortably aware of the defensive note in her voice. 'Or we would be if Papa would just let us marry.'

'He won't be able to say no when we get back from South Africa,' Margaret reassures her and Elizabeth sighs and touches Philip's photo one last time before turning away.

'I hope you're right.'

As HMS *Vanguard* ploughs on into the Atlantic Ocean, the swell gets heavier and the wind more brutal. It screams past the portholes, sprays the deck with sleet and whips up great waves that send the ship pitching and lurching. Long before they reach the Bay of Biscay, Elizabeth is miserably seasick. She lies in her bunk and keeps her eyes fixed on Philip's photo. If she dies, she will never see him again. That's all she can think, but sometimes the sickness is so bad she wants only to die anyway.

Margaret doesn't help by regularly bouncing into Elizabeth's cabin and demanding to know if she is better yet. 'Everybody's miserable except me and Peter,' she declares.

'Peter?'

'Yes, Peter. *Peter*.' Margaret stares at her. 'Gosh, you must be sick if you can't remember Peter! He's Papa's equerry, for heaven's sake!'

'Urghh.' It's the best Elizabeth can manage.

'Peter and I have been out on deck,' Margaret rattles on. 'It's not as bad as it was. I had to hold on to him when we first went out, the wind was so strong but it was fun. And then we were both starving so Peter asked if we could have some lunch and we had the most delicious shepherd's pie—' She stops as Elizabeth beckons her closer. 'What, Lil?'

'I hate you, Margaret,' Elizabeth says, weak but perfectly distinct. 'Go away.'

Margaret only laughs merrily and dances out while Elizabeth turns her face to the wall with a groan.

It is two days before Elizabeth can sit up, three before she can leave the cabin on shaky legs. It is like venturing into a new world. The wind has dropped, the seas have quietened and the sun glitters on a dazzling expanse of water. Whichever way she looks there is only space and light.

She stands at the rail, breathing in the ozone, astounded by the power of the ocean. *Vanguard* steams on, engines throbbing, while the breeze lifts her hair and her spirits rise in response. She can barely remember life before the war. Since then it has been a dreary world, a world of dim lights and grey weather and rationing and making do, even at Buckingham Palace. All this glitter, all this light, feels like a gift. Elizabeth feels as if she has been cut loose, untethered, and she grips the rail almost as if she might float away.

Was this what it was like for Philip on board ship? Did

he feel the same swell of the heart, the same expansion of the lungs? No wonder teaching at Corsham has seemed dull and unsatisfying. No wonder he hates the constriction of a tie and the stuffy culture at court.

Slowly, the rest of the household grope their way onto the deck as their stomachs settle and their legs steady. Elizabeth spends a whole day just sitting in a deckchair looking at the sea and marvelling at the sparkling swell and surge of the ocean. She misses Philip but she is not sorry to be here, overwhelmed by the power of it. Never has she felt so insignificant and yet so at ease. Never has she seen a horizon so vast. She is transformed by it.

Elizabeth hasn't expected this chance to let go of everything. Responsibility has evaporated in the sparkling air. Isolated on board *Vanguard*, she lets herself forget the bitter winter being endured by people at home. She forgets the frustrations of Greek politics and her father's intransigence. She doesn't forget Philip, of course, but the missing him is less raw on the ship. There is something about being out there on the ocean, knowing that there is nothing she can do, nothing she can say that will make any difference to anything until they get to the end of the voyage.

It's a kind of freedom.

Her parents, her sister, a household of ten travelling with them. And the officers and crew. There is nobody staring, nobody waving, nobody calling out intrusive questions. To her surprise, Elizabeth realises that Margaret is right: they can enjoy these three weeks at sea.

And she does. She and Margaret play tag and other silly deck games with the younger officers. They play deck quoits and badminton and take part in shooting contests. When they cross the equator, they enjoy the ceremony of crossing the line. Elizabeth writes to Philip about the crew dressed in wigs and skirts, about dunking other novices who have never crossed the equator before. She and Margaret are disappointed by the tameness of their own initiation, she tells Philip in the letter she writes to him that night.

The others were dunked in the pool and tormented in various ways but all we had to endure was having our faces dabbed with huge powder puffs. I feel sure that if you had been there we would have been made to sit on the greased pole and beat each other with pillows until we fell into the pool at the very least.

Chapter 31

South Africa, February 1947

Vanguard steams into Table Bay early on a fresh February morning. On deck, Elizabeth and Margaret shade their eyes against the early morning sun. They can see Cape Town and, beyond, the famous Table Mountain, its flat top draped in a cloth of dense white mist.

Although she is sorry to leave the carefree voyage behind, Elizabeth is wide-eyed at the colour and abundance in South Africa. January in London was bitter, tired, and grey. In Cape Town the sky is blue, the light is crystalline. The shop windows are full. The market stalls are piled high with fruit and vegetables: after the years of rationing, Elizabeth finds herself gaping at the redness of the tomatoes, the yellowness of the bananas, the bobbly green avocadoes. She is presented with a fresh peach and when she bites into the blush-coloured flesh, the sweetness explodes in her mouth and she smiles as she wipes the juice dribbling down her chin. It is nothing like the tinned peaches she has had before. It is the most delicious thing she has ever eaten, she decides.

The South Africans have built a special train for the tour. Elizabeth gasps when she sees it. With its fourteen carriages painted ivory and white, each decorated with the royal crest, The White Train gleams in the brilliant light as it streaks through the spectacular landscape. It curves around hills and mountains, arrows across the dusty veldt. She writes to Philip every evening.

We each have our own bedroom and bathroom. There is a drawing room and a dining room, and Papa has a study and Mummy has her own sitting room. All on the train! There is even a post office, which I will use to send this letter to you, and a telephone exchange which is connected at the main stops so Papa can keep in touch with events at home.

I know you have been to South Africa so I don't need to explain how beautiful the country is but I have never seen such light before. So different from the lovely Scottish summer light. Here it is diamond hard and it outlines every tiny thing so sharply that I keep having to blink.

Elizabeth pauses, her pen still in her hand, as she looks out at the veldt. It stretches away to a distant horizon where the sky is flushed a deep red barred with strips of purple cloud. Her bedroom on the train is furnished with a desk at the window and when the train has stopped for the night, as now, she likes to sit and write to Philip.

The view is distracting though. She keeps stopping to stare at the stupendous scale of it. The train has rumbled across endless stretches of golden grassland all day, broken only by the occasional acacia tree or the glimpse of mountains in the far distance. She and Margaret hung out of the window to watch a herd of zebras galloping away from the train.

Dipping her pen in the ink, Elizabeth returns to her letter to tell Philip about the wildlife they have glimpsed.

We saw some giraffes today, too. They are such extraordinary creatures and it was exciting to see them in the wild. They kept their distance but didn't seem too bothered by the train but turned their heads to watch us as we went by.

Sometimes we see people, too, just standing with their horses by the side of the track in the middle of nowhere, waiting to wave at us. Peter (do you remember Papa's equerry?) says that some of them may have ridden more than fifty miles to see us. I always feel terrible if we don't see them in time to wave back. Everyone in South Africa has been so very welcoming. If I didn't feel guilty knowing how much people at home are suffering in the winter, I would be loving it – although I do wish you could be here too.

I don't think Mummy and Papa are enjoying the tour so much. Everything is new and exciting for Margaret and me but for them it is quite wearing and poor Papa in particular finds it exhausting. He doesn't like the way the Afrikaner police order us around at times. He calls them the Gestapo. I'm afraid his temper is on a very short fuse.

She hopes Philip will understand that things are so tense that there is no question of raising the subject of announcing their engagement. She worries about her father. His nerves are so on edge that he seems unable to relax. Once, by the Indian Ocean, he ordered the train to stop by a broad beach. Looking out of the window, Elizabeth saw the police roping off a path across the sand between two vast crowds of people. She watched her father climb down from the train wearing a blue bathrobe and carrying a towel, watched him walk across the sand to the sea. It seemed to take a long time and by the time he reached the ocean he was a tiny solitary figure, jumping up and down in the surf. Elizabeth remembers the tightness of her throat as she watched him. He looked so terribly lonely.

With pity came a trickle of disquiet. Was that her future? Was that what being a sovereign meant? Always divided from the rest of the world, always watched, always alone?

But her father has her mother, Elizabeth reminds herself, just as she would have Philip. She wouldn't be alone any more than the King is. It was just a solitary swim, after all.

Elizabeth refills the pen with ink and remembers to tell Philip about their visit to Cecil Rhodes's grave in the Motopo Hills, set atop a bare hillside among strange round boulders.

Mummy set off in ridiculous high-heels, totally unsuitable for climbing a steep, rocky mountain. So like her! Of course they were soon pinching horribly and she could barely walk. I gave her my sandals in the end and I walked up in my stockinged feet, which was a novel experience for me.

The path had been dusty and she'd been able to feel the grit digging into the soles of her feet, but it had been strangely liberating too, to feel so connected to the hot earth.

There is so much to tell Philip! Every day there are new experiences. Elizabeth's favourite time, though, is the early morning when the sky is glowing with the gold of the sun hauling itself over the horizon and the air is cool. The train stops at night, and someone has provided horses so she and Margaret can ride before breakfast across the veldt or along some empty sweep of beach. Peter Townsend usually accompanies them, with one or two security guards following at a distance.

Elizabeth tucks the letter into its envelope, writes Philip's name and address carefully on the front and seals it up before sending it to the train's post office. She likes to write to him and feel the connection still. Her senses are so overloaded here, she is afraid she might combust, and thinking about Philip keeps her anchored. This trip is wonderful, but knowing she has him to go home to is the next best thing to having him here.

She is still thinking about Philip the next morning when she gets up early and jumps down from the carriage to find Margaret and Peter already waiting for her. Three young South African boys are holding a horse each and they smile shyly in response to Elizabeth's greeting. Elizabeth is given a frisky chestnut mare with dark, liquid eyes and a saucy toss to her head.

Elizabeth strokes the horse's nose and they take the measure of each other. The mare, she senses, is afraid that she is in for a sedate ride, and Elizabeth is able to promise her that there will be no holding back. She swings into the saddle, loving the responsive feel of the horse beneath her.

'Let's go,' she says, smiling.

The horses are fresh and they let them have their heads, hooves thundering as they gallop over the veldt. The sky is flushed an unearthly pink, and Elizabeth can smell horse and dry grass and dust as they race towards a lone acacia tree in the distance. She can feel the bunch of the mare's muscles, the easy power of her stride. For so long she has held herself tight, but in the hush of that African dawn, Elizabeth feels her chest loosen and unlock, and she lets out a whoop of exhilaration.

The mare responds to her excitement and powers ahead, leaving Margaret and Peter behind on their more sluggish mounts. A broad smile on her face, Elizabeth crouches over the horse's mane, her thighs clamped tight around the saddle, and her hair blown anyhow. She doesn't care what she looks like: she just wants to gallop forever towards the horizon, faster and further.

When they reach the acacia tree, Elizabeth pulls the horse up reluctantly to rest while Margaret and Peter catch up. Easy in the saddle, she surveys the empty horizon while the mare snorts and tosses her mane, well pleased by the run.

It is like being at sea, Elizabeth thinks. The same space, the same light, the same sense of being untethered. It makes her realise how confined her life has been until now. Oh, there is Balmoral, of course, and Sandringham, but for most of the war she was at Windsor Castle, where the horizon is constantly interrupted by towers or stone walls or shrouded in grey clouds.

There is nothing to break up the emptiness here, just this tree, stark against the great bowl of the sky. Elizabeth can feel herself changing, filling up the space. This trip has been eye-opening for her. She didn't want to come, didn't want to leave Philip, but it has been good for her, she can see that now. It has not just been about seeing a new country, interesting though that has been. These weeks with her parents and Margaret have given her a new insight into their family and what it means to be royal.

She has watched her parents and understands now what is expected of them, and what will be expected of her in the future. In particular, Elizabeth has a new appreciation of her mother. The Queen is unfailingly charming. Her smile never falters, no matter how tedious the dinner or how long the reception. She sits through displays of dancing and accepts bouquets with an expression of lively interest. And she always looks immaculate. Her hats are things of beauty, and her shoes designed to boost her height, although they are not always the most practical footwear.

Elizabeth has been watching and learning. She has seen how her mother makes every single person she talks to feel special, but she has seen, too, the harried expressions of the officials responsible for moving the royal party along and keeping to the punishing schedule. On more than one occasion Elizabeth has had to prod her mother's heels with the point of her sunshade to hurry her up.

This will be her future. It is less daunting than it once seemed. South Africa has given Elizabeth a new confidence. Her genuine interest in the country has helped her relax and it is easier now to talk to people. She will always be shy, but sitting on the horse under that acacia tree, Elizabeth feels a sense of purpose click into place, as if for the first time she fully understands the destiny that awaits her.

It will not be easy, Elizabeth thinks, her eyes on the far horizon, but she will be able to do it. She is nearly twenty-one, nearly an adult. She will accept the role that fate has given her, she vows. She cannot bear to think of a time when her dear Papa will be gone, but she will be Queen one day, and she will make him proud.

Chapter 32

The King's nerves are so frayed that in the end it is a relief to return to Cape Town in time for her twenty-first birthday. Elizabeth wakes on 21st April to the sound of unfamiliar birds peeping and whistling in the lush garden of Government House and she lies for a while, wishing she could escape for a gallop the way she was able to from the train. But the programme for her day has been agreed months in advance and Elizabeth will do as she is told.

That evening she is to broadcast a birthday message to five hundred million of her father's subjects across the British Commonwealth and Empire. The speech has been written for her, but it is so much what she wants to say that Elizabeth has tears in her eyes when she reads it. Now, on her birthday morning, she picks it up from her bedside table and reads it again, murmuring the words to herself: *an unwavering faith, a high courage, a quiet heart.*

That morning she is overwhelmed by gifts and congratulatory messages from all over the world, so many that

Margaret has to help her open them. The coffee table in front of her is littered with diamonds – earrings and badges and brooches and necklaces – all glinting in the sunlight between the opened telegrams. One gift though she keeps to last: something small and heavy that Philip has sent.

'Aren't you going to open it?' Margaret asks.

'Not now,' says Elizabeth, turning it between her hands, smiling at the thought that Philip has remembered her. She wants to keep it until she is quite alone. 'I'll take it upstairs with me.'

Leaving the diamonds on the table, she carries Philip's parcel upstairs and sits on the bed to open it. It is beautifully wrapped with a ribbon and a small card that she pulls out to read first.

Darling Elizabeth, this is for you on your birthday. There is only one piece of jewellery I want to give you, so until I can offer you a ring, the enclosed is a token to let you know that I am thinking of you with all my love, Philip.

Elizabeth opens the box and lifts the tissue paper to release the sweet smell of roses, lavender, and lily of the valley. Inside lie three perfect bars of soap, and she smiles as she lifts each to her nose, remembering how she had told him how much she longed for soap during the war. He has remembered. He hasn't forgotten her. He is thinking of her. That is all she wants.

Darling Elizabeth ... with all my love. They are just the things people say in letters, Elizabeth knows. It doesn't mean anything. But still, her heart lifts.

At six o'clock, she sits alone with Margaret and an engineer in a small, quiet room to read her message. Her heart bangs against her ribs as the engineer counts her down and then points to indicate that she should begin. Taking a deep breath, Elizabeth starts to read. Her voice sounds high and rushed at first, and she steadies herself for the second paragraph. 'Let me begin by saying "thank you" to all the thousands of kind people who have sent me messages of goodwill. This is a happy day for me, but it is also one that brings serious thoughts, thoughts of life looming ahead with all its challenges and with all its opportunity.'

The speech lasts for six minutes but it feels like much longer to Elizabeth. She keeps thinking of all those people, millions and millions of them, listening to her, to *her*, and when she makes her final declaration, the truth of it resonates through her.

'I declare before you all that my whole life, whether it be long or short, shall be devoted to your service and the service of our great imperial family to which we all belong.'

The words feel momentous. As she sits in front of the microphone, she realises truly, perhaps for the first time, what her life will be. When the speech is over, the engineer grins and gives her the thumbs up, and Elizabeth relaxes with a rather shaky smile. The broadcast is done but her task is just beginning. Her duty, her purpose, is to serve the country and the Commonwealth.

It is a vow she intends to keep.

Chapter 33

London, May 1947

'I suppose I know why you're here,' the King says in a resigned voice as he studies Philip over his desk.

'I imagine you do, sir.'

Philip is still smarting at having been refused permission to meet HMS *Vanguard* when she docked. Nor was he allowed to be part of the welcoming party at Buckingham Palace when the royal family finally returned from South Africa. It's true that he didn't want to greet Elizabeth in public, but his deliberate exclusion rankles.

All he has had is a brief phone call with Elizabeth while he was on duty at Corsham.

'It feels strange to be back,' she had said, and it felt strange to Philip too. Her letters have been full of South Africa and what she has seen, and he has been unable to shake the fear that the King and Queen may have succeeded in distracting her. He has done everything he can. He has written regularly and sent telegrams and remembered her birthday, but it has felt like a long three months and he has been scratchy and irritable with everyone. The unfortunate petty officers he's supposed to be training have quickly learnt to step around him very carefully.

He is so close to his goal, Philip thinks in frustration, but it's as if he takes one step forward only to be pushed back two.

'I wish I could have been there to meet you,' he told Elizabeth when she rang.

'I do too, but Mummy and Papa thought it would be better if we met in private.'

'That sounds good to me. I'm on duty, but the first chance I have to get away, I'll come up to London and ask to speak to your father again.' He had paused. 'If, that is, you haven't changed your mind?'

'No,' Elizabeth had said. 'I haven't changed my mind about anything.'

'Good. In that case, I'll see you soon.'

Perhaps not the most loverlike of farewells, but Philip was too relieved at her reply to think about a more affectionate turn of phrase until it was too late. When he realised he has missed an opportunity, he had shrugged. He's never been one for soppiness, and besides, Elizabeth doesn't want that. She made that clear enough.

Now at last he has leave and he has driven straight to Buckingham Palace.

'Elizabeth is twenty-one now,' he tells the King, standing

very straight, his hands clasped respectfully behind his back. 'We're both of the same mind as we were last August and we've waited for nine months. We'd like your permission to make our engagement public and set a date for the wedding.'

The King sighs, stubs out his cigarette and pushes back his chair. He hasn't even stood up before he is reaching for another cigarette, lighting it, and desperately drawing in the nicotine. Philip is a smoker, but he is nothing like Elizabeth's father. He is shocked by how ill the King looks, in fact. He is gaunt and grey-faced, with deep lines carved into his cheeks and forehead.

The King stands at his study window, smoking pensively, his back to Philip. Clenching his jaw in frustration, Philip reminds himself that he cannot press for an answer. This is the King and he will speak when he is good and ready. But it doesn't feel encouraging. Why not reach over the desk, shake his hand and tell him that he will tell Tommy Lascelles to make the announcement straight away?

When the King does speak, he seems to have ignored Philip's request. 'Lilibet's come on a lot over the last few months,' he says. 'I was very proud of her in South Africa.'

'I heard her broadcast,' says Philip. 'It was very moving.'

The King nods slowly, still looking out of the window. The smoke from his cigarette curls above his head, drifting in the sunlight. 'It was. For her birthday, you know, Lilibet was showered with diamonds, and I felt that was only right, because that's what she is: a diamond. She's strong and shining and clear and true.' He turns at last to fix Philip with his gaze. 'Do you understand that, Philip?'

'Of course I do,' Philip says, smoothing the impatient edge to his voice with an effort. He wants to marry Elizabeth, for God's sake. Why would he do that if he didn't understand how special she was?

'There's no "of course" about it,' the King says sharply. 'You don't know Lilibet the way we do.'

'I know her well enough to want to marry her.'

The King makes an impatient gesture with his cigarette and then his shoulders slump. 'For so long it's just been the four of us,' he says. 'I don't know how I would have got through if I hadn't had the Queen and my daughters.' He smiles fondly. 'Elizabeth and Margaret, my pride and my joy. They are so different, and yet we fit together, like pieces of a jigsaw. And now you want to take her away.' With a sigh he stubs out the cigarette. 'The puzzle will be broken. Do you wonder I don't want to lose her?'

'You wouldn't deny her the chance of a husband and a family of her own, would you, sir?'

'No, of course not, but she's young yet.'

'She's young but she knows her own mind,' Philip says. 'You said it yourself, sir. She's strong and she is true, and she is steadfast. She won't change her mind about me – and I won't change mine about her.' He pauses then says more gently, 'You won't lose her, sir. I know her well enough to be sure that her first duty will always be to you and to the country, to the Commonwealth, just as she said in her speech.'

The King only sighs.

Philip risks pushing harder. 'We have waited, sir. Longer than the six months you stipulated. And I have done my bit. I have renounced my rights to the Greek throne to help defuse anxieties about me being a foreign prince. I've given up my title.'

Focused on getting British nationality, Philip hadn't thought about what that would mean to him until it was too late. The moment he went to sign away his rights, he almost balked. The pen felt strange and unwieldly in his hand as he stared down at it and he found himself thinking about his father. What would he think about Philip rejecting the title of 'Prince' in favour of a mere 'Lieutenant'? The Greek dynasty was not a long established one, but their roots in the royal house of Denmark and their connection with royal families across Europe had always been a point of pride. Philip was turning his back on all of that.

'For the greater prize,' Mountbatten reminded Philip when he hesitated.

Philip knows his uncle is right. Giving up his rights of succession to the Greek throne was a practical decision. It was not as if he would ever have been King anyway. He hasn't expected to feel strongly about it, but rather like his father's death, the sudden realisation of what giving up his title would mean has caught him unawares.

He is a prince no longer ... so what is he? He is more

than a naval officer, whatever some lines on a piece of paper may say. Inside, where it counts, he is as royal as he has ever been.

He has lost a title but gained a name: Mountbatten. Philip is ambivalent about that. On the one hand, he needs to be practical and it is just a name. On the other, it is not his father's name. It is his uncle's. Philip doesn't begrudge Uncle Dickie that small victory but the knowledge that once again his father has been written out of his history niggles like a small stone in his shoe.

But what's done is done. What matters now is to get the King to agree to an announcement.

'And we've been discreet, as you know,' he goes on, 'but there are still rumours about an upcoming engagement. There seems little point in continuing to deny them.'

'No, I suppose not.' The King sounds defeated and Philip stiffens hopefully.

'So ... will you make an announcement, sir?' he asks, picking his words with care. The King is so skittish that Philip wouldn't put it past him to change his mind.

'Yes, yes,' Elizabeth's father says testily.

Philip just manages to resist punching the air in triumph. 'Thank you, sir.'

'I just hope it's the right thing.' To Philip's dismay, the King goes off on another tangent. 'I got some rather good pictures in South Africa. Would you like to see them?'

No, Philip wants to shout. *No, I don't want to see your holiday pictures. I want to talk about my engagement!*

268

'I'd be delighted,' he says instead through set teeth.

'Wait here a moment and I'll go and get them. I think you'll be interested.'

Dear God. Left alone, Philip drags a hand through his hair and stifles a growl of frustration.

The King's study smells of leather and old books and stale cigarette smoke. Philip wouldn't mind a cigarette himself right now, but it would be imprudent to light up, he decides. There is a red box on the desk. His eyes rest on it thoughtfully. One day it will be Elizabeth's job to work through the government papers, day after day, week after week. She will sit dutifully at the desk where her father sits now and she will never say she is bored or tired.

And what will he be doing? For the first time, Philip considers the matter and disquiet uncurls at the base of his spine. What *will* he do?

The sound of the door opening makes him turn, prepared to feign interest in photos of elephants and lions. But it is not the King who stands there. It is Elizabeth, holding the door handle as if she is not quite sure whether she wants to come in or not, an uncertain smile trembling on her lips.

Philip looks across the room at her and feels something in his chest click and unlock.

Elizabeth.

She has blossomed, is his first impression. She looks taller, more assured. There is a new glow about her, and those clear eyes are bluer than ever.

Philip clears his throat. 'Hello, you.'

Elizabeth closes the door with a quiet click. 'Hello,' she says breathlessly.

He doesn't think, he just opens his arms, and she walks across the room and right into them.

Chapter 34

'I missed you,' Philip tells her. They are walking in the palace gardens, hand in hand. It is a beautiful spring day, or maybe it only seems so because they are both euphoric. Birds twitter busily overhead, drowning out the distant sound of traffic around Victoria Station. The smell of cut grass with its tantalising hint of summer drifts in the air while Susan bustles ahead. Sunlight stripes across the path in between patches of shade as it winds around the lake. A duck chivvies her ducklings into the water.

It is true, Philip thinks. If he is honest, he has missed Elizabeth more than he expected to. At first he was mainly frustrated by the enforced separation which delayed their plans for marriage, but he didn't think he would miss her quiet presence quite so much.

David Milford Haven pounced as soon as HMS *Vanguard* had left for South Africa. 'You'd better make the most of these last months of freedom,' he announced. 'You'll have to behave the moment the engagement is announced.' He dragged Philip out to clubs and Philip told himself that he was enjoying it but at odd times he would find himself thinking about Elizabeth. Everyone in David's set – in his set too, he supposes – is so sharp and sophisticated. They are fun, yes, but sometimes too loud, too challenging. In comparison, Elizabeth seems tantalising, like a glass of cool water after too much champagne.

'I missed you too,' Elizabeth tells him, twining her fingers around his.

'Oh, come on, you had a wonderful time,' he teases her. 'Admit it!'

She laughs. 'I did, you're right. How could I not? Papa wasn't well,' she says, a shadow crossing her eyes, 'but we saw so much and met so many people. Everything was so different and exciting, it was overwhelming at times. On my birthday, the South African government laid on a ball. It was beautiful. I wore a white tulle evening gown, sparkling with diamante embroidery and sequins ... I know it sounds silly, but I felt like a princess. And then Field Marshal Smuts presented me with a silver casket. When I opened it, I found twenty-one perfect diamonds. They were so magnificent that I actually gasped.'

She glances at Philip. 'But I liked your present best.'

'I'm glad you did. I wasn't in a position to send you fabulous jewels, I'm afraid, but I wanted you to know I was thinking of you.'

'That's why I liked it.'

'The tour has changed you,' Philip says after a moment.

'In a good way,' he adds when Elizabeth looks uncertain. 'You seem ... more sure of yourself.'

'I think it made me realise that I could do the job,' she says slowly. 'A lot of the job is doing the same things and saying the same things over and over again. It's not always exciting,' she goes on in a dry voice. 'But I watched my parents. I saw how they dealt with everyone, and I saw what it meant to the people who came to see us, too. It didn't matter if they were at a ball or had ridden a horse fifty miles to wave as The White Train went by. It was ... humbling.'

'I listened to the broadcast on your birthday,' Philip tells her. 'You did well, Elizabeth.'

'Thank you.' Her face relaxes into a smile. 'I'm glad you were listening.'

'Me and two hundred and fifty million others, they say! It was a powerful speech. It made me feel hopeful.'

She turns to him eagerly. 'Exactly. That's what I thought. That's what I wanted to say. It feels as if we've all been marking time since the war, and now we should start looking forwards.

'And us?' Philip stops and looks down at her. 'Can we look forward?'

'We can now that Papa has finally said yes to an announcement. When will it be?'

'He didn't say. There's still a bit of him that doesn't want you to marry at all. I hope the announcement is soon, though. I don't see why it shouldn't be immediately. I'm

British now,' Philip says. 'I've renounced my Greek rights of succession, and now I'm just plain Lieutenant Philip Mountbatten.'

'Mountbatten? Uncle Dickie must be pleased,' Elizabeth says, her expression neutral, and Philip isn't sure whether the comment is pointed or not.

'Well, it was that or Schleswig-Holstein-Sonderburg-Glücksburg,' he says. 'It seemed a bit of a mouthful and not the handiest of names to have in a British passport.'

'I can see that.'

'Someone suggested anglicizing Oldenburg, which is where my family originated, but that made Oldcastle and the feeling was that was rather plebeian. Honestly, when it was suggested that I use my mother's name, I couldn't think of anything better, so Mountbatten it is.'

'But ...?' Elizabeth prompts.

'But nothing,' Philip lies, but her steady eyes on him make him continue. 'It's just ... I owe the Mountbattens so much, but it feels as if my father has been written out of my story somehow.'

'Couldn't you have kept his title?'

'I could but I want to be seen as British. While you were away, they published an opinion poll asking the public whether they think you should marry a foreign prince or not. Nobody showed it to me but I can read. Forty per cent of people don't want you to have anything to do with a foreigner.'

'That means sixty per cent don't mind,' she points out.

'True, but why risk the bad feeling? One of the reasons your father has hesitated for so long is my association with the Greek monarchy. Well, I've given that up,' Philip says determinedly. 'I can live without being called *Your Royal Highness* if it means I can marry you.'

Chapter 35

She doesn't need him to say that he loves her, Elizabeth tells herself. Love is just a word. It doesn't need to be spoken out loud. They are not in a romantic novel, after all. They are two members of a royal family negotiating a marriage that will be beneficial to both of them. Go back a generation or two, and she would have had little say in the business at all.

Philip has said he missed her. He's said he is happy to give up his title to marry her. Surely that is enough? And now that her father has finally given permission, they can be married soon and she will have everything she wants.

When her father told her to join Philip in his study, she almost ran along the corridor but at the last minute she hesitated, suddenly afraid he had changed and she wouldn't recognise him. In South Africa she had some-times closed her eyes only to panic when she couldn't immediately bring his face to her mind. Then she would pick up his photograph and trace the hard lines of his face with her fingertip, drawing reassurance from that bold stare.

She has felt herself changing while she was away, but what if Philip, too, has changed?

So she was shaky and faintly sick when she opened the door to the study and saw Philip standing there. For a beat, two, they just looked at each other and for Elizabeth it was a heart-stopping moment of utter clarity, because there he was, and everything she ever felt for him came rushing back with complete certainty at the sight of him: he is the one.

Her father has clearly passed on the word and a small gathering has been organised when they go back inside.

'Philip! Congratulations!' Her mother kisses him on both cheeks and then turns to gather Elizabeth into a scented embrace, while Margaret hugs them both. 'We must have champagne.'

Elizabeth's heart is light as she hugs her sister back and smiles at her father. 'Thank you, Papa,' she says fervently.

'Darling Lilibet,' he says and kisses her. 'I'm glad you're happy,' he adds, although he looks fretful rather than glad.

'This is so exciting!' Margaret claps her hands together. 'When is the wedding?'

'We haven't got that far yet,' Elizabeth says, laughing. 'Papa needs to make the official announcement of the engagement first.'

'I'm afraid that can't happen yet,' the King says, not meeting her eyes.

'Oh, *Papa*!' Elizabeth sees the smile drop from Philip's face like a stone, sees the effort it takes him not to explode. 'Papa, why can't you announce it straight away?' she says, dismayed to find her eyes pricking with tears of disappointment. 'We've waited nine months already!'

'Lilibet, it's not just your decision.' Guilt is making the King sound peevish. 'Your marriage isn't something we can just announce. It's not just about the two of you, however much you might want it to be. All sorts of people have to be consulted. I've been in touch with the Prime Minister and he tells me that the heads of the Commonwealth governments have been informed of your plans. I'm sorry to tell you that not all of them are enthusiastic about the idea of your marriage to Philip. The public aren't keen on the idea of you marrying a foreigner either.'

'I'm not a foreigner,' Philip grinds out. 'I went to school here, I only speak English and I served during the war. And now I've given up my hereditary rights and my title and am a British citizen. What more do people want?'

'I understand that, but you will have to give the country some time to come around to the idea.'

'Oh, for—!' Philip manages to swallow down the words in time, but her father is not impressed.

'I'm sorry if you don't like it,' he says coldly. 'I'm afraid you'll find this is the reality of marrying Lilibet. We'll make the announcement on 15th July. Until then, we'll start to include you both in engagements so that you appear in the Court Circular. You can be seen together but I'm not announcing anything until July.'

Her father's intransigence and Philip's ill-concealed fury takes some of the shine off Elizabeth's happiness, but she refuses to let herself be too downcast. The important thing is that they are still engaged and at least now they don't have to be furtive about their meetings. Philip is invited to a birthday lunch for Queen Mary and is included in the party for Royal Ascot to which he comes in spite of the fact that he doesn't share her love of racing.

'I hope you're not bored,' she says, biting her lip as she belatedly remembers his presence after a particularly tense race, won after an excruciatingly tight finish by one of the horses in the royal stud.

'I like watching you watching the race,' Philip says with a lazy smile. 'Your face is much more interesting than the horses. Anyway, I'm looking forward to dancing with you tonight.'

It is good to be back at Windsor Castle and to have a party for Royal Ascot after those lean war years. This year there is a ball in the Crimson Drawing Room. The carpet is rolled up and removed along with most of the elaborate gilt sofas and chairs commissioned by George IV. The tall windows are open to the soft June night and the great gilt mirror above the fireplace reflects back the dancers who circle in a kaleidoscope of colourful gowns punctuated with the crisp black and white of the men's evening dress.

'This is better,' Philip says, taking Elizabeth's hand and setting his free hand at her waist. 'At least we can dance together now. Remember when we weren't allowed to and I had to watch you over my partner's shoulder?'

'I remember watching you over *my* partner's shoulder,' she says. 'It always seemed to me that you were very well pleased with your partner.'

'I was just being polite,' he says virtuously. 'It was you I wanted to dance with.' He pulls her closer. 'And now I can.'

It is a happy summer for Elizabeth. She now has a private secretary of her own – Jock Colville – to advise her and manage her diary. She has her own car, a Daimler. She is busy with engagements, and now when she hears the shouts of 'Where's Philip?' she isn't distressed, because she knows where he is and that he wants to marry her.

She is even enjoying social occasions more than she used to. The visit to South Africa has given her more confidence, and she is more relaxed and better at talking to people. Her favourite times, though, are when she and Philip are alone. Whenever he can, he drives up from Corsham and parks openly in the palace courtyard. Sometimes, he pulls the roof of the sports car back and she ties a scarf firmly over her hair to stop it blowing around and they go out to Richmond Park. Wearing sunglasses, they can sit on a bench and nobody gives them a second look. They are just another courting couple enjoying the greenness and the space of the park.

Of course, there is green and there is space at Windsor, but there is something thrilling about the anonymity of the park, of pretending that they are just like any other couple. Philip rests his arm along the back of the bench behind her and his fingers graze her shoulder. He takes her to see *Oklahoma!* at the Theatre Royal, Drury Lane and he holds her hand in the dark. When he dances with her, he holds her close, and his nearness makes her hazy with longing.

Oh, Elizabeth knows it is tame stuff for many of her contemporaries but sitting close to him, feeling him male and solid beside her, is enough to make her blood beat low and heavy, to set up a fine quiver in her belly.

She longs to be married, but still her father insists that an announcement must wait and the strain is taking its toll on Philip who can be irritable and tense at times. So when he asks her if she will meet his mother, Elizabeth says yes straight away.

'Is she in London now?'

'She's staying with my grandmother at the moment. Rather her than me,' Philip says with a wry look. 'Grandmama's apartments are draughty and uncomfortable and she sits all day in her chair smoking and complaining.'

'What about?'

'Oh, everything. Mostly about her husband having to

renounce his – and her – royal titles in 1917. It's only been thirty years but my grandmother likes to collect grievances. My mother isn't like that at all, so I'm not sure how long the visit will last! I may have to help her to find an apartment of her own.'

Chapter 36

'How long is it since you've seen her?' Elizabeth asks. 'I was on leave in Athens during the war, in 1941, before the German occupation. She was living very simply then.'

Philip keeps his tone even. Talking about his mother always leaves him feeling ... complicated. He hates the way he had to work up to mentioning her to Elizabeth. It is ridiculous. He is a grown man, and it is not his mother's fault that she was ill. He knows that. He has always known that.

'She sounds like an interesting woman,' Elizabeth says. 'I'd like to meet her.'

It stings that she keeps her tone carefully neutral. Of course she has heard that his mother is eccentric, mad. A crazy woman confined to a sanatorium. Her own mother will certainly have told her in an effort to dissuade her from marrying him.

'You know my mother is going to be a problem,' he says

abruptly. 'Interesting is a kind word to use. She's not like other people. She's certainly not like any other royals.'

'I heard that she was amazingly brave during the war,' Elizabeth says. 'They say she fed people who were starving, hid a Jewish family from Germans, looked after orphans ... How many of the rest of us would have done half as much?'

'Yes, she would do anything for other people's children.'

Philip stops, appalled at the bitterness in his own voice. Elizabeth hears it, of course. She turns to look at him, but he won't meet her eyes. He scowls at a squirrel running up the trunk of a great oak. He doesn't want to talk about his mother.

He *isn't* going to talk about her.

'I went to look for her one day when I was on leave in Athens,' he hears himself say, 'and I found her at a soup kitchen she ran. She had this scrap of a boy clinging to her skirts while she berated some man twice her size about the way he'd been treating him. The man tried to argue with her but she wasn't having it. She threatened to have him arrested for cruelty and when he'd given up and gone away, I watched as she put her arms around that boy and told him she would look after him, that he would be safe with her. *Mon petit chou*, that's what she called him.'

All at once, there's a viciously tight block in Philip's throat, and his mouth twists with the effort of swallowing it down. He's still not looking at Elizabeth but he can feel her quiet eyes on his face.

'That's what she used to call me when I was small,' he says. 'My little cabbage.'

'How sweet,' she says and he can tell that she is smiling. 'I can definitely see you as a cabbage. A rather naughty one, I suspect.'

'I was very naughty,' he admits, grateful to Elizabeth for lightening the moment.

'Did she know you were there?' she asks after a moment.

'Oh, yes. When she saw me her face lit up, but I had to wait until she had arranged for the boy to be looked after. Then I took her out to lunch and she spent the whole time telling me what a terrible time the poor child had had, and how she would make quite sure he was properly cared for, and how sad it was that he was on his own. "He's only nine," she said.'

He breaks off again. Why in God's name did he start this story? This isn't what Elizabeth wants to hear!

'You were only nine when you were sent to school in England,' Elizabeth says quietly.

'Yes.' Philip lets out a long breath. 'It was different, of course, for me.'

'How?'

'I had Uncle Georgie and Uncle Dickie to look after me, and I was fine,' he insists. 'I was a boisterous boy, very self-reliant even then. I could look after myself. That poor kid was starving and beaten. That never happened to me.'

'I imagine boys of nine still need their mothers.'

'I was fine,' he says again, and he feels Elizabeth studying him.

'You keep saying that.'

'Well, I was,' he says defensively. 'I was like those children over there.' He nods in the direction of a gang whooping and yelling around a cluster of trees. 'When anyone tried to hug me or kiss me, I'd wriggle out of their clutches. I didn't want any of that.'

He remembers playing outside at Salem one hot summer day until his sister Dolla had dragged him inside. She fussed around, making him change his shorts and brush his hair.

'Please don't argue Philip,' she said tensely when he protested. 'Mama wants to see you.'

But his mother hadn't wanted to see him. Dolla took him to the sanatorium where Alice looked through him and played fretfully with the fringe of her dress. She barely seemed to know who he was while Dolla made determinedly cheerful conversation that Alice ignored.

'Kiss Mama goodbye,' his sister said at last. Philip didn't want to. The woman in the chair was a stranger, not the sweet, loving mother he remembered, who gathered him up and tickled him and called him her *petit chou*. But Dolla insisted and when he leant reluctantly forward and pressed his lips to his mother's cheek, he felt her flinch.

'I'm sorry,' Dolla said in the car on the way back to Salem. Her lips were pressed tightly together and he'd had the uneasy feeling that she was trying not to cry. 'I thought it would help.'

Philip never knew whether she had thought the visit would help him or their mother, but suspected that it just made it worse for both of them. He didn't get so much as a birthday card from his mother for five years after that.

He has learnt not to think about that day at the sanatorium. Easier to think about cricket or riding his bike instead. The memory is a bruise, one you forget until you press it by mistake.

Lost in his memories, he doesn't realise he has stopped talking until Elizabeth's hand slips into is. It is astonishingly comforting.

'I don't blame her,' he says. 'She was ill.'

'I know she was.'

'Everyone thinks I'm embarrassed about her but I'm not,' Philip says, as if she has contradicted him. 'I'm proud of her. She isn't afraid of anything. The rest of the royal family left Greece after 1941, but my mother stuck it out in terrible conditions during the occupation. In the last few months before the end of the war, she survived on bread and butter and she gave away every other scrap of food she could find to people she said needed it more than she did.

'It was even more dangerous in Athens after the liberation,' he goes on. 'The communists were fighting the British for control and there was a strict curfew but my mother insisted on going out anyway to distribute food to children.

She told me yesterday that the British forces tried to get her to stay inside because it wasn't safe. They were worried she might be hit by a stray bullet, but she just shrugged. Apparently she reminded them of the saying that you don't hear the shot that kills you. "I'm deaf in any case," she said, "so why worry about that?"'

'I'd forgotten that she is deaf,' Elizabeth says. 'It must be hard for her.'

'She lipreads very well but her voice ... she doesn't have the same tone as people who can hear,' Philip says. 'I never thought about it as a child, but I can hear it now. There's no getting away from the fact that she can seem strange, Elizabeth. She's not like other royals. My sisters can put on a show. They know how to be royal; they've been doing it all their lives. And you can rely on cousins like Sandra to put on tiaras and behave. But my mother?' He lifts his shoulders. 'No, she's different. If we ever get to a wedding, I'm warning you now that there'll be pressure to hide her away.'

'No.' Elizabeth's voice is quiet but firm. 'That won't happen, Philip, I promise you. She's your mother. She'll be there.'

Chapter 37

London, June 1947

The meeting between Elizabeth and Princess Alice goes better than Philip has expected. Proud of his mother he may be, but Elizabeth can never have encountered anyone quite so unimpressed by her position or so unconcerned with protocol.

But then, his mother is a great-granddaughter of Queen Victoria. She is not impressed by royalty.

Alice takes Elizabeth's face between her weathered hands and looks deep into her eyes. 'Yes, good,' she decides. 'You will do.'

'Mama ...' Philip begins, embarrassed, but Elizabeth gestures to him to be quiet and in any case, his mother hasn't heard him.

'Am I good enough for Philip?' Elizabeth asks, smiling, and Alice laughs as she drops her hands.

'Yes, you have true eyes. And you speak slowly and clearly. This makes me very happy.'

'I'm used to adjusting my speech to match Papa's,' Elizabeth says. 'Sometimes he struggles to get the words out and it's easier if we all slow down.'

Miss Pye, his grandmother's ancient maid, totters in with a tea tray and Philip gets quickly to his feet. 'Let me take that, Piecrust,' he says, using the nickname he and David have given her which always makes her tut with a mixture of pleasure and disapproval. Overriding her protests, he sets the tray safely on a table next to his grandmother who frowns at his interaction with her maid. She and Miss Pye are devoted to each other, but the Dowager Duchess of Milford Haven doesn't believe in familiarity with servants.

'I'll pour, Pye,' she says. 'You may go.'

The maid creaks out of the room after a shaky curtsey to Elizabeth. She is surely ready for a pension, but would be deeply offended if Philip suggested it, he knows. And who else would put up with his grandmother?

His grandmother pours and Philip is ordered to pass around the cups and saucers. Like everything else in this apartment, the tea service has seen better days. The once exquisite Meissen porcelain is cracked and chipped in places and he appreciates that Elizabeth doesn't appear to notice how faded and musty-smelling the apartment is, from the tattered curtains to the threadbare rug laid over the floorboards.

Uncle Dickie has frequently offered to help his mother financially, but the Dowager seems to like the heavy

Victorian furniture and general air of gloom and Philip refuses to be embarrassed by the contrast between Elizabeth, fresh-faced and glowing in her blue dress, and his decrepit relatives. The whole country is shabby at the moment, not just his grandmother. Judging by what he saw in Germany last year, things are not as hard here in Britain, but people still look tired and worn down. It makes him realise just how much Elizabeth symbolises hope for the future for so many people.

His eyes rest on her as she perches on the edge of the sofa, cup and saucer in her hand. Like his mother and grandmother, her back is perfectly straight. None of the women, he guesses, would ever dream of slumping into an armchair.

He likes the way she is careful to turn her head so his mother can read her lips. He likes the contrast between the discipline of her posture and the softness of her body, the passion that he senses is so closely guarded beneath her careful behaviour. It is a secret thrill to know that he will be the only one who will ever get the chance to unwrap all that restraint, all that control, and discover the warmth at the core of Elizabeth.

Her feet are placed neatly together, every hair is in place. It will be fun to muss her up a little, Philip thinks, letting his gaze drift up to her knees and to the modest cleavage. She has beautiful skin, clear and dewy, tantalisingly touchable, although obviously nobody is allowed to touch it. Her husband will be, he reminds himself with an inward smile. His eyes move on up the clean line of her throat to the curve of her mouth, the sweep of her jaw, the lovely clear blue of her eyes and the soft wave of her hair.

'Time you were married,' the Dowager says in the German accent she has never lost and he looks up with a start to realise that she has been watching him watching Elizabeth. 'High time,' she says with a minatory look and Philip has the alarming sensation that his tongue has been hanging out.

Swallowing firmly, he clears his throat. His grandmother can be alarmingly perceptive when she wants to be. He wouldn't put it past her to have seen exactly what thoughts were going through his mind, and the idea makes him cringe inwardly.

'The King doesn't want to make an announcement until July,' he says, uncomfortably aware of the dull colour in his cheeks.

'Pah, that is just politics.' The Dowager dismisses that with an abrupt wave of her hand. 'You should be moving things on anyway.'

'How?' Elizabeth asks. 'Nothing can happen while Papa withholds his consent.'

'It's not so long until July,' the Dowager points out. 'What about a ring? You will need to be ready as soon as the announcement is made.' She turns her steely gaze on him. 'What are your plans, Philip?'

'I was hoping you weren't going to ask that,' Philip says. He has been worrying about buying an engagement ring.

He has his lieutenant's salary, but that is it: how the hell is he going to be able to afford a ring fit for a princess? He's seen the jewels that she was given in South Africa; there is no way he could buy anything to compare and he can hardly offer Elizabeth a chip of a diamond.

Uncle Dickie didn't think about *that* when he was promoting the engagement, and now he's in India and not available to ask for advice the one time Philip would welcome it.

Alice puts down her tea cup. 'I have an idea,' she says.

'For once it's a good one,' the Dowager comments acidly as his mother shuffles out. 'Not like staying in a war zone to feed orphans or deciding to become a nun!' She shakes her head. 'What can we do with her?'

Philip doesn't answer. He is noticing how bent his mother is. Next to Elizabeth's glowing youth, she seems thin and worn out by the privations of war.

When Alice comes back, she is carrying an old shoe bag. Elizabeth's brows lift as his mother pulls open the drawstring and draws out what looks like a musty-smelling mess of yellowing cotton wool which she proceeds to pluck off until she is able to hold up a tarnished tiara.

'Use the diamonds from this to make a ring,' she says, passing it to Elizabeth who takes it, flustered. 'Oh, but we couldn't ...'

'What?'

Elizabeth clearly remembers the deafness issue. She looks into Alice's face. 'It's lovely but it's yours.'

'And how much use do you think I have for tiaras nowadays?' Alice's smile is sweet and Philip is ambushed by a memory of her crouching down in a dusty garden somewhere, holding out her arms for him, smiling just like that.

She takes the tiara from Elizabeth and hands it to him. 'What do you think?'

He turns it between his hands. The metal is tarnished and the diamonds dull, but you can see that it was once a magnificent piece.

'Your papa gave it to me,' Alice says reminiscently. Reaching over, she lays a gnarled hand on his knee. 'This is all I have left to give you, Philip. I sold everything else to help the children but this, this I kept for you.'

Chapter 38

'If it was cleaned up,' the Dowager says, 'it would look better. That central diamond is a beauty.'

Philip lifts his eyes from the tiara to his mother's face. His grandmother is right. The stones are very fine. This would solve the problem of the ring. 'Are you sure, Mama?'

'Of course I am sure. But ask Elizabeth. She will be the one wearing it.'

'Elizabeth?'

'I think it's a lovely idea,' she says warmly. 'I would love to wear a ring which has a connection with your family.'

Philip lets out a breath. 'Then, thank you, Mama.' He gets up and kisses her cheek and she lifts a hand to pat his cheek. 'I have not given you much, Philip. I am glad to be able to give you this.'

His throat is tight and he's glad when his grandmother takes charge. 'We'll ask a jeweller to come here and look at the tiara. We can tell him Alice wants the stones reset as a ring. No reason for them to know who it's for.'

They will probably guess, Philip thinks, but what is the

alternative? He can hardly go into a jeweller himself without alerting everyone to the prospect of an engagement. The rumours are flying fast and furious as it is. His grandmother is right; they need to get on with things. It's not long until July. He wouldn't be surprised if the King tries to delay things further. It's time to behave as if the engagement is established fact.

He looks from his mother to the Dowager. 'Thank you,' he says. 'Thank you both.'

Elizabeth decides that she wants a simple design. The jeweller Philip Antrobus is summoned to Kensington Palace and inspects the tiara.

'I told him I wanted the stones made up as a ring,' Alice tells Philip when he rings up to find out how she got on. 'His expression didn't so much as flicker but I fear he may have guessed that the ring was not, in fact, for me.'

'Oh, well, I suppose that was inevitable. Will he let you know when it's ready?'

'He says it should be done by the beginning of July.'

'Perfect,' says Philip.

It is a strange limbo time. He still spends the week on duty at Corsham, but it's hard to concentrate on training petty officers when his future is being decided by the government and Commonwealth leaders and a king reluctant to let his daughter go. In the long summer evenings Philip and his fellow naval officers play cricket and darts against the team at the Methuen Arms, where it has been a relief to discover that the locals know little and care less about royal politics. To them, he is just another naval type, down for some good-natured banter and renowned as a batsman.

The landlord, Dennis, is polishing glasses behind the bar when Philip goes in after his return from London. 'Not seen you for a while, Lieutenant,' he says.

'I've been in London.'

'You're always up there. You got a girl there?'

Philip smiles. 'I do, as it happens.'

'I thought so,' Dennis says tolerantly. 'No other reason to go up to the city when you could be playing cricket here, I reckon. I just hope she's worth it.'

'I think so,' says Philip.

'Well, that's all that matters. Now, what can I get you, sir? Your usual?'

It is a Tuesday when a naval cadet tells Philip that there is a telephone call for him. Hoping it is not bad news, Philip follows the cadet down to the office, where he is discreetly left alone with a phone. It is his cousin, David Milford Haven.

'I thought you should know that your mother was followed to the jeweller's when she went to pick up the ring this morning,' David warns him. 'Two of the afternoon papers have already published the story, claiming that the ring is for Elizabeth. Your mother didn't say anything to them but the press will be on to you next, so if you're going to deny it, you'd better have a story ready.'

That's it then, Philip thinks. He thanks his cousin, puts

down the receiver and then picks it up again to ring Elizabeth.

'The cat's out of the bag, I'm afraid.' he tells her.

'Perhaps it's just as well this has happened,' Elizabeth says. 'It's only a week ahead of Papa's deadline of 15 July. Surely he won't think there's any point in continuing to deny it?'

'I hope not,' says Philip. 'I'll ring him now, and with any luck he'll give me permission to drive up and bring the ring round this evening.'

The King isn't at all happy about being out-manoeuvred but reluctantly agrees that the engagement can now be formally announced. Feeling as if he has the wind behind him at last, Philip collects the ring from his mother and drives round to Buckingham Palace, parking at a jaunty angle in the courtyard and breezing past the footmen.

'I know my way,' he says and takes the stairs two at a time.

Elizabeth is waiting for him in her sitting room. She is wearing a deep yellow frock and her eyes are aglow with anticipation. Picking up on the excitement, Susan starts barking when Philip comes in and shuts the door firmly behind him.

'Susan, be quiet!' Elizabeth orders her, bending to shush the dog and when she looks up at Philip, her face is bright. 'Is this really it, at last?'

'At last,' Philip agrees with a grin as he pulls the ring box out of his jacket pocket and opens it to show her the diamonds which have been cleaned and reset in a cluster around the spectacular central stone.

It is not like him, but when he looks at Elizabeth's face, his triumphant smile fades and he finds himself going down on one knee and offering her the ring.

'Elizabeth, will you do me the honour, the very great honour, of being my wife?'

The moment is a little spoiled by Susan, who thinks he wants to play and jumps up at him, but Philip nudges her away without looking at her and watches instead the smile that blooms on Elizabeth's face.

'I will,' she says

Getting to his feet, Philip slips the ring on to her finger. 'It's beautiful,' she says, turning her hand so the diamonds flash in the sunlight.

Elizabeth has seen the design but hasn't been able to try the ring on before now and Philip frowns as he sees it slipping around her finger.

'It's too big,' he says in concern. 'We should have got it sized. Do you want to wait until it fits properly?'

'No,' Elizabeth says. She presses her fingers together to keep the ring in place. 'It'll be fine like this for the photos. Let's not give Papa another reason for a delay. We've waited long enough.'

Chapter 39

London, July 1947

'"Buckingham Palace, 10th July 1947",' David Milford Haven reads out in a suitably portentous voice. He is lounging on a sofa in Chester Street, making great play of studying the Court Circular in *The Times*. '"It is with the greatest pleasure that the King and Queen announce the betrothal of their dearly beloved daughter The Princess Elizabeth to Lieutenant Philip Mountbatten, R.N.," – that's you, cousin – "son of the late Prince Andrew of Greece and Princess Andrew" – then they add Princess Alice of Battenberg in brackets for the benefit of the hoi polloi who might otherwise wonder how she could be called Andrew – "to which union the King has gladly given his consent."'

'"Gladly" might be stretching it,' Philip says with a grim smile. 'The King could hardly bring himself to smile at the family celebration last night.'

David drops *The Times* onto the floor beside him. He is recovering from what he declared that morning to be

303

the hangover from hell. When Philip returned from the decorous celebrations at the palace, he crossed David on his way out to the Savoy. David urged him to go out with him, but mindful of his new role, Philip opted to stay at home – and then spent the rest of the evening wishing he'd gone out and belatedly considering the implications of getting married to the most visible woman in the country. Does this mean he is going to have to spend the rest of his life *behaving well*?

'Well, you did it,' David congratulates him.

'I did. Uncle Dickie will be pleased.'

David raises an eyebrow at the lack of enthusiasm in his voice. 'You're the one who ought to be pleased. You're engaged to marry the most eligible girl in the world.'

'Yes, and I'm just coming to realise what it will mean,' Philip confesses. 'Last night, we had champagne at the palace, and they were already talking about how I would need a detective and a valet and a social secretary and God knows who else to dance attendance on me! What am I going to do with a social secretary?' he demands. 'And then there was a lot of talk about protocol and duty.' He blows out a sigh like a horse.

'Come on, Philip, you must have known what marrying Lilibet would involve.'

Irritated by the fact that his cousin is right, Philip jerks his shoulder. 'Yes, yes, of course I did, but I wasn't thinking about that, was I? I was focused on getting the King to agree to the engagement.'

He has had his eyes fixed on the goal for so long, he realises, that he hasn't thought beyond it. Now that he has what he wanted, it is as if he has climbed to the top of a mountain and looked around to see that the only way forward is down.

'Cheer up,' David says. 'There are bound to be some compensations being married to someone who's going to be one of richest women in world one day. Maybe you'll be able to afford a decent wardrobe at last.'

'There have already been some rather pointed comments about that.' Philip tries to shrug off his ridiculously despondent mood. 'Apparently it's been noticed that my flannel trousers haven't been pressed, and horror of horrors, sometimes my sleeves are rolled up.'

'What about the fact that you stuff your hands in your pockets?'

'What's the point of pockets if you can't put your hands in them?'

'You don't have to jam them in so the jacket's all out of shape,' David points out and Philip scowls at him.

'We can't all be damned dandies!'

'You're going to have to sharpen up your act, cousin,' David says, smirking at Philip's discomfiture. 'You'll have to learn to tie your tie properly, pick up your clothes ... and buy some decent socks! Those things you wear are a disgrace.'

Philip's feet are propped on the coffee table. Lifting one, he regards the sock. It is liberally darned and his big toe is starting to poke through at the end again. 'Plenty of life in these yet,' he says. 'Besides, haven't you heard of rationing, David? We're supposed to be making do and mending.'

David rolls his eyes. 'I just hope you're not planning to wear that tennis shirt for dinner at the palace tonight?'

'That's what naval uniform is for,' Philip says.

A special dinner to mark the betrothal has been hastily arranged at Buckingham Palace for that night. It is going to be a glittering affair and afterwards he and Elizabeth will make an appearance on the balcony to wave at the anticipated crowds. It will just be the start, Philip knows. His life will never be the same again.

But there is no going back now.

Chapter 40

Buckingham Palace, July 1947

The crowds are already gathering around the Victoria Monument as Bobo zips up Elizabeth's white ball gown and twitches the long skirts into place. Elizabeth stands patiently, turning her engagement ring on her finger, but inside she is trembling with anticipation. Her betrothal dinner. It is really happening at last. She glances at the ring, turning her hand to catch the reassuring glint of the diamonds as she has done most of the day, just to convince herself her engagement is real.

Philip has sent her flowers, a simple, unostentatious bouquet that sits on the dressing table and reassures her almost as much as the ring itself. She saw his face last night when her father was informing him that Tommy Lascelles would sort out a private secretary for him.

Elizabeth is well aware of how hard it will be for Philip to adjust. He may be royal but he has no conception of how carefully regulated his life will become. It will be up

307

to her to make sure he doesn't regret his old life too much. She mustn't make any emotional demands, she reminds herself. She will need to reassure him she hasn't forgotten the agreement they made at Balmoral.

But still, they are betrothed. At last! While Bobo fastens her favourite pearl necklace around her neck, Elizabeth studies her reflection in the cheval mirror and sees an excited girl in a beautiful dress. She is wearing the white tulle gown that she wore in South Africa to the ball held on her twenty-first birthday. It sparkles with diamante and sequin embroidery, reflecting her mood.

'There now.' Bobo settles the fastening at the nape of Elizabeth's neck and stands back to admire her handiwork. 'You look happy.' She smiles at Elizabeth's reflection.

'I am.'

'I'm glad for you.' Bobo has been dressing Elizabeth since she was a little girl, since before Elizabeth knew she was a princess. She has an uncanny ability to tell what her charge is thinking. 'He's a fine man. Just be sure you make yourself happy, as well as him.'

'I will.' Elizabeth turns from the mirror and kisses her dresser on the cheek. 'Thank you, Bobo.'

Bobo pretends to shoo her away. 'Now go and enjoy your betrothal party.'

Philip is waiting with the King and Queen in her mother's sitting room when Elizabeth and Margaret join them. His expression when he catches sight of her makes Elizabeth's heart bump hard against her ribs, tangling up her breathing. There's a beat when the temptation to throw herself into his arms is almost overwhelming, but that isn't the way a princess behaves, particularly not in front of her parents.

She has to content herself with a decorous kiss on the cheek but allows herself to breathe in the distinctive smell of Philip – clean skin, clean linen – for a dizzying moment before she draws away.

Philip's eyes are warm as he smiles down at her and she lets herself hope that he has done the same and used that brief kiss to remind himself of the softness of her hair, the fragrance of her skin. When their eyes meet, it is as if they have had a whole conversation, as if he has told her she is beautiful, and she puts her hand on his arm as they make their way through the private quarters to the concealed door that leads into the White Drawing Room.

They pause at the door and Elizabeth takes a breath as she always does before an occasion. It is just a breath but it is enough to don an invisible armour over her shyness. But this time Philip is with her. His hand closes over hers on his arm and the warmth of his clasp seeps into her as she smiles gratefully at him.

Then the cabinet and mirror that disguise the door are swung open and they step into the noise and brilliance of the drawing room. Beneath the great chandelier, the room is a kaleidoscope of vividly coloured gowns while the animated conversation bounces off the gilded walls.

Elizabeth and Philip move together among the guests, accepting congratulations as they go.

For Elizabeth, it is as if all her senses are on high alert. Usually she is tense, concentrating fiercely on making conversation, but today, with Philip at her side, she is acutely aware of her body, of the way her dress rustles as she moves, of the warm weight of the pearls at her throat, the gleam of diamonds on her finger. And most of all, of Philip beside her, tall and proud in his shabby naval uniform.

As always, it strikes Elizabeth that he carries his own forcefield around with him. It makes everyone else dim in comparison to his vivid presence. He is not smooth or polished, but it is impossible not to take note of him. Whenever Elizabeth feels her shyness struggling back to the surface, she glances at him, and it is almost as if she has reached out and touched him. She doesn't, but he always knows exactly when to turn his head and meet her eyes with the merest flicker of a reassuring wink that makes her pulse jolt.

Her mother is standing with Philip's lively cousin, Sandra, and her husband, King Peter of Yugoslavia, when Elizabeth and Philip make their way round to them.

'So many congratulations,' Sandra says, kissing Philip. 'You've come a long way since you let those pigs out at Panker,' she tells him. She turns to Elizabeth and the Queen. 'Philip was such a naughty boy,' she says. 'There was a model farm there and we were fascinated by the pigs. It was Philip's idea to stir them up and unbolt the stalls. The next thing we knew there was pandemonium, with pigs stampeding all over the tea lawn. Tea things all over the grass, tables turned over, aunts and uncles screaming and shouting ...' She laughs merrily. 'Oh, it was fun while it lasted, wasn't it, Philip?'

'I don't remember anything about it,' Philip says.

'You *must* do!'

'I'm quite prepared to believe that I was a little devil, but I've got absolutely no recollection of squealing pigs on the tea lawn.'

'Talking of tea lawns,' the Queen interrupts smoothly before it descends into a cousinly squabble, 'there is a garden party here tomorrow, and the King and I think it would be a good idea if you came, Philip. It would be a good opportunity for you and Lilibet to appear together in public for the first time.'

Elizabeth sees Philip resist the temptation to grimace. 'Of course,' he says.

Peter winks at him. 'I see they're wasting no time throwing you to the lions, Philip!'

'Peter!' the Queen protests. 'It's just a garden party! Philip will have to learn that's part of the job.'

Remembering her vow to make things as easy for Philip as possible, Elizabeth tries to discourage the idea. 'We don't want to put him off too soon, Mummy,' she says, but Philip takes her hand.

'I won't be put off, Elizabeth,' he says, but he is looking

at the Queen with challenge in his eyes. 'You don't need to worry about that.'

Liveried footmen open the doors into the State Dining Room and as they take their seats around the mahogany table, twenty down each side and three at the ends, chants of 'We want Elizabeth and Philip!' can be heard from the gates at the front of the palace. Elizabeth pauses in the middle of unfolding her napkin, thinking about how long people have been standing out there in the hope of seeing her with Philip.

'Should we go now?' she asks her father across the table. 'They've all been waiting an awfully long time already.'

'Certainly not,' the King says irritably. 'We'll have dinner first.'

Knowing that so many people are waiting makes Elizabeth a little uncomfortable but it is a wonderful dinner even so. Rationing is still in force, but it hardly matters what they eat when the silver gilt gleams and glasses sparkle the length of the table. Floral centrepieces from the palace gardens scent the air and the gilding on the walls and ceiling is reflected endlessly in the grand mirrors while the shouting from the front of the palace is a good-humoured backdrop to the conversation at table.

After dinner, the King at last agrees that it is time to show themselves to public. They make their way to the room where they have waited to wave to the crowds on so many momentous occasions: her father's coronation, VE Day, VJ Day ... but this time they are waiting just for her.

And Philip.

Sensing movement in the palace, the crowd picks up the chant. 'We want Elizabeth and Philip! We want Elizabeth and Philip!'

'They don't sound too bothered about me being a foreign prince now,' Philip murmurs in her ear and they exchange a smile.

'They don't, do they?' Elizabeth moves to stand in front of the tall windows that open onto the balcony. Smoothing down the gown over her stomach, she touches the pearls at her throat in an unconsciously nervous gesture.

'All right?' Philip asks with a quick frown.

'I'm fine.' Elizabeth nods to the footmen, who pull open the windows while the crowd roars in approval. 'Ready?' It is her turn to ask Philip and there is something fierce in the way he nods in response.

'Ready.'

Together, they step out onto the balcony to be greeted by a cheer that rises up like a buffet of wind from the mass of people below. Hundreds of thousands of them are gathered around the Victoria Monument, clambering over the old queen's statue, pressed up against the forecourt railings and spilling up the Mall.

'Gosh,' Philip murmurs inadequately, and Elizabeth knows he is as moved as she is by the joyful crowd.

She follows the news closely. She knows people are still struggling to rebuild their lives after the long war. So many have died, so many lives have been devastated. Everybody has lost someone, a child, a parent, a spouse, a relative, a friend. Food is scarce, bombsites are still being cleared and everyone has suffered through the coldest winter anyone can remember.

And yet, still these brave, stoical people have come to show that they are happy for her and that they wish her well.

Elizabeth smiles and waves, wishing she could show what their good wishes mean to her. Perhaps she would not have chosen to be a princess, but that is what she is, and buoyed up by the cheerful, cheering crowd, Elizabeth renews the vow of duty she made on her twenty-first birthday. It is the price of her happiness, to serve these people who have suffered so much and who are looking to her to bring some joy to the nation's life.

With Philip beside her, she can do it.

Chapter 41

London, July 1947

'Why do we always have to shout at each other across the room?' Philip demands. He has just driven up from Corsham and has flopped into one of the armchairs in Elizabeth's sitting room. Margaret is sitting sideways in another, her legs slung languidly over the arm, one shoe dangling from the toe of her foot. Elizabeth herself is perched on the sofa, gently pulling Susan's ears. The dog's eyes are closed in bliss.

'We're not shouting,' Margaret says. 'You're the only one who barks at us as if we're ratings.'

'Rubbish!'

'There you are. You've just proved my point.'

Philip scowls at her before turning pointedly to Elizabeth. 'I'm just saying, it's not exactly cosy in here.'

'What's wrong with it?' Puzzled, Elizabeth looks around the room. It looks fine to her: pale pink and cream fabrics, a fitted fawn carpet, but then she's never been particularly interested in interior design. She'd rather be outside.

'It's so formal. Look at these two chairs, facing off across the fireplace. Anyone would think you were expecting an audience with the Pope. Why don't you move the sofa up in front of the fire, then we could sit cosily together?'

'Well, all right,' Elizabeth says with a placatory smile. 'I suppose we could try that.'

She means at some stage but Philip is full of restless energy tonight and leaps to his feet.

'Let's do it now. Come on, Margaret, up you get!'

'What for?'

'We're going to move the sofa. You take one end,' Philip says, pointing. 'It's not that heavy.'

Margaret gives him a flat-eyed look. 'I don't move furniture.'

'Why not? You've got two arms and two legs, haven't you?'

'We also have footmen to do that kind of thing for us.'

'Why call a servant when we can do it ourselves?' Frustrated, Philip swings round to Elizabeth. 'Please tell me *you're* not too grand to move a sofa a few yards!'

Elizabeth really doesn't care where the sofa is but faced with the challenge in those icy blue eyes, she gets to her feet. 'Where do you want to put it?'

Philip drags his armchair out of the way and takes hold of one end of the sofa while directing Elizabeth to take the other. Contrary to what he said to Margaret, it is too heavy to lift so they end up pushing and shoving the sofa across the room, watched by an incredulous Margaret. Susan keeps getting in the way and is shouted at by Philip when he trips over her, but once the sofa is in place and the armchairs have been rearranged, Elizabeth has to admit the room does look more inviting.

'There!' Philip announces, dropping into the sofa and patting the cushion beside him. 'Come and sit next to me,' he says, and Elizabeth sits down obediently. 'Isn't this better?'

'It is,' she agrees. 'It'll be lovely in winter, too. We can sit and watch the fire together.'

'Except we won't be here in winter, I hope,' Philip says, crushing her romantic picture of the future. 'Is there any news about us having Clarence House?'

'It's in a terrible state,' Elizabeth says doubtfully as she settles back against the cushions. It's a wet night and although it's not really cold, she is tempted to ask Cyril to lay a fire. But with the country still buckling under the rationing restrictions, it would be selfish to use up fuel for a whim in the middle of summer, however chilly the evening, she realises with an inward sigh.

'Clarence House was used as a Red Cross centre during the war,' Margaret points out. 'It will need a lot of work to make it habitable, let alone comfortable.'

'We have to live somewhere,' Philip snaps.

'I'll ask Papa about it again,' Elizabeth says hastily before they start sniping at each other. 'At least the wedding date has been agreed,' she tells him. 'They've decided on 20th November.'

'Who wants to get married in *November*?' Margaret asks. 'The weather's bound to be awful. Why don't you wait until spring next year?'

'Because we've been waiting long enough,' Philip says before Elizabeth can answer. 'Anyway, it's not about the wedding. It's about being married.'

'You're not the bride,' Margaret retorts. 'Perhaps Lilibet would like a lovely spring wedding with some sunshine?'

'I don't mind,' Elizabeth says, wondering why she always seems to get caught in the middle of their scrapping. 'Philip's right. We just want to be married now.'

Margaret sniffs. 'Don't blame me if it's grey and miserable on your wedding day!'

'I'm hardly likely to blame you for the weather.'

Elizabeth's tone is tarter than usual. Margaret been very scratchy lately. She doesn't like Elizabeth being centre of attention. Elizabeth understands that her sister is used to being the pretty sister, the clever sister, the talented sister, while her own role is just to be the elder sister. Of course Margaret's nose is out of joint with all the fuss about the engagement, but her carping can get tiresome, especially when, as now, Philip is also in a scratchy mood. The two of them usually get on well, but they are both forceful personalities and when they rub each other up the wrong way Elizabeth is stuck in the middle.

She turns to Philip and deliberately changes the subject. 'What was it like going back to Corsham?'

'Very strange,' he tells her. 'One minute I'm on the balcony at Buckingham Palace waving at hundreds of thousands of people, the next I'm letting myself in to my quarters in a tin-roofed Nissen hut! Do you know, the press had got into my room and taken photographs of fascinating items such as my iron bedstead, or the mess of pipes and family photos on the chest of drawers! Who on earth is interested in this stuff?'

'A lot of people, I'm afraid,' Elizabeth says.

'Did you see the papers?' Philip demands. 'I've been reading about myself as if I were some animal in the zoo,' he grumbles. 'People are stretching the vaguest connection with me. Apparently I'm bosom buddies with the local butcher and the undertaker and all sorts of other people I've nodded to once in passing. It turns out I have a green thumb, too. I bet you didn't know that,' he says with a sardonic look. 'The base grew some prize-winning potatoes and it seems that's all down to me too.'

He jerks his shoulders in a characteristically irritable gesture. 'It's all so ... *ridiculous*!'

'I'm sorry,' Elizabeth murmurs and Margaret glares at her.

'Why are *you* sorry? It's not your fault!'

'I can be sorry that Philip's having a difficult time, can't I?'

'Margaret's right.' Unexpectedly, Philip sides with her

sister. 'I suppose I should have expected the attention. I just hadn't thought it would be quite so … intrusive. I nearly didn't play cricket last week, even though I'm on the team. We've been happily playing cricket, skittles, and darts against the pub team ever since I've been there, and I didn't want to seem standoffish, so I went down to the Methuen Arms with the other chaps on the Navy team.'

'What happened?'

'There was dead silence when I walked in. Dennis, the landlord, was behind the bar and looked at me for a long moment before pulling a pint and pushing it across the bar to me. "This one's on the house, lad," he said.' Philip grins at the memory. 'Then there was a sort of cheer and a bit of back slapping and we all got on with the game, thank God.'

'Never mind,' Elizabeth says. 'We'll be in Balmoral soon, and there'll be no one to stare at you there.'

She can't wait to take the train north. She has been enjoying all the excitement of the engagement, of course, but the wedding plans are rapidly becoming overwhelming. She is yearning now for the quiet of the hills, to be out on a horse, or wriggling on her stomach through the heather. But something in the quality of Philip's silence makes her pause.

'You are coming, aren't you?' she asks anxiously.

'I suppose I must,' he says, pulling a face.

'I thought you liked it last year.' Elizabeth is dismayed by his lack of enthusiasm. Balmoral has always had a golden place in her memories but last year they took on an extra sheen. When things have been tense or fretful she has been able to take herself back to that morning by the loch, to remember the smell of the heather and the sound of curlew and the look on Philip's face as he lowered her into the heather and she has steadied.

Philip pulls a face. 'It's hard to like being eaten alive by midges.'

Perhaps the midges are a pest but there is so much else to enjoy at Balmoral. Elizabeth wants Philip to think about that day by the loch too, but why should he? He has never pretended to be romantic. She tells herself she doesn't mind when he is off hand with her, that the last thing she wants is to be pawed in public, but sometimes, secretly, she longs for him to tell her that their engagement means more than a dynastic union.

'You don't have to go stalking if you don't want to,' she tells him.

'Your father won't be happy if I'm not slaughtering some kind of wildlife,' says Philip morosely.

'You could try grouse shooting this year,' she offers. 'You always get a good lunch with that party.'

'That's something,' he says with a grudging smile that vanishes when Margaret tells him with a needle-sharp smile that he will have to take a kilt to wear.

'What? Why?'

'It's expected of members of the royal family, and that's what you'll be when you marry Lilibet.'

Philip turns an aggrieved gaze to Elizabeth. 'Is that right?'

'I'm afraid Papa is very particular about it,' she says and he glowers.

'God, that's all I need, to be forced to wear a skirt! Talk about emasculated!'

'It's a kilt, not a skirt,' Elizabeth says, quite sharply for her. 'It's part of Balmoral, Philip, and Margaret's right. If you're going to be part of the royal family, you're going to have to wear one.'

Chapter 42

Having longed to be in Scotland and dreamt of rediscovering the happiness of the year before, Elizabeth doesn't enjoy being at Balmoral as much as she usually does. This is partly due to Philip, who is deliberately making no effort to fit in as far as she can tell. He puts her father's back up on the first night when he appears in the kilt he insists on describing as 'cissy' and drops a curtsey. The King is not amused.

'It was a joke,' Philip says, exasperated, when Elizabeth remonstrates with him.

'Not a very funny one. Now Papa will be cross all evening. I know this isn't your idea of fun, Philip, but do *try* and fit in.'

'I can't fit in,' he says. 'I haven't been to the right school. If I'd been to Eton, I'd be able to toady along with everyone else. Is that what you'd prefer?'

'You know it isn't,' she says evenly. 'Nobody's asking you to be a toady. Just to be a little less ... brusque.'

'These old courtiers want me to sit quietly and not have an opinion. Why should I?' Philip demands. 'I've fought for this country. I'm entitled to a point of view!'

'Of course you are,' Elizabeth says, picking her words with care. 'Perhaps you don't have to voice it quite so forcefully though.'

Philip makes an irritable gesture. 'None of them want me here. They think I'm not good enough for you.'

'Oh, Philip that's not true! They just think your manners can be a little rough sometimes.'

'Do you know what Margaret told me?' he goes on, evidently not listening to her. 'That it was Peter Townsend's idea to invite me here last year to see if I could behave myself properly! What infernal cheek!' Philip paces around the room. 'Townsend! The ultimate in middle-class values and a dead bore besides! How dare he presume to judge how I'd fit in? My mother was born in Windsor Castle in the presence of Queen Victoria herself. You don't get to be more of an insider than that!'

Philip's prickly refusal to be conciliatory makes for an awkward atmosphere at times, but it is not all his fault. Elizabeth overhears plenty of subtle barbs and put downs and it is exhausting trying to keep the peace. After the disastrous kilt incident, her father recovers his good humour and her mother is invariably charming, but some of the other guests seem to go out of their way to make Philip feel unwelcome.

Her uncle, David Bowes-Lyon, is one of the worst offenders. 'I hear you've been rearranging the furniture at Buckingham Palace,' he says to Philip across the dinner table. 'How very domestic of you!'

'Only in Elizabeth's sitting room,' Philip says.

'Well, it's good to know you're making yourself at home.'

Sitting beside her uncle, Elizabeth stiffens at the snide note in his voice. 'Philip's good at making a home,' she says. 'I never notice furnishings or anything like that, but he does. It's wonderful the difference he's made to the feel of my sitting room.'

'Rather surprising,' David says, 'given that he's never had a home of his own.'

Her uncle means it unpleasantly, Elizabeth knows, but it is true nonetheless. Surreptitiously, she studies Philip who is attacking his meal with a kind of furious energy. His brows are drawn together over the bridge of his nose.

She needs to remember that he has never known the security of a home and make allowances for his prickliness. This isn't an easy situation for him, and if he can seem distant, well, when has she ever given him any indication that she would welcome more intimacy? That was not in their agreement. She can't comfort him publicly, and she knows he wouldn't want her to. But she can give him a home and a family of his own. She will ask her father again about refurbishing Clarence House.

As the days pass, Elizabeth lets herself relax. Philip goes grouse shooting with the King and wins her father's approval by turning out to be a good shot. Sometimes she goes with them and follows the shoot, enjoying the crisp air and the pleasure on Philip's face when he spots the lunch laid out in the rigged-up tent: venison pies and sausage rolls with Chelsea buns and sandwiches for tea.

There are picnics on the moors and a chance to walk through the pine forests. Sometimes she plays golf with Margaret and on wet days, there is a giant jigsaw puzzle set up on a table.

The one thing there is not is a chance to be alone with Philip. They might be engaged but the days are always fully planned and after dinner the fiddles and bagpipes strike up in the sitting room while a space is cleared for Scottish reels. If Elizabeth is lucky, Philip will grab her hand and swing her into the dance, but it is not as if there is an opportunity to talk and they are soon spun away from each other as they circle in time to the music. Philip doesn't seem to mind, and Elizabeth tells herself that it's enough that he is enjoying himself.

But one evening just before he is due to return to duty, they play games instead of dancing. 'Murder in the Dark!' the King announces to laughter and gaiety.

'What a good idea,' Philip murmurs. He is standing

close to her when the lights go out and she stifles a gasp as he pulls her deeper into the shadows and holds her tight.

'Gotcha!' he says softly, his mouth at her ear.

'Are you the murderer?' she whispers, dizzy at his nearness.

'I don't think so. But I've got you anyway.'

Chapter 43

Philip tries not to favour his knee as he climbs the stairs to Elizabeth's sitting room. He is still irritated with himself at the accident. A wet road, some autumn leaves and his camp record for the ninety-eight mile drive between Corsham and London has been blown. The twisted knee is a bore, but he is more worried about his precious car which came off the worst after its encounter with a hedge.

Thank Christ he'd been in his own car! If he'd been out in one of the cars from the Royal Mews, he would never have heard the end of it from the chauffeurs who cosset their vehicles like horses and shake their heads at the slightest dent or scratch. As it is, he has just had to endure some ribbing from the chaps in the Methuen Arms.

Elizabeth stayed in Scotland after his less than successful visit to Balmoral so he hasn't seen her for a while. Philip hopes they will be able to recover the closeness they had when they were first engaged. Since the formal announcement, it feels to him as if the court has gone out of its way to keep Elizabeth hemmed in by protocol and tradition – and away from him. It is as if they think of her as the precious brood mare and he is the stallion, reluctantly drafted in to service but otherwise of no use or interest whatsoever.

He barely saw her in Scotland. He spent his days shooting grouse with the King instead. Elizabeth's father seems obsessed with killing wildlife and given his evident lack of enthusiasm for the engagement, Philip thought it politic to make an effort to get on with him.

Much good it did him. Oh, the King was pleasant enough but the rest of the court made it plain what they thought of him. Philip was left feeling frustrated and out-manoeuvred. He was lucky if he got to touch Elizabeth's hand when dancing those endless reels. At least Murder in the Dark gave him the opportunity to get a bit closer, but he'd had to be quick.

The worst part of it, Philip acknowledges to himself, is not knowing what Elizabeth herself feels now. She has been schooled to keep her thoughts to herself, but he'd hoped he had got past that invisible guard she erects between herself and the world. Now, he's not so sure.

They just need some time alone together. Is that too much to ask? Philip grimaces as his knee twinges with every step. He hopes Margaret isn't there as she usually is for these palace suppers. Elizabeth's sister can be fun but she dominates the conversation and all too often Elizabeth lets her.

As with so much else at the moment, luck isn't with him. When Cyril announces him, the first person Philip sees is Margaret, lounging on the sofa in front of the fire and reading a newspaper. He bends to greet Susan who bustles to meet him, then lifts his eyes to Elizabeth. She looks tired, he thinks, and there are lines of strain around eyes, but she smiles and offers her cheek for a chaste embrace.

'I'm so glad you're all right,' she says.

'All right?' Philip bristles instantly. 'Of course I'm all right!'

Margaret waves the newspaper at him. 'We've just been reading about your accident.'

'Oh, good God, they didn't bother with that, did they? It was nothing!'

'That's not what this paper thinks,' Margaret informs him. 'They say you've got a reputation for speeding and they think you should be more careful.' She folds the paper to the right column. '"His well-being is essential to the happiness of the heiress of the throne,"' she reads out.

Philip throws himself down into an armchair. 'It would be nice if someone gave a fig about *my* happiness for a change,' he grumbles.

'But are you really all right?' Elizabeth asks as sits carefully in the armchair opposite. Typical of Margaret to appropriate the sofa so he can't even sit next to his own fiancée, Philip thinks sourly. 'It sounds as if it was a nasty accident.'

'It was nothing,' Philip says again. Irritated, he pulls out his cigarettes, extracts one and taps it on the packet. 'I skidded on a wet road and ended up in a hedge. Banged my knee up a bit but that's it. There's no need for anyone to fuss.'

'I worry about you driving so fast,' Elizabeth admits. 'And smoking,' she adds pointedly as he fishes out his lighter.

Deliberately Philip lights his cigarette and inhales. 'I didn't realise getting engaged meant giving up all my pleasures in life,' he says.

'You can see what heavy smoking has done to Papa. Call me a killjoy if you want, but I'd rather you didn't end up ill too.'

'Terrific,' Philip says sarcastically. 'No speeding, no smoking ... this marriage is going to be a barrel of laughs, I can see. Uncle Dickie arranged for me to have lunch with Winston Churchill just so the great man could impress on me what a serious business it is marrying the heir to the throne. As if I thought it was nothing but a joke!' He blows smoke at the ceiling. 'Not that it's been much fun so far.'

'I know.' It's Elizabeth's turn to sigh as she strokes Susan's head. 'I wish we could just be two ordinary people getting married at an ordinary wedding.'

'But you're not ordinary,' he points out, 'and we wouldn't be getting married if you were, would we?'

Elizabeth's fingers still on the dog at his bitter comment.

'No, I suppose not,' she says after a moment. 'I thought once we were engaged all our problems would be over, but it seems they're only just starting. I *hate* all the arguments about money,' she says. 'It seems as if there's no end to it: the cost of the wedding, doing up Clarence House ... Nobody can agree and you and I are the last people to be consulted.'

'It's not really *your* wedding, is it?' Margaret puts in. 'It's a state occasion. Poor old Lil,' she adds. 'You never have anything of your own, not even your own love affair and wedding.'

Elizabeth sighs. 'Thank you for that, Margaret,' she says. She turns back to Philip. 'The Government wants to keep things simple in view of the economic situation. With austerity it seems crass to have an extravagant wedding, but then there's the view that the country needs a happy event to look forward to and we should put on a show.'

'And what's your view?' Philip asks.

'I just want to get married,' she says, but she doesn't look at him. 'And for all the arguments to stop.'

'What else are they arguing about?'

'The guest list, for one thing.'

Philip stubs out his cigarette. 'Yes, I wanted to talk to you about that. Why haven't my sisters received an invitation? Sandra tells me she and Peter have had one, and Michael's coming from Romania, but Dolla, Tiny, and Margarita have heard nothing.'

'I'm sorry.' Elizabeth seems to shrink into herself. 'I did ask but it was decided it would be too provocative to invite them.'

'Decided by who? Tommy Lascelles, I suppose,' he says savagely.

'I'm sure he was involved but it was down to Mummy and Papa in the end.'

'And nobody thought to consult me? I *am* the groom and this is my family we're talking about!'

'I *know*.'

'What's the problem? Is it that my sisters are married to Germans?'

'Not just Germans,' Elizabeth says carefully. 'Germans who were senior SS officers.'

'You can't expect the country to welcome them,' Margaret says frankly. 'It's on its knees after the war with Germany. Everybody thinks it's wiser to play down your German connections.'

'Funny, nobody seemed that bothered about my German connections when they were cheering us on that balcony,' says Philip, tight-jawed.

'I'm sorry,' Elizabeth says again.

'Elizabeth, they're my *sisters*.'

She bites her lip. 'I don't think I can get them to change their mind. I'm sorry, Philip. Your mother will be there, of course.'

'Oh, big of them to invite her!'

'I think there is some concern about what she'll wear,'

Elizabeth goes on delicately. 'They don't want her to wear her nun's outfit.'

'I should think not,' says Margaret. 'She'll look absolutely mad ... oh, sorry, Philip,' she adds carelessly. 'I know it's a touchy subject.'

'My mother may have spent some time in sanatoriums, but she is not *mad*,' he grinds out. 'She's devout. She spent the war hiding a family at risk from the Germans. She sold her jewels to feed the poor. What did *your* mother do? Walked around a few ruins and smiled at people!'

'That's enough.' Elizabeth's voice is sharp as she gets abruptly to her feet. 'Margaret, you're not being helpful. Can you give Philip and me some time on our own?'

'Oh, all right.' Pouting, Margaret gets up from the sofa. 'Philip's so cross all the time I don't want to stay for supper anyway.'

Chapter 44

Elizabeth waits until her sister has flounced out before sinking down into her chair. She rubs her temples. 'I'm sorry about Margaret,' she says. 'She doesn't mean to be hurtful. She's just ... thoughtless. And I'm sorry about your sisters, Philip. I really am.'

Philip rose when she did but now he sits down again too. 'You look tired.'

'I didn't realise quite how much was involved in getting married.' She offers him a weary smile. 'Isn't this supposed to be a happy time?'

'That's what I thought, too,' he says with a wry smile. 'So, let's hear the worst of it. The cost of the wedding, the guest list ... what else?'

'Clarence House. They've estimated *fifty thousand* pounds to make it habitable. Can you imagine?'

He pulls a face. 'Well, it hasn't been used as a home for a while. It'll need gutting.'

'It's going to take at least two years, they think.'

'Two years?' Philip echoes in dismay. 'Where are we supposed to live in the meantime?'

Elizabeth hesitates. 'Here, I'm afraid.'

'Oh God, living with the in-laws!' Philip clutches his head in his hands.

'We'll have our own suite of rooms.'

'It's not the same as having a home of our own.'

'I know, but we'll have to make the best of it – just like everyone else is doing.'

Philip releases a long-suffering, spluttering sigh. If there's one thing he hasn't wanted to do it's to live at Buckingham Palace. It is cold, uncomfortable, inconvenient and stuffed with starchy courtiers and disapproving staff. Given the choice, he isn't sure he wouldn't rather live in the converted munitions hut which is his current quarters at Corsham.

'And now there are problems over Sunninghill as well.' It seems Elizabeth hasn't finished. 'You remember Papa gave it to us as a weekend retreat when we got engaged? The local council want to requisition it for conversion to flats for the homeless.'

'Oh, great,' Philip says in a flat voice. A weekend retreat versus homes for those made homeless by the war. Even he wouldn't have a problem making that choice.

'I really wanted us to have a home that we could build together,' Elizabeth says, 'but ...'

'... What can we do?' he finishes for her.

'I'm sorry,' she says miserably again.

'It's not your fault, Elizabeth. If there's one thing I learnt

from the war, it's that there are some battles you can't win
– and they're always the ones you're fighting on your own
side.' He stretches his arms above his head. 'Well, it looks
as if I'll be needing the Thursday Club even more.'

'The Thursday Club?'

'I'm a founder member,' he tells her. 'It's a stag club. Just
fifty or so chaps, and a place we can let off steam.'

Philip remembers how Baron Nahum had sold it to
him. 'You're going to have to have some kind of private
life that isn't controlled by the palace,' he'd said. 'Let's set
up a club with just a few trusted friends. Somewhere we
can meet, tell bawdy jokes without anyone calling for the
smelling salts, play games, dine, drink ... do everything
you'd like to do in your own home if you weren't afraid of
what your wife would say.'

'So no women?'

'Waitresses only,' Baron promised. 'All sworn to secrecy,
naturally. And best of all from your point of view, no
protocol.'

'What does "letting off steam" mean exactly?' Elizabeth
asks dubiously.

'It's just lunch,' Philip backtracks a little. 'We meet each
week in the top room of Wheeler's restaurant in Soho.
There's a set price for lunch, wines, and vintage port. Very
civilised. But we're all equals once we're there. I'm just
Philip at the Thursday Club. I can't tell you how refreshing
it is.'

He's not sure Elizabeth is entirely convinced but the

Thursday Club is one part of his life he's not prepared to give up. He's juggling his work at Corsham with an increasing number of private engagements and instead of making himself comfortable at Chester Street he has to make his London home at Kensington Palace with his grandmother. There are constant rows about the wedding arrangements and who is going to pay for what, endless starchy discussions about how he should or shouldn't behave in any given circumstance.

The only place Philip can really relax now is with his friends at the Thursday Club and he looks forward to it with disproportionate pleasure. Walking in, meeting smiles instead of pursed lips, discarding his cloak of 'prospective husband of the heir to the throne' at the door ... Who can put a price on that? Philip wonders. There is an unwritten code that nothing that goes on in the Thursday Club is ever discussed elsewhere. He is not the only member with a public profile who is glad of a reprieve from constantly having to watch his words. He defers to nobody, and nobody defers to him. The food is unpretentious and the décor even more so, although there is a cuckoo clock above the mantelpiece that provides endless amusement.

Perhaps some of the humour is a little schoolboyish but God, it's a relief just to have some fun for a change. Nor does he have to watch how much he smokes or drinks, although at times, he admits, this can lead to revealing more than he cares to normally.

One day, the other men are ribbing him about his

upcoming wedding. It's par for the course, and Philip is used to it by now. They're all drunk anyway.

'I don't know why you're not marrying Margaret,' one of members offers, gesticulating lewdly with his glass. 'She's much better looking than your girl.' He snorts. 'I wouldn't mind giving her one.'

Philip is seized by a cold fury. 'You wouldn't say that if you knew them,' he snarls back, sickened at the idea that this drunken oaf should dare pass judgement on Elizabeth. 'Margaret may be pretty but Elizabeth is sweet and she's *kind*.'

Spats like that are rare, though. Usually they just laugh in a way Philip can't remember laughing since he was a boy. They derive a lot of amusement from bets, just stupid things that distract them all from the grim reality of life outside the club.

'Baron, we've got a bet for you,' Philip and his cousin David call across the table one day.

Baron Nahum eyes them suspiciously. 'What is it?'

'Well, you're the great photographer. We bet you that you won't be able to photograph the cuckoo coming out of that clock there at precisely three o'clock.'

Baron looks from them to the clock as if trying to work out the catch. 'How much?'

'Five quid.'

'Done.'

With two minutes to go, Baron is poised with his camera focused on the cuckoo clock. Philip and David reach surreptitiously into their pockets and move towards the mantelpiece.

'Five … four … three … two …' The other members are counting down and waiting for the telltale whirring and clicking that presages the cuckoo's appearance.

'One!' they shout, and Philip and David throw the smoke bombs they have brought with them into the fireplace. They explode with a terrific bang just as the cuckoo bursts out of the clock and into a cloud of soot from the chimney which covers the entire company head to toe in soot.

'You arses, you've ruined my camera!' Baron Nahum bellows but he can hardly be heard above the raucous laughter of the other members, the shrieks from panicked customers downstairs and the pounding of feet up the stairway. The next thing they know, two policemen have burst into the room and are staring at the circle of well-dressed men with sooty faces.

'What's going on here then?'

'Ahh, officers …' Philip moves forward, belatedly aware of how ridiculous he must look. 'What can we do for you?'

'You can explain what caused that ruddy great explosion for a start … sir,' the policeman adds after a nudge from his companion.

Evidently realising how quickly the story could get out of control, Baron Nahum pushes Philip out of the way and sets about sweet-talking the policeman. *Just a friendly joke that got out of control. No harm done. Of course they'll make good any damages. Much appreciated if the officers didn't take matters any further. Sure they wouldn't want to cause any embarrassment.* And so on.

When the policeman eventually go there are a few moments of silence to make sure they have left the building before the whole company collapses into whoops of merriment.

Grinning, Philip slaps Baron on the shoulder. 'Good work, old chap. But you still owe us five pounds!'

Chapter 45

Buckingham Palace, November 1947

The King is permanently irritable these days, the touching outburst of joy at the announcement of the engagement has descended into scratchiness all round. Prime Minister Attlee is determined to tighten the country's belt yet another notch with new austerity measures that make it harder and harder to justify an extravagant wedding, and several members of the government are grumbling loudly about the cost as it is.

Every little detail is queried: has the silk for the wedding dress come from abroad? Tommy has had to write personally to Attlee to reassure him that the silkworms were Chinese – our allies – but that the silk itself has been woven in Scotland and Kent. The whole thing is ridiculous, the King complains, 'having to grovel to the Government for permission about your wedding dress. You're the heir to the throne! Bloody politicians. None of their bloody business.'

Between her father's short temper and Philip's frustration, Elizabeth feels as if she is walking on egg-shells and constantly soothing either one or both of them. Sometimes it feels as if she herself is only tangentially involved in the wedding. The Queen was delighted to approve Mr Hartnell's design for the dress when he showed them his first ideas.

'I've been inspired by Botticelli's *Primavera*,' he told them in his fulsome manner, snapping his fingers at an assistant who leapt forward with a print of the painting with a flourish. 'Particularly by Flora – here, you see – in her white garment.'

Another snap of his fingers and there is another assistant, this one producing a sketch of Hartnell's design. 'I see the princess's dress like *this*,' he said grandly. 'White satin, embroidered with seed pearls and crystals in a flower design incorporating roses – York roses, of course! – lilac, jasmine ...'

'Oh, Mr Hartnell, it will be magical!' The Queen was delighted and the designer beamed.

'Thank you, Your Majesty. As for the veil, I'm envisaging white tulle and a long train alive with the same flower motifs as the dress.'

'Exquisite,' the Queen said as she admired the sketch. 'A fairy-tale creation.'

'Precisely, ma'am. Because who amongst us does not need a fairy tale? I thought, too, a diamond tiara ...?' He glanced at the first assistant who hastily replaced the print with a photograph of the Queen wearing a tiara before the war. 'Something like this?'

'Oh, yes ... that would perfect.' Elizabeth's mother smiled sweetly. 'But Queen Mary has offered her own tiara for the day. Something borrowed, you know.'

Hartnell bowed deeply. 'Of course. What a marvellous idea.'

Only then did they both turn to Elizabeth. 'What do you think, Elizabeth?' her mother asked.

Elizabeth was thinking that in fairy tales the prince is in love with the princess. But she smiled, of course, because that's what princesses do, and told Mr Hartnell that his design was beautiful, which it was.

Remembering the scene a little sadly now, Elizabeth tells herself yet again to stop being so silly. She is marrying Philip. They came to an agreement and she has what she wanted. It is too late now to start getting sentimental or resentful about the fact that she still has to be back at the palace by ten o'clock at night, while Philip can drop her off and then roar off in his MG to meet his friends for late-night drinks and laughter. She said she would not interfere with his life as long as he was discreet.

But now it seems he is not being discreet.

It hasn't taken long for the story about the smoke bomb at the Thursday Club to reach Buckingham Palace. Elizabeth is told about Philip's exploit by the King and a deeply disapproving Tommy Lascelles.

'It's time the boy grew up,' snaps the King. 'Tommy's

had to work hard to keep the story out of the papers. God knows what people would think if they knew the heir to the throne is marrying someone who's carrying on like an idiot. I've asked him to come and see me,' he tells Elizabeth to her dismay. 'I'll try and knock some sense into him.'

Elizabeth can't imagine anything less effective but she's cross with Philip for causing yet another problem to be smoothed over.

'We warned you he wasn't one of us, Lilibet,' her father says. 'He doesn't have the same sense of humour.'

'While Your Royal Highness is here,' Tommy puts in smoothly before Elizabeth can respond, 'there *is* another matter it might be wise to discuss at this stage.'

Elizabeth suppresses a sigh. 'What's that, Tommy?'

'It's to do with the marriage vows. As you know, Lieutenant Mountbatten's rank is considerably lower than yours, particularly now that he has given up his royal title. You are, moreover, a senior officer in the services. Might it not be a little *incongruous* if you were to use the traditional vows for a bride which, as you know, are "to love, to cherish, and to *obey*" her husband?'

'No, Tommy,' Elizabeth says firmly and he pauses, his brows lifting in polite enquiry.

'Your Royal Highness?'

'No, I'm not going to change the vows,' she clarifies. 'I am to be Philip's wife so I intend to promise to obey him. There are few enough opportunities for us to have a traditional marriage, and it's important that he knows I'm happy to be a wife like any other. We cannot take this away from him as well.'

That afternoon she and Philip are due to view an exhibition of some of the presents that have been pouring in from all over the world. Some are spectacular indeed. Her parents have given her a magnificent double-string pearl necklace. The Shah of Persia has sent a beautiful Persian carpet, a wreath of diamond roses has come from the Nezam of Hyderabad. Elizabeth's secret favourite, a gift from the Aga Khan, is Astrakhan, a chestnut thoroughbred filly who for obvious reasons is not on display, though Elizabeth has already been to coo over her at the royal stud.

Other gifts are less grand but more useful. Twelve engraved champagne glasses and a fitted picnic case from Margaret. American towels and bathmats from Mrs Roosevelt. More touching still are the gifts from ordinary people whose generosity has left Elizabeth overwhelmed and humbled. They have sent handkerchiefs and nylon stockings, hand-knitted tea cosies and embroidered linen and clothing coupons to help with her trousseau. Knowing how hard so many people are struggling with austerity and rationing, Elizabeth is moved almost to tears by such thoughtfulness. All the coupons must be returned, though, as it is illegal to give them away, and she signs many letters of heartfelt thanks as they are posted back.

Together with Margaret, Crawfie, and her lady-in-waiting she has been opening most of the parcels as they arrive. Crawfie opened a round, heavy parcel with some trepidation. 'I hope it's not a bomb,' she said but when she snatched off the last piece of paper it turned out to be a lump of rock, sent by an elderly Welshman for luck. *A piece of Snowdon*, he said. Another parcel contained two soggy pieces of burnt toast, sent by two young women who were so excited at hearing news of the engagement that they let their toast burn to a cinder. As proof of their story they posted the charred toast together with a really charming letter of congratulation which made up for the disgusting mess that fell out of the envelope at first.

Now all the presents have been put on display in St James's Palace, and the royal family are due to inspect them with Philip and Queen Mary. At least Philip has put on a suit for the occasion, but his face is set and his manner abrupt. Elizabeth's heart sinks the moment she sees him. Increasingly, it feels as if he is regretting their engagement and looking for a way out and she doesn't know what to do about it.

The King is already cross about the smoke bomb, and matters aren't improved when Philip falls out with her grandmother over a gift from Gandhi. It is a fringed lace-work tray cloth made out of yarn spun by Gandhi himself on his own wheel, apparently at the suggestion of Mountbatten. Unfortunately, her grandmother mistakes it for a loincloth and is affronted.

'Such an indelicate gift!' she declares. 'What a horrible thing!'

Instead of making allowances for her mistake, Philip immediately goes on the attack. 'I don't think it's horrible at all,' he says. 'Gandhi is a wonderful man. A very great man.'

Queen Mary gives him a stony look in return and moves on in disgusted silence, which does nothing to improve Philip's mood.

Chapter 46

Elizabeth has a bright smile fixed to her own face as she goes around the display, finding a comment for whenever she stops. She admires a refrigerator and a Singer sewing machine, though she doubts very much that she will use either. There is a television set, a 22-carat-gold coffee service, a mink coat. Hand-knitted tea-cosies are displayed between antique furniture, pieces of crystal and china of varying quality, a duffle coat trimmed with beaver sent by a man in Milwaukee and more than two thousand other gifts, large and small.

Her head is aching with the tension of waiting for Philip to explode with some new irritation, and it is a relief to get to the end of the display. She needs some time on her own. It's a mild autumn day. She'll take Susan for a walk and clear her head, she decides, and for the first time ever even finds herself hoping Philip won't want to join her. Not that he would, she tells herself. He's probably longing to jump into his MG and drive off somewhere he can *let off steam*.

In the event, the King asks Philip for a word in a way that clearly brooks no refusal, and glad that she is not being asked to witness her fiancé's dressing down over the smoke-bomb incident, Elizabeth takes the opportunity to change into an old tweed skirt, a coat, and a scarf. Whistling for a delighted Susan, she waves off offers of company and heads off into the gardens.

The air smells of tumbled leaves and wood smoke and faint melancholy. Perhaps Margaret was right, and they should have waited until spring. Then perhaps there wouldn't have been such a rush and things could have been sorted out in a calmer way. But it is too late to change their minds now.

Beyond the walls Elizabeth can hear the ceaseless grumble of traffic. The grounds are spacious enough but tired and brown and wherever she walks, she comes across the high brick wall that surrounds the garden. It's not a prison, of course it isn't, but sometimes, sometimes it feels like one. She wishes she could be spirited away to Balmoral or Sandringham or even Windsor, somewhere there is space to breathe. There have been so many problems associated with wedding, so many decisions to be made, that it feels as if there has been little time to enjoy the engagement and she is left feeling tense and jagged around the edges. If only she could be sure she has done the right thing. It hurts to see Philip so unhappy.

As if the thought of him has conjured Philip up,

Elizabeth hears his voice calling her name and she stops and turns to see him striding along the lake path towards her. He doesn't look unhappy now.

He looks furious.

His face is white, his brows an angry slash across his nose, his mouth thin with rage.

'Your father and Tommy Lascelles ...' He can barely speak, he is so angry. 'I've just been dressed down like a damned schoolboy!'

Elizabeth opens her mouth to mediate as usual, to say something soothing. Instead, something quite different comes out.

'It sounds to me like you've been behaving like one.'

Philip's head snaps back as if she has slapped him; it feels as if she has. His eyes narrow. 'Oh, so you've been party to the let's-find-something-else-to-tick-Philip-off-for sessions too, have you?'

'If you mean have I been told that you and David made exhibitions of yourselves by throwing smoke bombs around, then yes, I have.'

'Oh, for God's sake! It was just a bit of harmless fun. Nobody was hurt.'

'I understand it caused a good deal of damage, not to mention embarrassment.'

'No one was *embarrassed*,' Philip insists, glowering, and Elizabeth looks him straight in the eye.

'*I'm* embarrassed,' she says. 'My future husband, my

future *consort*, thinks it's funny to drink too much and throw smoke bombs around, not caring about anybody who might be shocked or inconvenienced. Of course I'm embarrassed, and the King is embarrassed, and you should be embarrassed too.'

'Oh, right, so I can't even have a good time with my friends anymore?' Philip demands. 'I'm dogged wherever I go by bloody reporters. I can't do anything without that old monster Tommy Lascelles hauling me over the coals! What *am* I allowed to do, Elizabeth? Stand to attention like a stuffed dummy with my hands tied behind my back? What kind of life is that?'

'You knew what life as a member of the royal family would be,' she points out. Philip's anger is making her feel nauseous, but they need to have this out. She can't back down now.

'I didn't know it would be as bad as this!' Philip hunches a sullen shoulder. 'I didn't think it would be ... like this. Stupid of me.'

Elizabeth's hands are folded at her waist. She makes herself take a breath, keep her voice even. 'Do you want to change your mind, Philip?'

'I can't, can I?' He paces away from her, then back. 'You saw all those presents. People have made sacrifices for us. We can hardly send them all back and say, sorry, we changed our minds. It's all gone too far to stop now.'

It is not what Elizabeth wants to hear. All he needed to say was *no, I haven't changed my mind*, but instead he is feeling trapped. If he could change his mind, he would: *that's* what he is saying, and her throat burns with disappointment.

'It would certainly be awkward,' she says in a level voice even as the forbidden anger burns through her. 'But it would be better than being trapped in a marriage you will regret. I thought we had an agreement, Philip,' she goes on. 'I know you don't want to marry *me*. I know you don't love *me*. You've never pretended you did, and I've appreciated your honesty. You've made it perfectly clear you wanted to marry me because I'm heir to the throne. You wanted the position. Well, this *is* the position.

'No, wait,' she says, lifting a hand as Philip opens his mouth to remonstrate. 'Don't say anything yet. Take a good look at yourself and what you want. Think what being married involves,' she tells him, 'because after 20th November, there will be no going back. There will be no divorce and no chance of one, and you won't be able to follow your father's example and lead a separate life that suits you. That is not going to happen,' she says clearly, coldly, because that is more controllable than the anger roiling along her veins.

'So you can choose your freedom and we'll cancel the wedding – somehow – or you can step up to the position you said you wanted, and if you're going to do that, at least do it properly.'

She looks around for the dog who is snuffling in the undergrowth. 'Susan, come!' she commands and something in her voice has the corgi scrambling smartly back to the path.

Elizabeth looks back at Philip. 'Have a think and let me know what you decide,' she says, amazed at her own control, and she turns and walks deliberately away from him, leaving Philip gaping after her.

Chapter 47

London, November 1947

Philip's sense of grievance runs white hot for several days after being dismissed – yes, dismissed! – by Elizabeth. He has never seen her angry before and that glimpse of fire, usually so carefully banked down, has shaken him more than he cares to admit.

A lark that got out of hand, that was all it was, but they have all reacted as if he has committed some crime against the state! He's used to disapproval from the King and his advisers, but Elizabeth's reaction ... no, he didn't like that. She has always been so gentle and supportive that he is still stinging from her rebuff.

There was no call for her to be so ... cold.

I thought we had an agreement, she said. They *did* have an agreement. He has always been completely honest with her, Philip tells himself, aggrieved. Of course he didn't pretend to be madly in love with her. She would have seen through that in an instant! And it isn't as if Elizabeth has ever given him any indication she wants or expects any mawkish sentimentality from him. She made it clear from the start that an agreement was what it was, was what *she* wanted.

Still, he can't stop hearing her voice, can't stop seeing the shuttered expression in her eyes. *I know you don't love me.* The memory squats inside him, a heavy stone in his chest.

Would she have preferred him to act a part? Philip can't believe that, but round and round her words go in his head: *I know you don't want to marry* me. *You wanted the position. We'll cancel the wedding.*

They can't cancel the wedding. What a ridiculous thing to suggest! It is barely two weeks away. But Philip has no doubt that if Elizabeth says she would ensure something was worked out, something would be. She is not given to making promises she cannot keep. She has held open the door of the cage, and there is a part of Philip that is uneasily aware he can have his freedom if that is what he really wants.

And he is tempted. He would be the most reviled man in the world for a while, true, but he has his career. He could make a decent life for himself without all the protocol and the starchy traditions and the trappings of royalty. What a relief that would be!

But it would be a life without Elizabeth.

The thought of it is curiously bleak. It's not that he

loves her, exactly – didn't they agree that wasn't what their marriage would be about? – but he *would* miss her.

Yes, he would definitely miss her.

Philip snaps himself out of it. There is no question of missing her. He is going to marry Elizabeth. Anything else is unthinkable. Why has Elizabeth even suggested it?

Unless she has changed *her* mind?

She wouldn't do that, he reassures himself instantly. Elizabeth keeps her promises. She does what she says she is going to do, unwaveringly.

Unlike him, Philip realises with a wince of shame. He has wavered plenty. He has been losing his nerve and flailing out in frustration. He isn't used to the relentless speculation and observation. He's had a lifetime of being able to come and go as he pleases and all that has changed since the engagement.

His life is going to change completely.

Which is, he knows, an explanation but not an excuse. The realisation that he has disappointed Elizabeth clings to Philip's shoulders like a monkey all week, impossible to shake off. It leaves him touchy and jittery, unable to settle. He sends Elizabeth a stiff note saying that as far as he is concerned, he wants the wedding to go ahead as planned, but he knows he should go and see her himself. If only he didn't feel so confused and restless about everything. He'll only make it worse if he goes to see her in this state, he decides.

Meanwhile, planning for the wedding is continuing

remorselessly, inexorably, unaware of the fact that he and Elizabeth have stumbled. Sometimes Philip feels as if he is trapped in a nightmare, frozen like a rabbit in headlights. The knowledge that he has to do something leaves him frantic but still he seems unable to move. All he can do is go through the motions while his mind spins and spins without ever getting purchase.

When his chums at the Thursday Club originally suggested a secret stag do well away from any cameras, Philip thought it was a great idea. A more decorous event including Uncle Dickie has been arranged for the night before the wedding but the Thursday Club bash is supposed to be the real, relaxed event, a chance to let his hair down for the last time.

The occasion turns out to be as robust and ribald as he expected, and probably exactly what he thought he wanted at one time, but Philip is not enjoying himself. There is much drinking and guffawing and he is the butt of every lewd joke, which he expected too. But he feels disconnected from it all as he sits straight and white-faced as the reality of the situation he is facing crashes over him.

All the members of the Thursday Club are there. Philip hears the braying laughter, sees the drink slopping out of glasses as if from behind an invisible wall. Alcohol seems to shimmer in the air, distorting the room and the people in it. Debauched, dishevelled, they have all taken on the air of grotesques with red, glistening faces, their shirts straining over ample bellies. Philip's eyes fix on the stained tablecloth as he struggles to keep the disgust from his expression, and at that moment the image of Elizabeth rises before him: cool, clear, composed. He clutches at the memory of her clear eyes with a kind of desperation, and the need to be with her is suddenly so acute that it takes his breath away as revelation washes through him.

It is not the princess or the position he wants. It is Elizabeth herself. Elizabeth, with her warm smile and her kindness, her straight back and steady spirit.

I know you don't love me, she said. But she is wrong. He does love her, he just hasn't realised it until now.

Philip hasn't been looking for love, and he isn't prepared for it. Now, he feels aggrieved, almost foolish, caught unawares by the way it has crept up on him when he wasn't paying attention. His relationship with Elizabeth is supposed to be calm and practical. She is a princess, he is a prince. Their arrangement is not supposed to be about wanting or needing or loving.

Except now, somehow, it is.

He has been teetering on the brink of this chasm for months, Philip realises, and he has fallen over into love now that it is too late to do anything about it. And very uncomfortable it feels, too! He doesn't want this gnawing sense of need, this ridiculous feeling that he is off-balance without Elizabeth by his side.

He's been perfectly happy with the way things are up to now, Philip tells himself crossly. He doesn't want to be in love, but now the truth of it has hit him like a train, there seems to be no unknowing it and he is left feeling edgy and empty and uncomfortably aware that he needs Elizabeth more than she needs him.

Which means he will have to do something about it.

I know you don't love me. Elizabeth's words drum in his brain throughout the long, wretched evening. It is a relief when he can finally leave and sink onto his bed, dropping his aching head into his hands. He needs to tell her how wrong she is.

He needs to know if she can love him back.

Only then, Philip decides, will the world which has tipped so abruptly out of kilter settle back into place.

First thing tomorrow, he promises himself, he will go to the palace and put his happiness in Elizabeth's hands before he loses his nerve.

Chapter 48

Buckingham Palace, November 1947

Elizabeth is trying on shoes and hats for her going away outfit when Philip bursts in. Deeply discomposed by the interruption of someone so fiercely masculine and out of place amongst the array of frivolous accessories, Mr Hartnell and his assistants flutter ineffectually like hens confronting a fox in the coop.

Philip ignores them all. He looks angry and baffled and in spite of herself, Elizabeth's heart leaps.

'I need to talk to you,' he says to her.

'I'm rather busy, as you can see.' Elizabeth forces herself to stay cool. All she has had from him since their row is a stiff note indicating that he wants to go ahead with the wedding. Does he really expect her to welcome him with open arms? Why should she change her plans just because he is suddenly ready to talk? 'Can you come back in an hour or two?'

'No.' Across the room in two strides, Philip takes hold

of her wrist and tows her back to the door, scattering assistants as he goes. 'I really need to talk to you now.'

Elizabeth is still in her stockinged feet. The footman outside the door stiffens when Philip appears with a breathless princess. He steps forward as if to intercept them, but Elizabeth shakes her head and he falls back. If Philip is so determined to have his say, he had better have it.

She is practically running to keep up with him. 'Where are we going?'

'Somewhere we won't be interrupted,' he says curtly, striding past doorways with footmen standing to attention. He keeps opening doors at random, only to be confronted by startled faces. 'How can this bloody palace have seven hundred rooms and still nowhere we can be alone? Ah, what about this one?'

He pulls her into the room and releases her so he can turn and shut the door firmly behind him.

'This is where we feed the *dogs*,' Elizabeth says, looking around as she rubs her wrist. It isn't sore exactly, but she can still feel the imprint of his fingers on her flesh.

'It's empty,' says Philip. 'That's all that matters.'

Elizabeth is feeling distinctly ruffled. She feeds Susan herself, after the footmen have set out the food in stoneware dishes, so she is familiar with the room. It is just a narrow kitchen, with the neatly washed dog dishes stacked on the draining board. 'Is there any reason we can't go to my sitting room instead of hiding in the dog kitchen?'

'Because there'll be some lady-in-waiting or Miss

Crawford or *somebody* there and I want to speak to you alone.'

'Well, we appear to be alone now.' Her heart is slamming painfully against her ribs. Philip looks so agitated. Is he really going to break things off? Would he really do that to her? She composes her expression, inwardly bracing herself. 'What is it that can't wait?' she asks in a chilly voice.

'I had to see you. I had to tell you ...' Having got her here, Philip seems at a loss as to how to proceed. Breaking off with a smothered curse, he drags a hand through his hair. 'I thought this would be easier,' he mutters.

'Tell me what?'

She can see him pull himself together with an effort. 'I keep thinking about what you said,' he begins again.

'What did I say?'

'You said you knew I didn't love you.'

Elizabeth keeps her chin up, her guard up. 'And?'

'And you said you liked the fact that we'd always been honest with each other.'

'That's true.'

'The thing is, Elizabeth ... the thing is, I wasn't honest. At least, I *was* honest, or I thought I was ... *Christ*, I'm making a mess of this!' Philip clutches his head with both hands before dropping them and looking directly at her for the first time. 'I don't think I was being honest with myself,' he says more clearly.

Stepping closer, he takes hold of Elizabeth's hands. 'I *do* love you,' he says quite simply after all. 'I just didn't know it.'

The breath seems to have evaporated from her lungs and she feels giddy from the lack of oxygen. Her fingers tighten around Philip's for support. 'I ... I thought ... you said we would be friends and partners, not lovers.'

'I thought that's what *you* wanted,' he says.

'Well, I could hardly tell you I had been madly in love with you since I was thirteen!' she says almost crossly.

There's a pause. 'Thirteen?' A smile is hovering around his mouth.

'We played croquet at Dartmouth. You were showing off terribly.'

His smile is spreading. 'You fell in love with me then?'

'Well, not really.' Her eyes slide away from his, suddenly embarrassed. 'I was only thirteen, after all. But I was ... fascinated.'

'And later?'

She looks at him then. 'Later, I realised you were the only man I would ever love. The only man who would ever see me for myself. The only man I would ever want beside me.'

'Well, you kept *that* to yourself,' Philip says, pretending astonishment, but he is grinning now. 'How was I supposed to know that?

'It was perfectly obvious to anyone except a bone-headed idiot,' Elizabeth says but the tartness in her voice is betrayed by the smile curving her own mouth.

'I'm sorry,' he says, suddenly serious. 'I'm sorry I didn't realise, Elizabeth, and I'm sorry it took me so long to come to my senses, but now I have, can we agree that we can be friends and partners *and* lovers? Can we forget all the pomp and the politics and make this wedding about us?' he says. 'I don't mean cancel all the plans – God forbid! – but just that when we're standing there at the altar in Westminster Abbey, it'll be just you and me? Everyone else can watch a princess marry a prince – well, a mere lieutenant now – but I want to marry *you*, Elizabeth. Not a princess, not an heir to the throne, just you. And I'd really like it if you would marry me, Philip, bone-headed fool that I am, not Mountbatten's nephew or an ex-prince of Greece or that cocky boy who showed off at Dartmouth. Just me. Will you do that?'

Elizabeth's throat is clogged as she takes her hands from his to lay them on his chest and move closer with a trembling smile. 'Just you and just me,' she agrees as his arms come around her. 'Yes, let's do that.'

Chapter 49

Buckingham Palace, November 1947

A throng of bejewelled and bemedaled guests has turned the ballroom into a cheerful muddle of colour and noise. Chatter and laughter bounce off the gilded ceiling and merge with the music from the band tucked away in the gallery. The ball at Buckingham Palace is the last and most glittering of a series of celebrations before the wedding itself. Over the week, guests from around the world have been gathering in London and the last few days have been a whirlwind of social events that have left Elizabeth feeling breathless.

What a difference Philip's declaration has made! Sometimes her happiness is so acute it almost hurts. Knowing he loves her has somehow made everything fall into place. All the petty tensions in the wedding plans seem to have evaporated and the palace, so tired and dreary after the war, has come alive again and for the past week has been buzzing with good-humoured preparations. Staff flit around, swathed in aprons, ferociously dusting and cleaning chandeliers and polishing silver. Stacks of gilt chairs line the corridors, ready for refreshments for the ball tonight, and then for the wedding breakfast. The scent of huge floral displays drifts in the air, mingling with that of furniture polish, while the sound of hoovering and musicians tuning up has become the norm.

Nobody can hear themselves speak and the dancefloor is a crush but everybody seems to be enjoying themselves so Elizabeth counts the ball a success. True, there have been a couple of incidents, but no good party is without those, or so they say. Elizabeth herself was dancing with Uncle Dickie when the plump Princess Juliana of the Netherlands slipped and fell to the floor where she lay, upended like a turtle, while the band trailed off and everyone froze. Elizabeth didn't dare look at Mountbatten: she could tell he was trying not to laugh and if he did, she wouldn't be able to help herself. There was an excruciating silence until the princess's partner, the Duke of Gloucester, managed to help her, not without difficulty, to her feet and the band hastily resumed.

'Good of your father to lay on some comedy as well,' Mountbatten murmured provocatively and Elizabeth had to press her lips firmly together to stop laughing.

'Stop it!' she muttered.

'No, really. Everyone's having a terrific time. Did you hear about one of our Indian friends who has been taking advantage of the plentiful champagne?'

'No,' she said with foreboding. 'What happened?'

'He took exception to the Duke of Devonshire for some reason. Or maybe he did have a reason. Poor old Ted took a punch on the nose.'

'Oh, dear.'

'He's all right,' Mountbatten told her, his eyes gleaming with amusement. 'The Maharajah in question has been escorted off for a "rest",' he added and then leant closer. 'We're far enough away from dear Juliana ... I think we're allowed to laugh now, don't you?'

The memory is still making Elizabeth chuckle when Philip comes up beside her later. 'Hello, you, what are you giggling about?'

She tells him about Princess Juliana's mishap. 'It sounds so unkind, but it *was* funny!'

Philip grins. 'Uncle Dickie's right about the comedy. You know Beatrice Lillie?'

'The comedienne?'

'She outdid herself tonight. Apparently, she'd been told she wasn't allowed to smoke in the royal presence – a message that seems to have passed your father by – but she was desperate for a cigarette. Of course, Margaret chose that moment to stop and talk to her and poor Beatrice didn't know what to do with her cigarette. There were no ashtrays nearby and she could hardly grind it into the floor.'

'Gosh, what did she do?'

'Only stuffed it down the front of her dress!' Philip's

solid body shakes with laughter. 'I was watching as Beatrice tried to make polite conversation with Margaret while smoke drifted up from her cleavage. Some enterprising chap doused her with a glass of water. It did *not* go down well!'

Elizabeth puts a hand to her mouth to stifle her giggle. 'I wish I'd seen that!'

'And I've just overheard Field Marshal Smuts trying to charm Queen Mary. Talk about brave!'

'What did he say?'

Philip puts on a creditable South African accent and strikes a pose. '"You, Your Majesty, you are the big potato,"' he quotes Smuts, pretending to shake a finger in Elizabeth's face. '"All the other queens here are just small potatoes, but you, you are the big one."'

Imagining her grandmother's face at being compared to a potato, Elizabeth collapses into helpless laughter. When she looks up at him, smiling and wiping the tears of laughter from her eyes, Elizabeth surprises an arrested expression in Philip's icy blue eyes. 'What?'

'I was just thinking that you're to be the big potato yourself one day,' he says.

'Even big potatoes need someone by their side,' says Elizabeth and Philip's face relaxes into a smile.

'I'll be there,' he says, 'reminding you just what a wonderful potato you are.'

'I hope so. A potato should go well with the little cabbage that your mother calls you.' Tucking her hand into Philip's arm, Elizabeth smiles as she surveys the crowded room. 'Everyone seems to be enjoying themselves, don't they?'

'They do. Even the big potato is in a feisty mood. That's the good thing about weddings. It's a chance to get families together. Half my relatives came over from Europe on the train ferry together and are all staying at Claridge's. I went round to say hello the other night and the noise was unbelievable,' Philip says with an affectionate grin. 'They were all talking at the same time, as usual. They took over half the restaurant and spent the whole evening table hopping, drinking out of each other's glasses, gossiping ...' His smile fades a little. 'I couldn't help thinking how much my sisters would have loved being there.'

Elizabeth leans into him in wordless sympathy. 'I wish they could have been, Philip.'

'I know.' Philip squeezes the hand on his arm and makes an obvious effort to push the momentary sadness away as he brightens his voice. 'But you'll be glad to know that Uncle Dickie has at last persuaded my mother to abandon her nun's habit for the wedding.'

'Oh good. What is she going to wear?'

'Don't ask me,' he says unhelpfully. 'A grey dress, not a nun's habit, that's all I know.' He eases his arm away so he can take her hand in a firm grip. 'Now, come on, let's go and dance. I've done my duty with every queen and princess in the room, and now I want to dance with my fiancée.'

Elizabeth pulls a face. 'I've still got so many duty dances to do ...' she begins to protest, but she doesn't pull her hand away as he steers her towards the ballroom.

'Let them wait,' says Philip.

Chapter 50

Philip studies his reflection as he shaves carefully. In his vest, boxers, and socks – new ones for the occasion! – he hardly looks an imposing figure, but appearances can lie. No longer is he Lieutenant Mountbatten. Unable to contemplate Elizabeth becoming a mere Mrs Mountbatten, the King touched him on the shoulder with a sword the previous afternoon and created Philip, Baron Greenwich, Earl of Merioneth and Duke of Edinburgh. Not only that, he is now a Knight Companion of the Order of the Garter, a sonorous title with ancient associations of unswerving loyalty to the sovereign. He is bound tight now, part of the royal family whether he likes it or not.

The King was trying to put a good face on it, but it is obvious he hates the idea of losing his daughter. Philip is uneasily conscious of a kind of primitive satisfaction. The King has lost, and he has won. He's not proud of the feeling, but he is honest enough to admit it, if only to himself. Elizabeth is his, and the knowledge that she loves him – has loved him all that time! – is at once remarkable to Philip and insensibly steadying.

His valet, John Dean, is in the other room, picking invisible specks off Philip's regulation blue uniform. 'How are you feeling this morning, sir?'

'Not too bad, considering,' Philip says, running a hand over his jaw to check for stray bristles. 'I wouldn't mind another cup of tea, though.'

'Certainly, sir.'

Dean bustles out to get the tea while Philip buttons his shirt slowly. He can hardly believe the day has come. Uncle Dickie was emotional at the stag party last night ... at the second private one anyway. The official one at the Dorchester ended at half past midnight with a ceremonial smashing of photographers' flashbulbs, which had felt bloody good, Philip had to admit. The snappers took it in good part, not that they'd had much choice. Having shaken off the press, a smaller, select group including Uncle Dickie and his cousin David had continued partying until the small hours so Philip hasn't had a lot of sleep. Thank God he was sensible and didn't drink too much, he thinks. He wouldn't have wanted to face Westminster Abbey with a massive hangover.

As it is, he has only a vaguely nauseous feeling and a churning gut.

He is nervous.

But when Dean comes back with the tea, Philip brushes

aside anxious queries about how he is feeling. 'I'm fine. Raring to go.'

He is ready far too early. Even spinning out breakfast and then donning his uniform doesn't fill the allotted time, and he is driven mad by Dean fussing around him and fiddling with his hair.

'All right, pack it up,' he says impatiently at last. 'Let's get this sword on.'

Gingerly, Dean hands him the Battenberg sword lent by Uncle Dickie. It is a magnificent thing, a jewelled, ceremonial sword and symbol of the Battenberg dynasty. To wear it while marrying the heir to the throne is a momentous thing, Philip realises that. He is fulfilling his uncle's dream, yes, but he is doing this for himself too, and because he wants to marry Elizabeth. He won't forget that.

With the sword strapped to side, it is not easy to sit down, and Philip is too restless anyway. He paces around the apartment until David, who is to be his best man, begs him to stop.

'Here, have a smoke,' he says, proffering the packet.

Philip eyes it longingly but shakes his head. 'I've given up.'

'You've *what?*'

'I've given up smoking. I promised Elizabeth I would. It's a vow – and this isn't the day to start breaking vows.'

'Dammit.' David rolls his eyes as he taps the cigarettes back into the packet. 'Well, let's have a G&T instead.'

'It's only ten-fifteen!'

'So? I don't know about you, but I need something to steady my nerves – and I'm not the one marrying the heir to the throne in front of two hundred million people! If we can't have a fag, let's at least have a drink.'

Philip looks at his watch. The car isn't due to come for them until five to eleven. That leaves more than half an hour to hang around wondering what in God's name he's let himself in for.

'All right,' he says to David. 'Better make it a small one, though.'

Chapter 51

The sound of bagpipes has woken Elizabeth as usual at six thirty. 'What's the weather like?' she asks Bobo when she brings her a cup of tea.

'Dreich,' Bobo opined, drawing back the curtains. 'But what do you expect for the end of November?'

'I'm worried about all those people who have slept out. They must have had a cold night.'

'Aye, well, I don't doubt they'll be glad of it when they see you pass by.'

'Oh, Bobo, I can't believe it's really happening!' Elizabeth puts down the cup and saucer and takes the flesh on her arm between her thumb and forefinger. 'This is my wedding day.' The day that seemed as if it would never come is here. The day she has dreamt about for so long. Philip loves her and they are getting married today. 'I have to keep pinching myself!'

Bobo is never one to lose her head. 'I'll go and run your bath,' is all she says.

Breakfast arrives with a bouquet of white carnations from Philip. Her favourite flower. Elizabeth holds them to her nose, her mouth curving with pleasure at the scent, at the thought.

Still in her dressing gown, she peeps out of her window. Her rooms overlook the Mall, which is already a solid mass of people, with mounted police riding up and down on splendid horses to keep the processional route clear. It's obvious that huge numbers of people have slept on the pavements and are now having picnic breakfasts, cooking bacon, she guesses, on portable stoves and brewing up coffee. Elizabeth can smell it when she eases open the window. Women are washing their faces, pouring hot water from vacuum flasks into little bowls, and putting on make-up in readiness for the day.

Touched by the efforts they are making to help celebrate her big day, Elizabeth smiles as she turns away from the window. She keeps smiling as she stands patiently for an hour or more while the Hartnell team start the long process of dressing her, checking that every stitch and seam sits perfectly.

They melt away when Monsieur Henri arrives to do her hair, only to reappear to fit the veil, but disaster strikes when her grandmother's diamond tiara snaps in two as they adjust it on her head.

The crack splinters the buzz of excitement in the room

and is followed by an appalled silence. For the first time, Elizabeth's smile falters.

'It just came apart in my hands ...' The assistant in charge of the tiara lowering is white-faced and near to tears.

'Can you fix it?' Elizabeth asks.

The assistant just looks at the two pieces of the tiara in her hands.

'Mummy ...' Elizabeth looks helplessly at her mother who steps forward and attempts to calm everyone down.

'There's no need to upset yourself, Lilibet. One thing we're not short of here is tiaras. I'll ask my dresser to find another. Remember the one Mr Hartnell suggested originally?'

'No, I want this one. Granny lent it to me for the wedding.' It's not like Elizabeth to be fretful but all at once, it seems impossible to be married without Queen Mary's tiara.

The thought of her grandmother, the Big Potato as Philip calls her now, brings ridiculous tears to her eyes.

The Queen exchanges a look with Bobo. 'Call the court jeweller,' she says quietly. 'Get him here straight away.'

Smiling, she turns back to Elizabeth. 'There's plenty of time – two hours until you're due to leave for the Abbey.'

'Yes, of course.' Elizabeth takes a deep breath and makes herself calm down.

'You look like a fairy-tale princess,' her mother tells her. She really does, Elizabeth thinks. The dress is as beautiful as Mr Hartnell promised. It shimmers with seed pearls and tiny crystals that catch the light. 'It needs the pearl necklace.'

'This one?' Still in calming mode, the Queen picks up Elizabeth's favourite strand of pearls from the dressing table. They're the ones she usually wears, but it's not the necklace she has in mind for the wedding.

'No, the double strand you and Papa gave me. Bobo, where is it?'

Bobo and the Queen exchange another look. 'It's still on display in St James's Palace,' Bobo says carefully.

'Someone can go and get it.' Elizabeth has made up her mind. 'Ask Jock Colville to come in.'

Her private secretary is summoned but looks dismayed when Elizabeth asks him to fetch the necklace.

'From St James's Palace?' he repeats cautiously.

'It's not that far.'

He hesitates. 'Not usually, no, but there must be a hundred thousand people crammed between here and there this morning.'

'*Please*, Jock.'

'Certainly, Your Royal Highness.' Clearly daunted, Jock withdraws with dignity but the moment the door is shut behind him, they can hear him charging off down the corridor at speed.

Fortunately, the court jeweller arrives just after her secretary has left, presumably having passed Jock on the stairs, and doing his best to look dignified in spite of being distinctly breathless. He purses his lips when shown the tiara and is told the bride is due to leave at eleven but manages to retain an air of avuncular calm. 'I cannot promise a perfect job in view of the time,' he begins, only for Elizabeth to interrupt.

'I don't mind as long as I can wear it,' she says. 'I *must* wear it!'

The jeweller bows. 'Then wear it you shall, Your Royal Highness. I will be as quick as I can.'

'Now,' says the Queen when he too has gone, 'let's all calm down.'

Elizabeth's earlier feeling of serenity has completely deserted her, but she knows her mother is right. She thinks about Philip and how he would react to a broken tiara, and instantly feels steadier. He is what is important today, she reminds herself, pressing her fingertips to her chest to slow her breathing.

It enables her to stand still while they deal with earrings, and shoes, and the long, beautifully embroidered veil is carefully pinned to her hair awaiting the crowning touch of the repaired tiara, but as time ticks on and there is no sign of either Jock or the jeweller, Elizabeth begins to fret again. She wants to pace but she can't with the veil on. She twists her hands together instead. What is she going to do with her hands during the walk up the aisle?

'My bouquet!' she exclaims, suddenly realising she hasn't seen it yet. 'Where is it?'

There are glances of consternation around the room.

Nobody knows. 'It's been delivered,' the Queen says, 'I'm sure of it.' Although she doesn't sound sure. 'It must be somewhere.'

Summoning a footman from the corridor outside, the Queen sends him to organise a search for the missing bouquet, and Norman Hartnell delegates two of his team to help them. Elizabeth can hear the sound of footsteps running along the corridors and doors being unceremoniously flung open.

There is still no sign of the bouquet when the jeweller comes back. Everyone lets out a simultaneous sigh of relief as he slides the tiara safely onto her hair, followed by another as a panting, red-faced dresser returns with news that the bouquet has been found in the porter's lodge icebox.

'A footman put it there to keep it cool so it could be given to you at the last minute,' the dresser says. 'But then he went off duty and forgot.'

'Now we just need Jock with the necklace.' Elizabeth's hand keeps straying to her throat where the pearls will nestle.

'It's almost time,' the Queen says anxiously. She is wearing a flattering dress in an apricot-coloured silk brocade. 'I need to go, I'm afraid. They'll be waiting for me downstairs. I'm going in the car with Margaret.'

'All right, Mummy.' Elizabeth kisses her mother. 'See you at the abbey!'

'Best of luck, darling.'

The bridesmaids have been getting ready in another room and they can be heard chattering and laughing as they go past the door on their way down to the entrance where a fleet of Daimlers are lined up to take them to the abbey along with the rest of the royal party. Elizabeth and her father will leave last.

Outside, the crowd are stirring in anticipation too. Singing and sporadic cheering drift up from the Mall.

'You should start heading down too,' Bobo says in a practical voice after the Queen has gone. 'You can't move very fast with that train.'

'The necklace—'

'I daresay Mr Colville will be able to find you when he makes it back from St James's Palace.'

'All right.' Elizabeth starts to nod and then thinks better of it with the tiara and veil. 'I think we're ready, aren't we?'

'As ready as we're going to be.' She beckons to one of the Hartnell dressers to help with the train. 'Here, we'll take the veil, you just concentrate on walking in the dress.'

They have almost reached the top of the stairs when Jock Colville comes running up them. Elizabeth stops.

'Did you get it?' she asks eagerly, and Jock's smile is triumphant as he pulls the pearl necklace from his pocket.

'Sorry I took so long, ma'am,' he says. 'I commandeered the King of Norway's Daimler before I'd given the king a chance to get out, but in the event, we couldn't get through the crowds in the car, so I got out and ran, fighting my way through everybody.'

He hands the pearls to Bobo, who undoes the clasp and puts them around Elizabeth's neck.

'When I got to St James's, it was deserted. Everyone is already at the abbey and there was only one aged retainer who had no intention of letting me in. Of course, I left in such a hurry, I didn't have any way of proving who I was! There is a police guard and they tried ringing here, but the switchboard operators have been given the day off.'

'What did you do?' asks Elizabeth, thrilled to be able to pat the pearls into place at her throat.

'Eventually I had the brainwave of showing them the wedding programme with my name on it, but even so two policemen insisted on coming back to the palace with me. I don't think they quite trusted me!'

'Well, I'm very grateful, Jock. Thank you.'

'My pleasure, ma'am.'

The pearls have steadied her. She is ready now, nervous still but it is a simmering low in her belly, not the frazzled, fluttery feeling in her chest she had before.

As Elizabeth makes her way slowly down the stairs, she can see the Life Guards on horses trotting out through the arch. For the first time since the war, they are in their ceremonial uniforms rather than battle dress and they look splendid in their plumed helmets, scarlet tunics, and steel cuirasses. It lifts her heart to see them and judging by the roar of approval from the crowd on the other side of the gates, they have the same effect on everybody. The Queen and Margaret follow in a sedately driven Daimler, followed in their turn by an escort of the Horse Guards in all their ceremonial glory.

The horses look wonderful, Elizabeth thinks. They are all groomed to a gleam, their manes and tails carefully dressed, and their harness glittering.

Her father is waiting for her, looking emotional but managing a smile as she reaches the bottom of the stairs. 'Lilibet ... you look beautiful.'

'Thank you, Papa.'

'I just pray that you and Philip will be as happy as Mummy and I have been.'

'I hope so too,' she says.

Pulled by four superb Windsor Greys from the Royal Mews, the Irish State Coach has moved forward under the portico. The horses stand patiently, shaking their manes occasionally. Elizabeth catches the eye of Cyril in his full scarlet and gold livery. He has been her footman for ten years and she invited him to the wedding in the abbey, only for the idea to be vetoed by the sergeant footman.

'He says I'm on duty,' Cyril told her. 'I've got to go on the carriage, he says. At least I'll get a good view!'

Elizabeth likes knowing he will be close, and when he lowers an eyelid in a wink, her face relaxes into a smile.

A roar on the other side of the arch indicates that the Queen and Princess Margaret have come into view.

'Our turn,' the King says, sounding strained.

Very carefully, Elizabeth is helped into the coach, the dressers piling the billowing train in after her. The King gets in beside her and there is a little jolt as the coachman gives the horses the word to walk on, a further escort of the Horse Guards falling in behind them.

'We're off,' says the King. 'It's not too late to change your mind,' he jokes.

'Oh, Papa!'

'Do you think anyone would notice? We could just tell the c-coachman to put the horses to the gallop and head up to Balmoral.'

The fact that he is half serious makes it all the more touching. Elizabeth laughs a little unsteadily. Margaret has always been the demonstrative one, the one who flings her arms around her father. Elizabeth is more reserved, but now, just as they are hidden in the shadow of the archway, she leans against him.

'You're not losing me, Papa. I'll always be here.'

The King squeezes her hand. 'Thank you, Lilibet, for making me so proud. For doing your duty so well and so uncomplainingly. You don't know what a comfort you are to me. All I want now is for you to have the happiness you deserve.'

'I will have it with Philip, Papa, I know I will.'

'In that case,' her father says with a twisted smile, 'we'd better get you to the abbey.'

As the carriage comes out from under the arch into the forecourt, the roar from the crowd swells to a deafening volume that only increases as the coach moves out into the Mall. The faces on either side are a blur, the noise they make beats at the panels of the carriage. It is exhilarating and oppressive at the same time to be isolated from and yet the focus of such sound.

Elizabeth feels strangely detached from herself but still hyper aware of everything: the warm, smooth weight of the pearls at her throat; the prickle of the crystals on her skirt where her hands rest under the bouquet of flowers whose scent mingles with the faintly musty smell of the old leather seats; the mesmerising sway of the elderly carriage.

The journey is a sensory blur, so much so that she is almost disorientated when the coach stops outside Westminster Abbey. A footman opens the door, her father descends first, and turns to help her out. A team of assistants materialise to lift the train carefully out of the carriage after her and twitch it into position.

Margaret and the other bridesmaids are waiting for her, smiling, with her two little pageboys in kilts, Prince William of Kent and Prince Michael of Gloucester. As Elizabeth and the King arrive, the bridesmaids dip into curtseys in a rustling blur of organdie.

A final adjustment to the veil, and her father holds out his arm. 'Ready?'

She swallows. 'Ready.'

There is a moment of absolute silence as they stand framed in the ancient doorway, both momentarily blinded by the blaze of colour and light ahead of the them. Under its soaring ceiling and arches, the abbey is crammed with guests in a multitude of costumes: there are turbans and chasubles, sheikh's robes and surplices, red and blue uniforms decked with gleaming medals, gorgeous dresses and a plethora of diamonds, rubies, emeralds, and sapphires, all winking and glittering in the ceiling lights.

But she can't see Philip. A red carpet stretches the length of the nave, into the distance. To Elizabeth, standing dazzled in the doorway, the altar seems twice as far as in the rehearsal but somewhere up there he will be waiting for her.

When we're standing there at the altar, it'll be just you and me.

Ahead of the King, the Royal Standard is ceremonially dipped to the floor. This is her cue. Out of nowhere, Elizabeth remembers the dizzying fear of waiting to go on stage in the Waterloo Chamber all those years ago. She remembers peeking through the curtains to see if Philip had arrived and the bitterness of her disappointment at realising he wasn't there.

The memory makes her hesitate and then she forces herself to step forward to a tremendous roll of drums and a heart-shaking trumpet voluntary that resounds in the great cathedral.

There is a momentary jolt as one of her pageboys – William, she thinks – gets flustered and treads on her train. Someone hisses at him to get off, and she can move forward again, walking slowly up the long, long aisle with her father beside her. The congregation rustles into bows and curtseys as they pass while the choristers' voices soar over the sonorous sound of the organ.

And then Philip steps out and turns to watch her coming towards him, and Elizabeth forgets the pageboys, forgets the guests. Forgets that millions are listening on the wireless or watching on television or waiting outside.

He smiles at her as she reaches his side and her heart swells with a strange mixture of joy and relief, as if coming into safe harbour at last.

He is there.

Acknowledgements

It's always a pleasure to get to the end of the book and to thank all those without whom I would still be staring at a blank screen. First and foremost, my thanks to Charlotte Ledger, who was thinking about this book before I was. I am so grateful to her for the idea and the opportunity to write it, and to Bethan Morgan and the rest of the team at One More Chapter for their unfailing enthusiasm and support. Many thanks, too, and as always, to my tirelessly supportive agent, Caroline Sheldon.

Before the Crown is my imagining of how this most famous of relationships may have developed. It is, obviously, a work of fiction but it is based on fact, and I have drawn on a number of published biographies and accounts of the events that led to this most iconic of royal weddings.

I found the following books particularly useful: Philip Eade, *Young Prince Philip*; Anne Edwards, *Royal Sisters; Queen Elizabeth II and Princess Margaret*; Queen Alexandra of Yugoslavia, *Prince Philip: A Family Portrait*; Charles Higham and Roy Moseley, *Elizabeth and Philip: The Untold*